She waved a hand at me, as if dispersing gnats. "Don't drag me into this. All you care about is the goddamn *mystery*. What's important to me is that last night this woman, as you call her, *this woman* was bright, beautiful and alive. Today she's a corpse." A shudder ran through her.

"See," I said, stepping around her to block her path to the door. "That's where we differ. For me, what's important is that a murderer is walking around today congratulating himself on a job well done."

She made a sound under her breath.

I wanted her to understand. "Okay, try this. Somewhere in this city, some psycho woke up this morning with the biggest goddamn smile on his face. The first thing he did was turn on the news. Then he went out. Maybe he stopped for a cup of coffee. Maybe not. But without question he bought the first local newspaper he could find, and there —" I snapped up the *Times-Picayune* from where K.T. had tossed it and waved it at her. "He found this. This is his performance review and it's an absolute rave." I read to her from the article. " 'Gruesome murder . . . a phantom wreaking havoc in the middle of the night, while we and our children slumber . . . her body twisted at horrifying angles . . . the killer lurks among us unknown.' This story turns him on, K.T. He sees all the attention he's getting and he's high. It's better than sex. Better than anything. And he's going to want a repeat performance . . ."

# OLD BLACK MAGIC

The 6th Robin Miller Mystery

## JAYE MAIMAN

THE NAIAD PRESS, INC.
1997

Copyright © 1997 by Jaye Maiman

All rights reserved. No part of this book may be reproduced or transmitted in any form or by any means, electronic or mechanical, including photocopying, without permission in writing from the publisher.

Printed in the United States of America on acid-free paper
First Edition

Editor: Christine Cassidy
Cover designer: Bonnie Liss (Phoenix Graphics)
Typesetter: Sandi Stancil


**Library of Congress Cataloging-in-Publication Data**

Maiman, Jaye, 1957 –
    Old black magic : a Robin Miller mystery / by Jaye Maiman.
      p.    cm.
    ISBN 1-56280-175-9 (alk. paper)
    I. Title.
PS3563.A38266043   1997
813'.54—dc21                                      97-10004
                                                                       CIP

*For the miracle boys,
Evan Alexander and Jacob Lev*

## ABOUT THE AUTHOR

Jaye Maiman has written five romantic mysteries featuring the private investigator Robin Miller: *I Left My Heart,* the Lambda Literary Award winner *Crazy for Loving, Under My Skin* and Lambda Literary Award nominees *Someone to Watch* and *Baby, It's Cold.* A native of New York City, Jaye Maiman enjoys an amazingly maintenance-free and delightful existence with her partner, playmate, editor, co-neurotic and magic-maker Rhea.

## Note to the Reader

Writing a series is immensely satisfying and infinitely infuriating. No matter how many Twinkies and Yoo-Hoos she consumes, Robin Miller never gains weight as easily as I do. More maddening yet, she ages more slowly. In *I Left My Heart*, the first book in the Robin Miller series, my protagonist is 29 years old and the year is 1989. *Old Black Magic* takes place four years later, in 1993. The gap between my age and Robin's, meanwhile, has grown to a full six years. Despite these trespasses, I remain fond of her. Back by popular demand in these pages is K.T. Bellflower, the sexy chef with a southern accent. Many of you have asked — no — *ordered* me to bring her back, so here she is in all her butter-scented glory.

*Old Black Magic* is set in New Orleans, Louisiana, and New York City. I owe much thanks to Beth Miller, Robin Martin and Manina Dolores Duborca, who showed me the best of the Big Easy, while graciously allowing me to portray the worst. I have taken some liberties in describing that exuberant city. Similarly, anyone who knows Brooklyn and travels via the subway will instantly recognize the creative license I've taken in describing the Carroll Street train station. My apologies to anyone who takes exception.

As usual, I must thank the incredible universe of people who make my life so rich and magical: my dearest friends (if you don't know who you are by now, shame on you!), my family of origin and my extraordinary powerhouse of a partner, Rhea, whose hope, love, commitment, kindness and passion bring me to tears of astonishment and gratitude.

This book will also forever be linked in my mind with the loving memory of Teaka Balboa Cleopatra. One name could never have described you. Enjoy the mint garden, sweet queen.

This is a work of fiction. Names, characters, places and incidents either are the product of the author's imagination or are used fictiously. Any resemblance to events, persons or pets, living or dead, is entirely coincidental. Any inaccurancies in portraying real locations are entirely intentional, or so I claim.

# *Prologue*

He'd been following her so long, her perfume had soaked into the fabric of his shirt, mingled with his sweat. This would be the best one yet. He'd take his time, do it right. Maybe it wouldn't even happen at the hotel. He could've done her right outside the restaurant, after she stopped yapping with that copperhead. Oh, he could've done them both right then, the two of them whispering like they were queens of the earth. But no, she had to be alone. Patterns had to hold. He chuckled to himself. What fools they were.

She dropped a cigarette and ground it beneath her

heel. Their eyes almost met for an instant as she turned the corner, and he grew hard in response. This one had long legs, thick calves. But she didn't walk fast. She walked like she had time on her hands, like life was waiting for her. Maybe they'd end up near Congo Square, Armstrong's armpit, oh, it'd be so right. He could carve "Widow of Paris" on her back.

No, that would be too much, too soon. The game had to be played right.

The knife was cold in his pocket, the statue the perfect size. He hefted it in his hand and floated after her shadow.

# Chapter 1

*Monday, May 3*

Sunlight cut through the shutters and ran soft, hot fingers over my cheeks. I half-opened an eye and smiled. From the room service cart at the foot of the bed rose the spicy aroma of last night's Café Brûlot. I could still taste the rich combination of cloves, cinnamon, citrus, cognac and strong, black coffee. I burrowed my face into the sheets and remembered the abandon of the last twelve hours.

In the French Quarter of New Orleans, sensory

overload is a daily mandate. Days begin with a deceptive quiet: a click of solitary heels on flagstone, clear and distinct. The cough of a solitary car motor. The squeak of a window pressed open against the damp morning air, which instantly beads up on the cold glass and leaves glistening trails, each as slender as a frog's tongue. By early afternoon, Bourbon Street begins to percolate again, a slow boil that builds into a scalding, inescapable steam. Moody jazz, pounding rock and exuberant zydeco collide into one another and make music of a fifth dimension. The air smells of stale beer, fried oysters and sweat.

New Orleans is at once one of the most exhilarating and one of the most depressing cities. It is the experiential equivalent of cocaine: a narcotic that dulls pain and induces paper-thin elation. The city fools even the most sex-phobic men and women into believing they have the potential for bestial eroticism. The first hit of the city is intoxicating, producing a thrilling sense of abandonment. You have the sense you've entered the biggest party of your life, a Disneyland of decadence. But then the high wears off and you see the squalor, you feel the emotional void at the center.

Lovemaking takes on a different heat. Frenzied, desperate and unbridled, people fall into bed and grind limbs as if passion itself existed only here, in the dark, throbbing heart of the French Quarter. As if sunrise threatened to slice through the fervor and expose the hollowness beneath. I should know. I've been under the knife a few times myself. On my last trip here, many years ago, I fooled around with a woman on a park bench in Jackson Square, both of us so drunk it didn't matter whether we climaxed or not. Neither of us expected to remember sensation by morning. My father had just died and my lover, Mary, had announced her decision to leave me and move out West. My grief and outrage at the time loomed too large for Yoo-Hoos and Twinkies to vanquish. New Orleans had provided me with a black hole in which I could lose my discontent, or at least zone it out.

Since then, I've found that there are different kinds of happiness. One you can apply superficially, like a coat of gawdy cosmetics, and another that your body, heart and soul assimilates like nutrients drawn from food. New Orleans supplies people with a feel-good sensation akin to cheap, dime-store cosmetics. Now, cosmetics don't always look as good to others as you think they do. And after a day, even the best makeup job looks like crap. But as my L.A. buddies would say, that was then and this is now. And now felt a lot closer to Elysian Fields than I'd ever been.

I was in New Orleans to celebrate the debut of Les Enfants, the new restaurant run by PBS cook K.T. Bellflower and the renowned Cajun chef Winston Hawkins. In truth, K.T's only contribution to Les Enfants was a lockbox of coveted recipes, two former sous chefs and a check that carried more 0s than you need to win tic-tac-toe.

It was nearly noon, which meant we must've had less than six hours of sleep. K.T. was already in the shower, humming some God-awful country tune. I couldn't be sure, but it sounded as if she was singing about the hubcaps of her heart. She'd been doing that a lot lately, singing. Yesterday it was "Let Me Entertain You," sung with a rose clasped between her teeth, a scarf her only adornment. K.T.'s a big *Gypsy*

5

fan. Me, I'm just learning to appreciate the score. By the way, K.T. did not need a gimmick to get applause.

I should point out that my relationship with K.T. didn't have one of those picture-perfect launches, the kind of stranger-across-a-crowded-room romances that causes the eyes of close friends to roll in mock disgust. The truth is, witnessing someone else's unbridled new love can make even the strongest stomach kick around a few olive pits. Panic fists into your brain as you clamp down a second too late on the question: Did I ever feel that way about ———? Go ahead, fill in the blank. We've all been there. Not that I didn't suffer whiplash from my first glance at K.T. I did. But we had danced one of those dysfunctional tangos, tripping all over each other's best intentions, until finally, the band packed up its instruments and went home. I came to my senses in the dead of winter, just as I was about to nail a kidnapper and succumb to pneumonia. Days later I woke up in a hospital. K.T. reentered my life just as my I.V. drip ran out.

Maybe it was the rattle in my lungs she found irresistible. Or it could've been the way my skin took on the sheen of overcooked tuna. Whatever it was, K.T. fell back in love with me while I was stretched out butt-naked on a hospital bed. At any other time, I would've resisted. But there's something amazingly sobering about those little plastic name tags hospital clerks snap onto your wrists to distinguish you from other chattel. Somewhere around three in the morning, in a dim hospital room that smelled of dead flowers and dirty linen, I realized that the harder I ran, the faster I ended up where I began. So Robin

Miller, one-time famous romance writer and now fearless private eye, decided to settle down.
There was a snag, of course.

The bathroom door opened and K.T. emerged, a teal towel wrapped around her torso and another turbaned on her head. Under the guise of sleep, I scrutinized the woman I'd been seeing exclusively for eleven weeks. She stood before a floor-length mirror, delightfully unselfconscious, and shook out her hair. It's naturally curly, shoulder-length and the color of lion fur in an African sunset. Her eyes are hazel and her nose freckled. She has strong, square shoulders and farmer-stock hands. At that moment, the skin covering her five-seven curvaceous frame had a just-scrubbed luster. Ah, but when she dropped the second towel, the snag revealed itself.

Her belly had the slightest swelling, one that I might not have noticed if last night had been our first time together. More telling yet was the color and size of her nipples: dark as coffee beans and very pronounced. K.T. was almost exactly twelve weeks pregnant.

We had just started round two of our relationship when the EPT dipstick turned blue. If you think I kicked up my heels in jubilation, you probably believe in fairy tales and J.F.K.'s monogamy. I went absolutely slack-jawed. Sure I knew K.T. had been trying to get pregnant. She'd been trying all the months we'd been separated. Seven, to be exact. Long enough for her to start worrying that it was never going to happen. Long enough for me to pretend everything would stay the way it used to be. After all, at thirty-seven and counting, K.T.'s no young puppy, at least in terms of fertility. But fate has the humor of a bad *Saturday Night Live* skit. Just one week into new-relationship heaven, an embryo dug into my honey's uterus and thumbed its nose at me. Sure, I could've booked. But I was, and am, hopelessly in love. So K.T's going to be a mother, and I'm going to be something as yet undetermined.

She patted herself dry and reached into the closet for her jeans. I propped myself up on one elbow and said, "Hey, no underwear?"

Those leaf-green eyes smiled at me. "Honey," she said, "this is the Big Easy, remember?" Her voice normally carried a mere trace of her West Virginia origins, but when she wanted me to melt, she turned it on like a roaring campfire.

I said, "Come back to bed." The purr I tried to emit sounded like a '64 Chevy idling. My mouth needed toothpaste and coffee, preferably in that order.

"Can't. I'm on a mission." She spiked her arms into an Opera in the Park T-shirt. "I woke up craving beignets from Café du Monde. And I am bound and determined to get us some."

"You're hungry?"

"First time in ten weeks, so you can understand why there's no time for donning undies."

I threw aside the sheets as she wiggled into her sandals. "Wait for me. I'll come with you."

"With you looking like that? No way. Besides, I'm feeling energetic this morning. If I wait even half a second, I may revert to my previous slug state."

I edged onto my knees and checked out my reflection. I'm five-nine, olive-skinned and, at thirty-four, not as tautly muscled as I used to be. The two months I'd spent in bed while recouping from pneumonia had added a stubborn ten pounds to my frame. My dark hair is cut in short, choppy locks, all of which were pointing straight up at the moment. My breasts bore imprints of the sheets. Capping the picture, the ragged scar above my left eye had sunburned on yesterday's paddleboat ride down the river.

K.T. almost cackled. "I love you, but I don't want to be seen with you. At least, not yet. Shower. Order some coffee. Become human." She opened the door, knelt down and tossed me a copy of the New Orleans *Times-Picayune*. "I'll be back before you finish your first cup of café."

I scampered to the door, tucked myself to one side so my naked butt wasn't visible to the hall, and grabbed her by the waist. Our kiss was sweet, the good-bye kiss of an established couple.

"Save some room for me," she said with a wink.

If I had known what was coming, I would've never let her out that door. But that's how life works. One minute, you're humming a tune and basking in sunshine, and the next minute, splat! You're crud under someone else's shoe. I don't care if you call that someone else God, kismet, your ex-lover or a serial killer. All I know is that when the drop comes, you go down hard.

Some people are terrified of roller coasters. Not me. At least you know when you're going to take a nosedive. What terrifies me is happiness.

I called room service, took a quick shower and put on a pair of shorts and a tank top. The coffee arrived a minute later. I sprawled on the unmade bed, took a hefty sip of the chicory-laced brew and spread out the newspaper. The entertainment section featured a full-page spread on Les Enfants. K.T. and Winston looked exuberant, clinking together vintage Flintstones glasses bubbling with sparkling cider. The restaurant reflected the owners' personalities. Both had contributed items from their individual collections of toys from the Fifties and Sixties. Every table had a Slinky or an Etch-A-Sketch. The menu featured new spins on old classics: clumpy mashed potatoes laced with rosemary and whole cloves of garlic, an amazing gumbo that smelled of sassafras and andouille sausage, wood-oven roasted lamb shank with sundried tomatoes, Creole ratatouille and a Bananas Foster equal to foreplay. I should have stopped with the rave review, but instead I flipped back to the main section.

**DEAD HERO COP'S EX FOUND SLAIN IN HOTEL ALLEY**

The headline caught my eye immediately. Blood rushed into my belly as I read on. The woman's name was Lisa Rubin, 39, a journalist from Berkeley, California. She was in town to settle the estate of her ex-husband, Peter Strampos, a local beat cop. He'd been killed a week ago while attempting to stop a thirteen-year-old from raping his next-door neighbor. Rubin was found tucked between garbage cans in an alley behind the Hotel Roi, on the outskirts of the French Quarter. She was sodomized, clubbed, then stabbed to death. An egg was cracked open on the back of her head.

My hand shot to the phone. I dialed so fast the first time, I got the wrong number. The next time, I got the station.

"He's not here," a civic drone informed me.

I hurried to the closet, retrieved my address book, then dialed his home number. "Ryan, is that you?" I blurted when I heard a click on the other end.

"Let's see, you call my house, then quiz me on my identity. I must be talking to a master detective." He sucked in his breath. "Robin Miller, I presume."

If I didn't know better, I'd say he was drunk. But Detective Thomas Ryan has been stone sober since his wife was brutally murdered in a San Francisco hotel nearly nine years ago. Given his years in Homicide, the safer bet was that he was drop-dead exhausted. I took a breath and said, "I think it's happened again."

Through the wires, I heard a distant foghorn. The sound instantly transported me back to San Francisco and my first anguished investigation: the death of my ex-lover, Mary. Ryan had been the thorn, then the balm in my side. Somehow, over the past four years, he'd come to be a close friend, a rough-edged bear of a man who treated me more like a daughter than my own father ever had — which wasn't hard considering that my father ceased talking to me when I was three years old, after I accidentally discharged a gun and murdered my sister Carol.

"Are you still in New Orleans?" he said at last. "Shit, you have to be. Only the local rag's covering this. What'd you read?"

I was too stunned to respond.

"Hey, Miller, I need an answer. What does the *Picayune* say?"

I shuffled back to the bed and read the article to him in full.

"Morons." Ryan snorted. "Even when it's one of their own kind. A cop would never do that. Give me the byline."

I read it to him.

"Not that some dumb-ass editor's gonna understand why announcing so many fuckin' facts could screw the case up so good, no cop's gonna be able to unravel it. Hell, a story's a story, right?"

"Ryan, cool down. How'd you know about this? It only happened last night."

"Last night was a long time ago, hon."

My coffee cup was empty. I filled it to the brim, took a sniff and waited for him to continue.

He said, "So maybe Serra's taught you something after all, huh?" Tony Serra's my partner in the detective agency. Ryan set us up years ago. "Look, Robin, my Mary's been dead for nine years. There's not a month that goes by that I don't wonder if this is the case that's gonna fish out the scumbag that did my wife. Not a month. I got a buddy working with me who's got contacts in the FBI, every major police department in this country. First Monday, every month, one or both of us make the rounds. At this point, if we stopped making the calls, most of our contacts would call *us*. 'Cept the FBI, those uptight suckers still don't see the connections. Too many inconsistencies, right? Bullshit. They got a murderer who's smarter than all their stiff blue asses combined, that's the problem."

"Ryan."

"Yeah, right. Time's blood. I just got off the phone with Remillard . . . he's the only Fed who'll give me half a second these days. And even Remy keeps telling me he needs more. What more does he need? A woman gets raped or sodomized in a hotel, murdered, and somewhere near her body, the investigators find eggshell. How many times can they say it's coincidence? This makes six."

"The MOs *do* differ."

"Don't you start —"

"I'm not."

"Miller, you're still a juvie to homicide, right? But tell me this, if you wanted to commit a series of murders, would you repeat the same pattern again and again? Hell, no. You'd make sure there were enough variations so no one could nail you down."

"But then why does he keep choosing hotels?"

"And planting fuckin' eggshells? Because he's a fucking sick asshole, 'cause he wants to give us just enough to get the blood going, to get someone thinkin', maybe, maybe, there's a connection. This guy's laughing at us, Miller. I swear, sometimes at night, I can hear this fucker. These murders are a joke to him."

"Is there anything I can do?"

His answer was abrupt. "Yeah, like I've told you and Tony for years, stay out of it."

"I'm down here, Ryan. I can —"

"Stay out of it. You think you're hot shit because you've handled a murder or two. You're a pissant novice. I got someone on this for me. If it pans out, I'll fly down myself if I have to. You wanna do something for me, go back to New York. Check on my daughter. She's dating a defense lawyer. Now, there's a snake you can wrestle."

"Ryan, I'm not as green as you think. I can look into this without getting in over my head."

"I said, I have someone on it."

"Give me a name."

"No."

"Okay, I'll call Tony and get the name from him."

"Aw, crap. Can't you leave this alone?"

I took a breath. "I owe you. It's time you let me and Tony pitch in." Without Tom Ryan's help, I never would have resolved the murder of my ex-lover. I'd still be churning out tawdry romances with titles littered with words like *flaming, churning* and *untamed desire* and wondering why I began and ended each day with a hollow ache in my belly. With Ryan, I glimpsed what it might've been like if I'd had a father in my life instead of a brooding, silent phantom who reversed directions anytime he encountered me. I didn't just want to help him out, I *needed* to.

"Ryan," I said, "police headquarters is right across the street from where I'm staying —"

"Oh, no you don't. The NOPD is a ripe old men's club. You stick your head in and they'll blow you *and* the investigation away, just for the hell of it. They are strictly Sweeney's territory."

"Okay, okay, but at least let me in on what's happening. I'm telling you that one way or another, I'm going to check into this. Now, if you're smart, you'll take this opportunity to have some modicum of control —"

"Nothing like a friendly threat."

"Seriously, I *can* help out, even if it's only from the sidelines. K.T.'s tied up with the restaurant opening, and I could use the distraction. Besides, I'm wired to the max. Serra Investigations has gone hightech. I've got a laptop, modem, fax, subscriptions to databases of every size and shape. I even have a few research CD-ROMs with me. Give me a name in a published telephone directory anywhere in this country and I can get you an address, birth date, voting record, you name it."

"You made your point." There was a weighty pause. "Well, I gotta admit, Theo's a damn good foot solider, but he's a Luddite. I can barely get him to use the phone." He sucked in his breath. "Maybe this could work. You'll let him handle the field work, right? Exclusively."

I grunted.

"This guy's good, Miller. He used to work with me on the force, and he's stuck to this investigation all these years just out of loyalty to me. Half the time I think he's as skeptical as anyone else, but he stays on top of what's happening no matter what. He doesn't need you up his ass when he's on the streets, got me?"

"Ryan, you're as clear as glass. What's his name?"

"Theobald Sweeney. Make fun of the name and you're talking to dead air."

"No comment, sir. You've mentioned him before. Anything else I should know about him?"

"Like I said, we go back a long time. We started out as drinking buddies. *Heavy* drinking buddies. Then we took the sober road together . . . nothing like traveling to hell and back with somebody to forge a bond. Him and his wife separated, then she passed away, this was almost a year before Mary. Actually, Celeste killed herself . . . Man, Sweeney was wrecked by that. You wouldn't guess it by seeing him now, but when he was in love, he was an absolute pussycat. After Mary's murder, I finally understood the kind of guilt he had to be carrying in his gut. I dragged him to AA with me. Shit." Silence buzzed in my ear. I couldn't begin to imagine the nightmare

Ryan must be remembering. I waited for him to continue.

"Anyway," he said. "I gotta warn you, he's rough around the edges. But his bark's much worse than his bite. You gonna think he's the biggest right-wing asshole you could ever meet, but meanwhile his wife Celeste was black. Talk about guts. Try to imagine what life must've been like for him, a good old Southern boy marrying out of his race. In *Louisiana*. In the *Sixties*. Despite what he may say to you, he's as liberal as anyone I know who was born and raised in the bayou. And when it comes to detective work, Rob, he's the best."

Ryan's description made me think twice about offering to partner up with this guy. Reluctantly I asked, "Does he work out of San Francisco?"

Ryan laughed. "He works out of his car, most of the time. He has a fishing cabin up near the Russian River, his uncle still owns a place down in New Orleans, he winters with his sister in St. Louis and spends part of the year in New York. He's a nomad, which has served my purposes just fine. You'll hate him."

"Thanks for the warning. Wonder how you describe me."

"You don't want to know."

"Gotcha. Can you e-mail me information on the murders?"

"A summary, maybe... the rest is hard copy. I'll put it in the mail."

"I'm at the Royal Orleans." I read off the address and number from the phone base.

"Okay, Miller. I'll have him call you."

"Sooner rather than later," I injected.

"When he needs you. Stay safe, Miller. And let Tony know I'll pay your standard rates. No freebies, okay? This way, if I have to fire you, I can do it without guilt. Tell Tone to send me a contract right away."

"He'll love that." Tony's an ex-cop with a penchant for quoting the Bible, stacking pennies in tall, neat rows and finding lucrative corporate clients. He also would've charged his own mother if she wanted us to conduct a credit search. He's just that kind of guy.

"So how's the old bastard doing?" Ryan asked.

"Not so good." My partner contracted HIV nearly a decade ago. For the most part, he'd been remarkably symptom-free. Until last summer. To make matters worse, he suffered a minor stroke a few months back. "Tony's working from home most days," I said. "His new command central. On the other hand, he's finally allowed me to pull in a new crew of temps, whom he dispatches with the grace of Patton. The man won't go without a fight."

"Good for him. Me, I'd've blown my brains out years ago."

"Bullshit."

He laughed. "Maybe you're right. Well, tell him I said, 'Fuckin' A,' for what it's worth." Ah, the cryptic language of men.

It wasn't until he hung up that I glanced at the clock on the nightstand. K.T. had been gone close to an hour. Café du Monde wasn't that far. I threw open the shutters. The balcony overlooked the corner of Royal and St. Louis. I leaned out, hoping to see K.T. trotting back with a grease-stained bag of beignets. The street was crowded with tourists wandering between restaurants and antique shops. I started to breathe harder and caught the stench of manure from the horse-drawn carriages parked in nearby Jackson Square. Bitter, coffee-tinged juices surged up from my stomach and singed my throat. Where the hell was K.T.? I clenched the iron railing, suddenly remembering how careful I'd been not to rest my weight on her belly when we made love last night, how she murmured into my neck, "It's okay, honey. You won't hurt me." Despite her assurances, I hoisted myself up on my elbows and knees, thinking, *the baby can feel me.*

"Hey, you, whooee!"

My head jerked in the opposite direction. K.T. was approaching from Bourbon Street. She waved a bag at me and winked. In an instant, every muscle in my body sagged. I waved back. Then an abrupt motion behind her caught my eye. A man wearing gray slacks and a white shirt had been matching her gait too closely. When she stopped suddenly, he caught himself, pivoted and crossed the street. Then just as suddenly his pace slowed, became deliberately casual. He even paused to window-shop. I knew the tactic. I've used it myself to recover from a tail I'd blown. The stab in my chest was no longer heartburn.

The bastard had been following K.T.

## Chapter 2

"Where the hell have you been?" A growl crept into my voice as I tugged K.T. into the room by her elbow and glanced down the hallway behind her.
"Wow, what a welcome."
I locked the door and spun around to hug her.
"Whoa, darling, you'll crush the beignets." Her smile melted when she saw my expression. She glanced at her watch, puzzled. "Was I really gone that long?"
"There was a man following you."
"Oh Lord." She laughed and nudged the room

service cart out of her way with a bump of her hip. "What do you get when you combine the flaming imagination of a romance writer with the paranoia of a private eye? Take a gander in the mirror. You look like Edgar Allan Poe on steroids. C'mon, hon, let's eat these while they're warm." She waved the oil-stained paper bag at me, then shuffled out to the balcony and shook the beignets onto paper plates. Powdered sugar exploded into the still, humid air. K.T. winked at me. Her cheeks were flushed and moisture beaded up on her upper lip. She poured a half-pint of milk into a wine glass and absent-mindedly stroked her belly.

The gymnast in my stomach stuck its landing. I sat down on the edge of the bed. "K.T., I'm serious. I saw someone following you."

She smiled coyly. "Wouldn't you?"

"Oh, for God's sake, listen to me. A man in gray slacks and a white shirt was right behind you, following you step for step until you called up to me. He had deep olive-toned skin. He may have been Hispanic."

"Did he have slick, blue-black hair, like Reggie in the Archie comics?"

Surprising myself, I laughed. "You are impossible. Hon, I don't know if it was blue-black or just dark brown."

"I met a guy down by Café du Monde who needed directions to Bourbon Street. He seemed very sweet and was incredibly polite. I walked him up there... I needed the walk, anyway... then I came right on back." She appeared to reconsider her remarks. "Well, maybe he *was* dogging me... He did ask me if I'd join him for dinner. But, come on, you know how scary this city can be for the uninitiated. Especially if you're from some small town. If this guy was following me, believe me, it was innocent. I'd lay odds his only crime was hoping my down-home friendliness might extend to more than just providing directions. Or maybe he was after my beignets, which any person in her right mind would be." She wiggled her eyebrows at me as she bit into a pastry.

I shook my head and joined her on the balcony. I have to admit that in my field unfettered suspicion is an occupational hazard. I tore off a sticky corner of a beignet and said, "You have to stop being so nice."

She planted a kiss on my cheek, then sat down heavily. "I moved from West Virginia to New York City. What more do you want?"

"Low blow." The beignet practically melted in my mouth.

"If you'd like . . ." She lowered her voice to a whisper, stroked the length of my thigh. My knees went soft. "That's better." She continued stroking. My body tightened in response. "Now, why don't we talk about our plans for today."

I latched onto her hand, held it against my body. "Guess what I want to do?"

"Too easy. Give me a harder one."

Leaning over her, I countered, "Let's try the body paints."

She laughed, not the response I hoped for. "Sweetheart, I'd love to fingerpaint your luscious skin, but I do need to tend to business this afternoon. Winnie and I agreed to scout some of the local markets, and then we're going back to Les Enfants. I wasn't pleased with the étouffé last night . . . did you see the color of the sauce? Mud's more appetizing. And that pre-pubescent sous chef took some liberties with my recipes that I did not appreciate." K.T. took her food seriously. I felt bad for Timothy, the twenty-two-year-old sous chef who looked like he'd be more comfortable behind a jack hammer than wielding a chef's knife.

"So when can we spend time together?" I asked.

"I want to be at the restaurant when we open for dinner. Win said he could use me up to eleven, but I'll try not to stay that late. Maybe I'll be able to get free by ten."

"Wow. I get you as early as ten?"

"I didn't hear you complaining last night."

I smiled at the memory. The cravings of pregnant women extend far beyond pickles and ice cream. I went in for a kiss. Her mouth tasted of powdered sugar and warm milk. "When do you have to meet Winston?" I asked.

She averted her eyes. "I should've been there about fifteen minutes ago." She barreled past my expletives. "Hold it, tadpole. I warned you my schedule would be tight. I promised Win I'd help him get the place humming and I intend to do just that. Our deal was I'd feed you well, take exquisite care of your libidinous urges and provide you a warm butt for spooning each and every night."

"Sure, but you extracted that deal while I was hooked onto a respirator, fearing for my life."

I loved the sound of her laugh. "Robin Miller, you are impossible. Why don't we meet back here around four. It's my usual nap time, but you never know, you could get lucky."

"Well, if I have to, I'm sure I can keep myself

busy until then." I fingered a crumb off the green metal café table and wondered how long it'd take for Theobald Sweeney to contact me. K.T. and I planned to be in town for another week, plenty of time for an investigation. *If* Sweeney called right away. Maybe I'd just look him up first.

There was a sharp rap of knuckles against metal. "Hello?" K.T. said, half-teasingly. Then all at once, she narrowed her eyes at me. "What's up, Robin? You have that scary, gone-big-game-hunting look. Did you get a call from Tony or Jill?"

This is the part of relationships that unnerves me. I don't like anyone reading my thoughts, not even me. I got nice and indignant. "No way. This is a pleasure trip. I'm just trying to imagine how I'll manage without you today."

She slapped me playfully. "Yeah, right. Well, you can keep your secrets, Ms. Miller. Just remember, I have mine as well." She gulped down the remainder of her milk, leaving a filmy mustache behind. I licked her upper lip. There was a moment then, when our eyes met, that my need for this woman stunned me, an electric prod in the flank of an intractable cow. She moved me to places I wasn't entirely sure I wanted to go. And yet any other path was absolutely unacceptable. With a fist of anxiety in my belly, I watched her walk inside. I didn't want to feel this much, be this vulnerable.

I did what I always do when my mind drags me down roads I don't want to travel: I wolfed down the remainder of my beignet and went to retrieve a chilled Yoo-Hoo from the stash I'd stored in the hotel's mini-fridge. K.T., meanwhile, was stuffing her backpack with home-made granola bars, frozen slices of lemon and recipe notes. All of a sudden she stopped short and gasped.

I turned around so fast, Yoo-Hoo sloshed onto my feet. K.T. was staring at the newspaper I had left on the bed, one hand over her mouth and her eyes wide with shock. My stomach soured instantly. "What is it, K.T.?"

She pointed at the newspaper. "I talked to that woman just last night. Outside the restaurant."

I took a step toward her, keeping my tone measured. "What about?"

Watching her from behind, I could almost sense the speed and sweep of her mental calculations. For some reason, she made me think of a chickadee who's just spotted a cat stalking toward her nest. With her head cocked to one side, still not facing me, she asked in a deadly monotone, "Why is the paper opened to this page, Robin?"

The best response was none. Or so I thought.

She spun around. "Good Lord," she said, "can't we go on a trip without you weaseling into some homicide investigation? New Orleans is a city of life and celebration, but you —" She snatched up the paper and tossed it at me. "You find this, this *shit* wherever you go."

"New Orleans is the murder capital of America, K.T."

"Fine, Robin, fine. Why do I bother?" She zipped her backpack and swung it sharply to her shoulder. The waist strap clipped my chin.

"So," I said, rubbing the scrape with exaggerated distress. "What did you talk about? Had you ever seen her before?"

She waved a hand at me, as if dispersing gnats. "Don't drag me into this. All you care about is the goddamn *mystery*. What's important to me is that last night this woman, as you call her, *this woman* was bright, beautiful and alive. Today she's a corpse." A shudder ran through her.

"See," I said, stepping around her to block her path to the door. "That's where we differ. For me, what's important is that a murderer is walking around today congratulating himself on a job well done."

She made a sound under her breath.

I wanted her to understand. "Okay, try this. Somewhere in this city, some psycho woke up this morning with the biggest goddamn smile on his face. The first thing he did was turn on the news. Then he went out. Maybe he stopped for a cup of coffee. Maybe not. But without question he bought the first local newspaper he could find, and there —" I snapped up the *Times-Picayune* from where K.T. had tossed it and waved it at her. "He found this. This is his performance review, and it's an absolute rave." I read to her from the article. "'Gruesome murder...a phantom wreaking havoc in the middle of the night, while we and our children slumber...her body twisted at horrifying angles...the killer lurks among us unknown.' This story turns him on, K.T. He sees all the attention he's getting and he's high. It's better than sex. Better than anything. And he's going to want a repeat performance. You say I'm only interested in the mystery." A chill breeze swept over me. "That's bullshit. I know I can help save a life. You know what that means to me?"

Her hand was already on the knob, but she shot

me a fiery glance. "Very noble, Robin. But why you? Why not the New Orleans police force? Or the FBI? Why you? I'll let you in on a secret. No matter how hard you try, no matter how many strangers you save, you'll never forgive yourself for your sister's death. You'll never forgive yourself for not rushing out to California to be by your ex-lover's side in time to stop *her* death. Your guilt is etched in here." She pounded her chest and then flinched as her own words settled in. "Oh, chew on a pig's tail," she muttered as she yanked the door toward her. "I don't want to argue. Do what you want. You will anyway." She swung the backpack onto her shoulder. "Try to stay alive until I get back."

    I didn't stop her, although I should have. I should have taken her in my arms and told her how much she meant to me, how much I needed her. Instead, I locked the door behind her. Of course there was truth in what she said, but it didn't matter as much to me at that instant as the relief my work brought me. Ever since I'd become a detective, the locust of guilt buzzing inside my head had become a little less voracious. What K.T. didn't understand and I'd only started to is that saving lives had saved mine, uncovering secrets made mine easier to escape. Tom Ryan had started me out on this path to sanity. Nailing his wife's murderer would be more than justice; it'd close a chapter in my life.

    I stomped to the closet and unpacked my laptop. As I plugged in the modem cord and clicked the CD-ROM into place, I noticed that the base of my fingernails were blue. The damn air-conditioning was on too high. I found the thermostat, whipped the dial to Off and opened the balcony doors. The heat slammed over me like a sixty-pound dog hell-bent on dinner. I felt it lap my skin, and a strange calm settled in. With my usual finesse, I'd pushed myself into another zone, the one in which analysis replaced emotion, distance annihilated intimacy. The place was safe, but damn lonely.

Down to business. My screen flickered at me as I opened a new investigative file. I was in the same city as the madman who'd killed six women, including Mary Ryan. A tremor shook me. Why the hell was I so cold? I rustled through the dresser until I found a sweatshirt, then I dialed in and retrieved the file Ryan had sent me. His wife's murder was listed first. Under a grainy photograph of a woman who reminded me of my fourth-grade teacher was a caption, startling for its brevity:

> Mary Jean Ryan, age 42, red hair, blue eyes, 5'2", freckles across bridge of nose. Murdered at approximately eight p.m. on Friday, August 3, 1984, in The Pink Clam, a residency hotel located at Jones and Eddy in San Francisco.

I read through the document with the taste of iron in my mouth. Ryan's biographical sketch was antiseptic, perfunctory, written by a man devoid of emotion. I knew the real story.

Mary and Thomas Ryan married when they were just sixteen years old. My immediate assumption when first hearing this was *shotgun wedding,* but Ryan had been quick to correct me. The marriage hadn't been pregnancy-induced. Amazingly, the lovesick teenagers didn't even sleep together until their honeymoon night. They were simply kids in love, who mixed equal parts of romanticism and mischievousness, conformism and rebellion. As an end product, they conjured up the concept of marriage. They manipulated their parents into believing a child was on the way, with the anticipated results.

Tom's mother took them in and waited anxiously for the birth of her grandchild. She waited just a hair longer than originally expected. Mary gave birth to a daughter eleven months later. The little girl was named Shawn after Tom's father, who had been a police lieutenant. The little girl had Mary's flame-red hair and Tom's sense of adventure. With doting parents and grandparents, Shawn was destined to grow up a spoiled brat. But she didn't.

At age three, she drowned in a lake during a family reunion. Within a week, Tom Ryan succumbed to his first alcoholic blackout. Three years passed before Mary became pregnant again with their second daughter, Casey.

At the time of Mary's murder, she and Tom had been married for twenty-six years, although they had separated a year earlier. Ryan readily admitted that the break-up was nine-tenths his fault. He'd been an ugly drunk, nasty, abusive and brooding. Eventually the drinking wasn't enough. He tacked on a few prime vices, waiting for Mary to draw the line. In less than a year, he managed to throw away their entire savings on bad OTB bets and hookers he'd met on the force.

When Mary finally drew the line, Tom was shocked to find out how deep it ran. She moved into a cheap residential hotel, the Pink Clam, and told

Tom she fully intended to live there until he agreed to a divorce. Her choice was meant to humiliate him. The Pink Clam had been the site of his last liaison with a streetwalker. He refused to sign the papers and continued drinking. Living in a bourbon haze, he managed to delude himself into believing he could call Mary's bluff. He waited for her to give in and come back home. By August, 1984, the game folded. Mary Ryan, the woman who Tom once described to me as having "the face of Ireland and the fiery heart of a dragon," had been robbed, sodomized repeatedly and brutally clubbed to death.

Ryan crashed the crime scene. Only later did he recall kneeling in a pool of egg yolk and broken shells as beat cops tried to drag him away from his wife's corpse. The chief investigator later speculated that the intruder had attacked Mary as she was putting away groceries.

Tom's alcoholism came to an abrupt end. The day he buried his wife, he dug a two-foot-deep trench in his backyard and buried a case of Maker's Mark, Kentucky's finest bourbon.

I scanned the files on the other murders. Despite Ryan's insistence, the connections among the cases were thinner than surgical thread. The two consistent, and possibly coincidental, elements were the presence of eggshell and the proximity to a hotel. Three of the six murders were committed inside a hotel room, one in a hotel staircase and the other two in hotel alleys. I spent the next hour jotting data into a pocket-sized notebook. In the last file, Ryan had inserted a quote from a letter he received from the FBI after the last "eggshell murder."

*With all due respect to your professional reputation and distinguished career with the San Francisco Police Department, we conclude that your particular involvement in the 8.3.84 homicide has diminished your investigative capacity to assess any correlation, or lack thereof, among the cases in question.*
*Thank you for your inquiry.*

I took a bathroom break, then rang my office. Jill Zimmerman answered with her typical efficiency.

"So are you stuffing yourself with rich, butter-soaked food while I run this damn agency for you and Tony?"

Jill's style is inimitable. She'd started with us as a part-time clerk and had quickly become integral to the business. She made no secret about her desire to become a full partner, but Tony kept his hands tight on SIA's reins and liked it that way. In truth, my partnership in SIA has more to do with the funds I have invested carefully in stocks, bonds, real estate and money market accounts than with my investigative experience, a fact Tony periodically points out to both me and Jill. Since partnership was not a current option, Jill took peculiar delight in tormenting us with her well-earned stance as the underappreciated and indispensable underling.

"I have a new assignment. For Thomas Ryan."

"Oh, boy. Tony won't like this. Another murder?"

"Bingo. Here's the dirty." We got down to business quickly. Jill and Tony were as familiar as I was with the basic circumstances of Mary Ryan's murder. The three of us had spent many hours speculating about the case. Usually, we ended up talking about how unhealthy it was for Ryan to dedicate his life to investigating a homicide no one was likely to solve. "I want you to get me as much info as possible on the other murders. News clippings. Police reports. Interview transcripts. We have some of that in the files, the rest you'll need to dig up. Get one of the new techno-kids to do a fresh search. We've all settled into a rut on this stuff. Overnight what you've got as soon as you get it."

"You sure you want to get involved in this thing? Ryan's been pretty adamant about keeping us out of the line of fire."

"That's why I want to move fast, before he changes his mind. This is the first time I've been in the right place at the right time. A fresh trail may make all the difference in the world."

"That's what I'm afraid of. Does K.T. know about this?"

"Love ya too, hon," I said quickly, shutting down this new line of questioning. "Check in on my cats, will you? My feuding housemates seem to be preoccupied these days. I checked in with Beth yesterday and between Carol's colic and Dinah's peevish rampage in the background, it sounded like round-up time at the O.K. Corral. I'm afraid my babies may be getting the short end of their short stick. And you know what Geeja's like when she doesn't get her daily dose of stroking and adulation." I laughed, picturing my slick, black cat stretched out on my bed, stabbing a six-toed paw at me disapprovingly, her eyes narrow and demanding. When Geeja wanted to be petted, you didn't disagree.

Jill and I took care of a few more housekeeping details, then I hung up and got back to work. The laptop purred under my fingertips. Next best thing to being home, I mused.

Just then, a crash in the hallway jerked me out of my seat. I smirked at my startle reflex. Too much mayhem on my mind. I logged off the computer and seconds later heard the sharp rap of knuckles on the door. Maybe my vigilance wasn't silly after all. "Yeah, whatcha want?" I figured it couldn't hurt to sound like a New York truck driver.

"Room service."

I glanced through the peephole. The guy on the other side looked legit, but I hadn't ordered anything else from room service. "Must be a mistake."

"No way, sir. Says right here, room four-two-two. Eggs Sardou. Decaf. You Robin Miller?"

Opening the door the width of the chain lock, I peered out. "Let me see that."

After rolling his eyes, he flashed the order. I still wasn't convinced. I'd used the room service ploy myself. "Okay, lift the lid."

"You want this or what?" he asked, annoyed. Strange how someone from New Orleans can sound so Bronx-like.

I repeated my request and this time he complied. The eggs looked swell. Wielding a wood hanger as a potential weapon, I let him in and signed for the food. Then, just to be safe, I called down to room service. I was told that the other guest in my room had ordered the food on my behalf. Finally satisfied, I sat down to eat. Just as I wiped a rivulet of Hollandaise from my chin, the phone rang. I vaulted around the room service cart.

The voice on the other end sounded like Harvey

Fierstein. "How many Fats Domino hits can you name?"

"Excuse me?"

"You even know who Fats Domino is?" The voice was thick with the southern Brooklynese accent so common to New Orleanians.

"Who is this?"

"Theo Sweeney. Ryan told me to call. What a joke. For years, he insists I fly solo and suddenly he's throwing you at my propellers. You gonna help me and you don't know nothing about de town . . . I thought you used to do travel writing. What's a Zulu coconut?"

I counted to ten. "Are you telling me coconuts and blues singers are critical to this case, or are you practicing for a Trivial Pursuit tournament?"

"Ha. You got a sense of humor. That's real important when you're working homicide. But to me you're still a *cochon de lait*. Understand? Sure you do."

He had just called me a milk something. I knew enough to know I was supposed to be offended. "Look, Sweeney, I am not interested in honing in on your case or your fee —"

"My fee? Hey, babe, you know who you're talking to? I was Ryan's fucking partner. I walked the streets of San Francisco with him. When a bullet came looking for my organs, Ryan was the one who tackled my ass and let that bullet slap brick. This man's my brother and you're talking *fee*? Christ. If he offered me a buck, I'd burn it. *Fees*."

The word sounded dirty in his mouth. Maybe I shouldn't have been so fast to accept Ryan's offer to pay. "The bottom line," I said, stumbling over my blip of conscience, "is that we're on the same side. I owe him, too. Ryan's like my father." The silence on the other end gave me time to change into jeans and sneakers. I had a feeling Sweeney wasn't going to be real flexible about time.

"Yeah, he says that about you, too. Calls you his *other* daughter. Okay, here's what I'm gonna do. Be downtown riverside, at the steamboat *Natchez* in fifteen minutes. Get there before the calliope finishes 'Alexander's Band,' and you're in. I'll be at the ticket booth."

"Where are we going?"

"*I'm* going to check on a real bad ass," he said at last. "*La ripopée*. White trash to you. Should be a real education, hon. Be there in fifteen, or I'm gone."

Before I dropped the phone back on the base, I heard him shout my name. "What?" I asked.

"You carry?"

"A gun? No."

He laughed and hung up.

# Chapter 3

Sweeney may have sounded like Harvey Fierstein, but he sure didn't look like him. He was five-seven, at most, with a thick waist, muscular forearms and a Burt Reynolds hairpiece. Olive-skinned, with thin lips and an incongruously aquiline nose, he wore faded jeans and a stained dungaree vest over a pristine Hawaiian-print shirt. Around his beefy neck dangled a brass medal that had probably seen polish sometime in the previous century. Through the grime I made out the image of some macho saint brandishing a sword and playing he-man bronco-buster. Ryan had set me up with another winner. I almost turned tail, but I was too beat from sprinting the distance from the hotel. With the steam rising from my sweaty limbs, I could've run the calliope myself. I bent over from the waist and gasped for air.

"What happened to New Orleans' beautiful spring weather?" I managed to say in a wan attempt at small talk. The humidity was at August levels.

Sweeney grunted. "You're late." He tapped a Timex that looked like it'd been in one of those commercials I remember from childhood. *It takes a licking and keeps on ticking*. Actually, the same might be said of Sweeney. The man had a poorly healed puncture wound on the left side of his jaw and a thick thread of scar tissue along his forearm.

I'd barely had time to catch my breath when he took off again. Questioning my sanity, I scrambled after him toward the parking lot.

"Frogsticker," he said as he slammed into the driver's seat of his rental car.

"What?" I asked, my butt dropping into the car one second after he revved the engine.

"The scar. I saw you looking at my arm. Some perp in Houston stabbed me with a pocket knife."

"Oh."

"You shoulda seen what I done to him."

We lurched out of the lot. Sweeney drove with a heavy foot. I belted myself in and asked, "What were you doing in Houston?"

"I'm a traveling man, sweetheart. I've chased lowlife scum from Dan to Beersheba."

"Oh, for God's sake, why do you keep talking like that?"

An ugly grin spread over his face. "Pisses you off,

doesn't it?" The Cajun twang disappeared instantly and he sounded at last like a San Francisco cop. "I was born down here. Amazing how fast it comes back to you. And how good I am at pissing off little tidbits like you."

He popped in a cassette and turned up the volume. Zydeco. Raucous accordions and washboard music. I actually liked it. The best part was that Sweeney clearly had expected me to be irritated. I finger-tapped the dashboard with more zeal than I felt and asked, "So where are we going and why?" To myself I added, and for how long? I'd already decided that compared to Sweeney, a visit to the dentist would be a welcome respite.

"I met with the lieu in the sector where the woman was killed. We've had our share of *les bonne temps*. He dropped enough hints for me to come up with the name of this jailbird I been tracking for years. The man's got a camp out in the bayou, which is where we're headed now. The cops got no legit reason for questioning him, so in a way I'm doing them a favor. See if the fish is stinkin'."

The bayou? I checked my watch. Damn. There was no way I'd be back in time to meet K.T. I switched on the beeper I wore on my waistband. At least she'd be able to page me.

Sweeney glanced my way and said, "Uh-uh. Shut that off. I seen a man blown away 'cause of one of those contraptions."

I started to protest, but he cut me off with a wave of his hand and said, "Mind if I stop for a bite?" Not that he waited for an answer. He pulled up to a Popeye's drive-in window with the finesse of a drunken New York cab driver. Lava rock studded the outside walls. As Sweeney rolled down his window, heat rolled through the car like a fireball. He swung his arm out and depressed the order button. My hand went immediately to the door handle. I should have enough time to call the hotel and leave a message for K.T.

"Where you going?" Sweeney asked.

"I need a phone."

"You get out of the car, you also gonna need a lift." The automatic door lock clicked into place. "While I'm ordering, you want anything?"

I grunted my response. Working with Sweeney was the cost of helping out Thomas Ryan, I reminded myself. The price was high, but I owed Ryan a hell of a lot more.

A few minutes later Sweeney retrieved a basket of fried chicken legs and french fries. "You still find the best Popeye's in the black neighborhoods," he said, gunning the ignition, "but even they're past their heyday." Heyday or not, Sweeney tore into a leg with the gusto of a medieval landlord. Within seconds the car stunk of grease, with an undertone of cloying air scent. I leaned over, shut off the air-conditioning and rolled down the window.

We reached the city limits and he floored the gas. Between mouthfuls, he asked, "How much you know about the other murders?"

I told him about the research I'd done earlier in the afternoon.

"Chicken piss," he snorted, shoving a fistful of fries into his mouth. "Look in there. I brought you a present." He nodded at the glove compartment.

Inside I found a manila envelope. I untied it and

dropped the contents onto my lap. My stomach heaved instantly. "Shit, what is this?"

I felt him glance at me. "What do you think? You gonna grind the beans, babe, you better be able to drink the coffee."

My gaze drifted back to the image of a battered naked woman, her limbs twisted into a position resembling a swastika. Blood caked on the back of her head. The other photos were worse. I turned them over slowly. He rattled off the names. Eileen Anderson. Hope Williams. Betty Galonardi. Andrea Allen.

"How the hell did you get these?"

"Connections."

"Are these from all the crime scenes?"

"Every one that Ryan's called me on. That bottom one is his wife. Go ahead and look." Again, the small smirk. He was daring me.

Mary Ryan rested on her back. There was no resemblance to the beautiful woman depicted in pictures Ryan had showed to me. Bloody pulp obliterated her face. Her body...

I stuck my head out the window and heaved.

"Knew it." Sweeney's laugh was high-pitched.

"Fuck you." I rummaged in my backpack for a tissue and Life Saver.

"Ryan told me you'd only done pretty murders. A nice poisoning or two. Here...drink the rest of my Coke."

I declined the offer and said, "If you think I'm such a soft-weight, why'd you invite me to ride along?"

"Ryan thinks you got smarts. That says something. Still, I'm reserving opinion. So far, I can't say I'm real impressed with your credentials. Or your guts. You wanna tell me how you're gonna track a serial killer if you can't stomach a few nasty photos?"

I didn't bother to respond.

Neither of us said another word until we drove by an assembly facility for NASA, where they build the rocket section of the space shuttle. Sweeney pointed past my nose. "Pride and joy of Michoud. Personally, I don't think we got business in space. Earth's fucked up enough." He polished off the last fry, licked his fingers and flicked the garbage into the back seat. A few minutes later the smell of coffee wafted in through the car window. Finally, a welcome aroma. I stuck my head out and took a deep whiff.

"Hera International got its headquarters here," he explained. "Company wanted to be right neighborly to South America. Why else would they move out to this boony. Unless it's 'cause labor's so cheap here in the po' South. Ain't that what you Northerners think?"

He was testing my sore spots, a sadistic dentist digging for cavities. This guy made Thomas Ryan look like English gentry. I made a cup with my hand and let the wind blow hard against my palm. Anywhere but here, I thought. The man's bitterness was almost palpable. I wondered what made him tick. "So, Sweeney, how long ago did you leave New Orleans?"

He threw me another sideways glance. The man was sharp. He had recognized my unspoken criticism. *"N'awlins.* Sweet N'awlins," he sang. "Well, at least you pronounce it right. If you'd a said New Or-*leans,* you'd be eating tire dust right now."

"You worked with Ryan back in 'eighty-four?"

"I worked with Ryan from nineteen-seventy-five to 'eighty-five. Ten years. I'd been up North twelve years before that. Twenty-two years. Then I decided to chuck the force and go out on my own. Want my es-es number?"

I ignored his jibe. "Why'd you quit the force?"

"Pigs shouldn't wag their tails in the farmer's face, especially when he's got a hankering for pork."

"Are you saying you don't want to answer my question?"

"Gee, you *are* quick. I'll tell you this much, sister, I was pissed at how they treated Ryan after his wife's murder. When you got a rep as a drunk, it don't ever leave you. The straight and narrow boys look at you from the corners of their eyes, waiting for you to slip. Life under a fuckin' microscope. I'm amazed he's stayed on this long. After I left, I never looked back and I gotta say, I've done real well working for myself. Meanwhile, Ryan's rotting away in that foggy-assed city."

A few minutes later, we reached the twin spans. The air rolling off Lake Pontchartrain reminded me of Cape Cod. I took a deep breath and closed my eyes. Three nights ago, Winston drove K.T. and me to a seafood shanty out here called Vera's. K.T. had reveled in teaching me to snap off the heads of crawfish, pinch the tail and suck out the sweet meat from the heads. We'd giggled like kids, played footsie under the table while Winston pretended to not notice. Later, in the drive back to town, K.T. fell asleep on my shoulder, strands of her hair brushing across my cheek like silk, our hands joined tightly over her swollen belly.

"Nap's over, Miller," Sweeney said, snapping me

back. "I need the companionship. And you need info." He stabbed a finger toward my side of the car. "This area's called the Irish Bayou. Good, solid folk. The perp of the day was raised out here." We were passing little fishing villages. "Them camps just blow away during a good hurricane. I saw it happen once when I was just a boy. Thought it was the most exciting thing I'd ever seen, but that was before homicide. Nothing compares to that, now ain't that right?" He poked my side. "I still got cousins out here. Clover Lee just bought himself a two-bedroom condo 'round here for forty-five grand. The place is a good thousand square feet with its own boatslip. Tell me where you can get that up North."

We were about forty minutes out from the city. I wondered how much longer I'd have to listen to his travelogue.

"Tell me more about this guy in the bayou."

The car jerked forward. We were cruising at close to eighty. I clasped the door handle.

"Barry NeVille and if ever a man were born on crazy creek, it's him. Let's see . . . he's thirty-five. Some folks 'round here would still call him a quadroon. He's five-nine, dark-skinned, got weird blue-gray eyes, black hair. Good-looking guy. Grew up in foster homes. Been in and out of jail since he was sixteen. Convicted rapist and burglar in three states. I came across his name first on Mary Ryan's murder. Acts dumb, kills smart. I like him for the murders, but no one's paid me much attention. They will, though, when I nail the sucker."

"What's the connection to this case?"

"Jimmy, a buddy of mine on the force, says someone matching NeVille's description was made at the hotel just hours before Rubin kicked. But the connection goes way back. Ryan arrested him on the first rape. This was back in 'seventy-five. NeVille was seventeen, a bum camped out in Berkeley, getting stoned and messing with chicks from the university who found his po' boy history oh-so-romantic. The pinko liberal ass judge let the scum go with little more than a kick in the butt. Problem then was the same one we have now... no sperm, no pubic hairs, not a single goddamn forensic trace. Ryan went crackers. Turns out NeVille and his little girl Shawn were born two days apart. Made the man crazy to think his daughter died, but this bastard got to live. The two of us got him down in an alley, gave him a private lesson in law. He was still living in flophouses down on Mission when Mary was killed. Started roaming 'cross state the next week."

The thought of Ryan as a vigilante disturbed me. The guy I've come to know plays by the rules.

Sweeney must've read my mind. "Ryan was booze blind when we jumped the kid, case you're wond'ring."

"Why'd NeVille wait nine years to get revenge?"

"Who said he waited? I think opportunity just knocked him in the face. The place he was crashing in back in 'eighty-four was a stone's throw from the Pink Clam. Knowing Mary, she might've seen the kid and swept him under her wing. You know, giving him money, bringing him food. I figure somehow NeVille found out she was Ryan's wife. Coincidence can be mighty cruel, sometimes."

"How does he link to the other murders?"

"I found a strong *link* in your own backyard, darlin'. Betty Galonardi, the *I*-talian woman." I remembered the case. Betty was forty-seven when she was killed. A school teacher with no significant relationships outside work. "June thirteen, 'eighty-eight," Sweeney crooned on, then checked my expression. "You surprised I can remember the date, huh? I see it on your face. Well, let me remind you, I've been foxing this here trash since he took out my partner's wife. These murders are engraved in my mind. They found Betty with a hard-boiled egg stuffed in her mouth. Take a gander at the shot there."

The photo stung my eyes.

"Immediately, I thought of NeVille, so I started scouting the flophouses. Sure enough, the man was in town. Found out old Betty had been throwing him some odd jobs. Car washing, groceries, shit like that. I thought I really had him, but it weren't no turkey shoot. I trailed him back to the camp we're aiming for right now, but by then some Bronx psycho confessed to the murder and everyone assumed the case was signed, sealed and delivered to the D.A. Later on they found out the perp was freakin' nuts... he kept insisting he was fuckin' Jack the Ripper — the original, mind you. Asshole couldn't even pick a contemporary killer. Turned out the guy hadn't even been in New York City the night of Betty's murder. He was released a few weeks later, real quiet-like. All that time, no one bothered to talk to me or my man. Morons. Now, NeVille's either been real good or real careful since then, 'cause Betty was the last kill I heard about until now."

"Didn't Allen come later?" I tapped the stack of crime-scene photos.

"So you been paying attention? Good. You passed

test one. Now let's see how you handle the tough part."

He two-wheeled onto a dirt road. The trees closed in around us, scratched the side windows. Deep shadows covered the road. I shivered again, despite the heat. "How can you be so sure he's here?"

"Like I said, this ain't my first visit. One thing I know about NeVille is no matter where he roams, he always ends up back home. In that way, the son of a bitch ain't much different from me. Better hold on, it gets bumpy 'round 'bout here."

As if to punctuate his words, the car heaved in and out of a ditch, then collided into a thick mound of underbrush.

"Rock and roll," he muttered, utterly absorbed in sailing through the obstacle course. Mosquitoes and gnats buzzed around my ears. I rolled up my window. "There she be." He stopped short, in the middle of nowhere.

Almost instantly, the car started to smell mossy. I glanced around. We were surrounded by massive oaks. The filtered sun tinted the air green. "Where the hell are we?"

"Hell is right. Step on outside." He pushed the car door open against a thorny bush, then scampered onto the hood and leapt off. Stretching his arms wide, he smiled at me.

My heart thudded. What did I really know about this man? How could I be sure he was even who he purported to be? I thought about the man following K.T., the room service I hadn't ordered. Suddenly, I felt like a fool. I was in the backwoods of Louisiana, without a weapon and without information.

"C'mon sweetheart. The bayou's calling." He sucked air in through his teeth and winked.

The crime-scene photos still rested in my lap. I flipped through them in disgust, then shoved them back into the glove compartment. Without movement, the car had grown oppressively hot. My hands, however, remained stone-cold. I took a deep breath and stepped outside. Instantly my sneakers plunged into brackish mud. A tree limb slapped my neck. I elbowed my way around the corner.

When I reached the front fender, Sweeney hooted. "The Northerner's in her element. Ha. C'mon. We're just getting started."

He disappeared into the thicket with the purposeful gait of a bear tracking salmon. I cursed and followed him. Sweat beaded up on my brow and trailed down to the corners of my lips. Insects swarmed around my head. I hesitated for an instant, considered heading back to the car. There was no way to tell how long Sweeney would be gone. I glanced down at my watch. Humidity had fogged the face. I wiped it clean and cringed. It was way past three. K.T. would worry about me when she didn't find me at the hotel. I should've left her a note. For both our sakes.

I followed Sweeney more by sound than by sight. Branches cracked. Mud sucked around our heels. Birds flitted from the bushes with each step forward.

Suddenly, Sweeney shouted, "Did I mention New Orleans got over half-a-million 'gators. Biggest concentration in the country. Once saw a ten-footer swallow a Doberman whole."

The son of a bitch was having fun. I picked up my pace. In another minute or so, we emerged on the banks of a river. A corroded rowboat lay on its side. He trudged over and stroked the rim as if it were a cat stretched out in the sun.

"The Pearl River yacht."

"How'd you know that was here?" I asked.

He stalked over. "What's wrong, missy? You feeling peculiar?"

"Just answer my question."

A hand shot inside his vest. Too late I noticed the shoulder harness and the blue-black hammer of a forty-five. I swung away as he slapped thick fingers around my wrist.

"My identification." He flipped a billfold under my chin. "Theobald Sweeney, licensed private investigator in four states, a current California driver's license. Photograph of me with Ryan and his mom. Want more?" His ugly puss was so close I could smell his aftershave and the perspiration glistening at the base of his neck.

I stepped back. "You still haven't explained the boat."

"It's my cousin's. And without it, we can't get to the perp. You in or out?" His back was to me now as he turned over the boat and eased one end down the bank. The oars slid into place. I uttered a silent prayer and stepped in.

We pushed into the current, slicing through a rich, moss-green carpet. I gingerly dipped a finger into the water.

"Duckweed," Sweeney said. "It covers a good portion of fresh-water swamp. Now hush. We don't want to scare him up until we're ready." Out in the middle of the river all shade disappeared. The sun scorched my scalp. I dug a baseball cap out of my backpack and slipped it on. Squatting opposite me, Sweeney shook his head. "No rainbows here."

I scrunched my eyes at him, puzzled by the reference.

"Ryan told me you were a dyke," he continued. "Never married. That's fine with me, better'n lezzies who break their husband's heart and shrivel their organs by eating a neighbor's puss. But out here, you better be straight and narrow, so take the damn cap off."

I checked the hat. Sure enough it was from a gay march. I tucked it back in the bag and briefly considering kicking Sweeney into the murky water.

"Here, try this." He dropped one oar and retrieved a classic red bandanna from his back pocket. "Tie it on like a scarf."

I complied, knowing I'd look like an idiot. At least my head stopped frying. Since Sweeney was occupied with rowing, I leaned back and took in the view. The river was silent, except for the splash and squeak of oars. Along the banks, grayish green Spanish moss dangled from massive oaks in threadlike streamers. The moss reminded me of massive dried herbs, as if we were gliding by the Green Giant's private apothecary. I felt transported back in time, adrift in a foreign world. To have sacrificed an afternoon with K.T. for this was pure insanity. Why was it so important for me to prove myself to Ryan, I wondered.

"The moss is epiphyte," Sweeney said quietly. "It's kinda like a parasite, don't need soil, just feeds off another plant. An agricultural bloodsucker." Sweat splashed from the tip of his nose. His tone unnerved me. "My great-grandparents used to use it in bedding, mattresses and shit. That's where people got the expression, 'Don't let the bed bugs bite.' Of course, they did." He made a chomping noise.

My body tensed. "You're just a fountain of information."

The oar creaked against the rings. We took a hard right and sliced into a narrow canal. A breeze kicked in as we cut back into the shadows. The swamp we'd entered was pierced by Cypress knees, angular stumps with tips the color of newly minted pennies. They reminded me of the trolls my friend John collects, plaster-cast statues of big-nosed imps with mad, gleaming eyes. The water seemed to pulse around them.

Sweeney paused to survey the landscape. I couldn't figure out how the hell he knew where we were. Three-hundred and sixty degrees of indistinguishable swampland surrounded us. My end of the boat caught a sudden eddy and crashed into a tree with coarse gray bark and a swollen buttress. I felt as if I'd been dumped in a Grimm's fairy tale. All that was missing was the evil witch. My focus snapped back to Sweeney as he braced an oar against a stump and slewed the boat around. Maybe the nightmare was complete after all. If he'd offered me a glistening apple right then, I swear I would've leapt overboard and taken my chances with the alligators.

"How far is this place?" I asked nervously.

Sweeney shushed me. He'd begun rowing in slow motion. The oars made less than a hiss as they sank into the still, black water. Lily pads bobbed in our wake. We drifted into another tight channel, sunlight reduced to a dim green haze. Big flopping leaves, the shape of elephant ears, slapped the sides of the boat. Sweeney's hair piece was dotted with dusty sprigs of wild rice, which grew along the edge of the bayou on tall, lacy stalks.

A rumble sounded nearby, followed swiftly by the sound of someone running toward us. In an instant Sweeney had exchanged an oar for his handgun. I dove for cover and stayed there until I heard him chuckle. He said, "Boar," and tapped me on the back of my head.

I followed the grunting noise to where the wild boar stood. The creature snorted and stamped at us as we sailed deeper into the bayou. "Okay, Sweeney, enough is enough. Where are we going?"

"If you'd shut up and pay attention, you'd know exactly where I'm headed."

He had to be joking. As far as I could tell, we were doing crazy eights, weaving in and out of claustrophobic canals and deranged swamps, scuttling along dank marshes. There hadn't been a single sign of human habitation for miles. I took off the bandanna and used it to wipe the sweat from my upper lip. It smelled of tobacco. Strange. I hadn't noticed that earlier. I sniffed again. No. The bandanna didn't smell like tobacco. Someone was smoking and it wasn't me or Sweeney. I stared into the brush ahead of us. Gradually my eyes made out the lines of a shack.

The canal curved and then opened up again. Sweeney made the boat yaw and we scraped up onto the bank. In a whisper, he said, "The rest is on foot. Watch for sinkholes, gators, snakes. And this time I'm not shitting you. When we get there, keep your mouth shut. You're an observer, period. Open your mouth and my protection won't mean crap." He took the safety off on his gun. My lips trembled. I took a deep breath, steadied myself and followed him in.

Again, he disappeared almost immediately. I crossed my arms in front of my face and barreled into vegetation that stood a good seven feet high. At one point I sank up to my knees in water that smelled only slightly better than sewage. I almost called Sweeney's name out loud. Damn him for leaving me behind. The foliage overhead eclipsed the sun, making it impossible for me to find my bearings. Panic crawled over me like a parade of spiders. I squatted and bit my bottom lip. I could hear things moving in the grass. A mosquito the size of a cat took a nip from my wrist. I swatted it and watched my blood ooze from its body.

How far was I from the shack? Then it struck me. Follow the smell of tobacco. I sniffed my way back through the reeds, then edged along the bayou. Finally I saw Sweeney's silhouette. He had his gun drawn and aimed at the head of a man I assumed to be Barry NeVille. I crab-walked toward him, then stopped short. Between us lay a rivulet and an alligator about the length of a double bed. The snout was broad and flat and lucky for me, its eyes were closed. I started to retreat, stepped on a snake and screamed. Fay Wray in the arms of King Kong. I knew I'd blown it even before I heard the gunshot.

Sweeney shouted, "Roll left," but no one had to instruct me on how to avoid the gator's gaping jaws. I charged through the reeds. My lungs were still in sad shape from the recent bout of pneumonia, but I went at full sprint. Just as I started to wheeze, I heard feet pounding right behind me. I kept running. With effort, I stayed close to the canal, praying I'd stumble onto the rowboat. Glancing down, I realized my arms were drenched in blood.

I stopped and leaned against a tree, dizzy from exertion and fear. Had I been shot? Everywhere I looked I saw blood.

Sweeney hollered to me, "For crissakes, stay where you are."

I slumped down and waited to be found.

## Chapter 4

"Sawgrass got you bad."

I winced as Sweeney daubed a wet rag against my arm. We were in NeVille's shack and Tom Ryan's brusque ex-partner was ministering to the deep cuts on my arms, neck, hands and ankles with the gentleness and skill of a sixty-five-year-old nurse. I don't know how he'd managed it, but somehow he had clamped handcuffs on NeVille, shot the alligator and tracked me down all within the span of fifteen, maybe twenty minutes. The guy was a creep, but Ryan was right. He was amazing in the field.

"Lucky for you, NeVille's well equipped." He slapped on a seventh bandage and stood up. "Ready for the inquisition?"

I gulped Gatorade from a mud-caked bottle and followed him outside. The shack was built from corrugated steel, old tires, beer cans and Coke bottles. A section torn from a Marlboro billboard served as the floor. The cigarette I was walking on was four-feet long. Out front, he'd strung Christmas lights, Chinese lanterns and fishing nets. Bizarre animal traps dangled from a fender tied to the roof with climbing rope. I'd never seen anything like it in my life. On the other hand, I'd seen hundreds of men just like NeVille, but never in settings like this. He was square-jawed, clean-shaven, with eyes the color of stormy summer skies and dark curly hair. A regular boy next door. Right then, Sweet Face was cuffed to a cane rocker.

"Why don't you go first, Miller?" Sweeney asked without turning around. He squatted in front of NeVille and braced his hands on his thighs. "I'll just watch the boy squirm."

I had no idea where to begin. The two men turned their attention to me. After a short century or two, I asked, "How long have you lived out here?" The question was lame and the gleam in Sweeney's eyes announced amusement.

NeVille glanced at Sweeney, apparently waiting for a cue.

"Go ahead, boy," Sweeney said, rubbing his damn brass medal with satisfaction.

"Most my life, I s'pose," he said, finally. The man's voice shocked me. His speech was halting, almost slurred. I shot a silent query at Sweeney. He closed his eyes and shook his head, dismissing my hesitation. NeVille tugged on his bottom lip and said, "You need a doseta Salapatekie."

I cocked my head at Sweeney, who blurted, "Cut the crap, Barry."

"Where were you last night?" My heart wasn't in the question. Something was wrong here.

NeVille bit the inside of his cheek. "Outta the river. Gets so quiet 'times jere, I hears Coke fizzing in my mout'. Las' night, it was like I caught ahold of a 'squeeter."

Sweeney stood up, blocked my view of NeVille. In an exaggerated accent, he said, "You pushin' fire in the quarta last night, boy?"

"No fire, no way. What you got your neck poked out fuh? You wan my swimp, dat it?" He nudged a bucket of squirming gray creatures. "Swimper caught six-tousand in one drag on Lake Pont, who gonna miss one buck?"

If my heart hadn't been pumping so hard, I might've laughed. NeVille thought we were after him for stealing shrimp. We weren't barking up the wrong tree, we were kicking a potted fern. I'd had enough. "Take off the cuffs, Sweeney. This can't be our guy."

"You falling for his con? Maybe you should go back to your suite at the Royal Orleans and order yourself some sweet nothings. Sweet Jesus, you're dumber than I thought. This is a fuckin' act." He kicked the leg of the chair in which NeVille sat. The man barely reacted.

"Well, then, he's damn convincing. Let him go."

"This your idea of an inquisition?" Sweeney asked, pounding NeVille's back with his fist.

"I didn't count on an *inquisition*," I almost

shouted. He raised his hand again and I caught it with my own. "Are you nuts? Leave him alone!"

"Oh, you think he's worth pissing me off for? Fine, lady." He shook me off roughly and leaned into NeVille's shoulder. "Boy, you wanna touch some sweet titty? Whatcha say? See how ripe?"

I exhaled sharply. What the hell was he up to now?

"You can touch titty, maybe cuff some snatch. Just tell me what I wanna know."

NeVille's eyes locked on my breast. The hunger was unmistakable. I felt naked and pissed off at Sweeney for exposing me to this.

"You tree that pretty girl last night?" He drove on. "Now I don't want no *menterie*."

"I ain't done nut'in," NeVille whined. "Come see, *chère*." He was talking to me now. I stepped closer, then noticed he was gesturing at his lap. He had an erection.

"Aw, shit, Sweeney." I turned around. The key clanged against the handcuff. Son of a bitch. I spun on my heel. Sure enough, NeVille was up and stalking toward me. I stared in disbelief as Sweeney casually pocketed the cuffs. Backing up, I said, "Barry, you can go inside now," as if I were talking to a twelve-year-old. But he was no miscreant teenager. In a long-legged stride, he caught up and latched onto my breasts. I struggled to pull him off, one finger at a time. I bent one so far back, I heard it crack and still he held on. "Sweeney!"

"Boy's faster than I thought. Let her go, boy. I promised one squeeze, that all. And I ain't heard you bark."

NeVille didn't even appear to hear Sweeney. He

grunted and bumped his penis against my thigh, his eyes rolling back in his head. "I'm gonna wild crazy," he said, slobbering at my neck. "Big I and little you." He started to unzip.

Suddenly, Sweeney was behind him. The pistol whipped across his ears and he went down.

"Bastard doesn't know how to keep a deal," he said, smiling at me.

"Are you crazy?" I sputtered.

Stepping over NeVille's limp body, he blurted, "Listen up, your job here was silent partner. Silent. Not a fuckin' screamer. Look over there..." He shoved me toward the front door. "See that whiskey barrel. Now, what's that sticking out?" He answered his own question by storming over, lifting out a sawed-off shotgun and waving it at me. "Idiot could've blown my head off while you were shouting over a stone-still gator. So I figured you owed me. If you'd've been on the force, you'd understand what it means to be a decoy."

I shook my head, stunned. Sweeney was pissed at *me*. I leaned down and felt for NeVille's pulse. It was rock steady. I lifted his head slightly and rested it on my backpack. The pistol had left a welt on the back of his head, but hadn't done much physical damage. His groan was reassuring. At least, I wouldn't be an accessory to murder.

Sweeney snorted at me. "While you worry about the scumbag, I'm gonna ransack his camp."

As soon as he was inside, I collapsed on the rocker. I must've been insane to get into this, I thought. I closed my eyes and thought of K.T., how wonderful last... Oh shit. I checked my watch. It was close to six. She'd be gone by the time I got back to town. If I got back. I heard furniture being thrown, plates crashing.

"Nothing in there," Sweeney announced when he emerged. "Let's get going."

"What about him?" I pointed at NeVille. His eyelids fluttered, then grew still again. Sweeney dug his hands into NeVille's armpits and dragged him inside. I retrieved my backpack and checked for bloodstains. There were plenty, though I figured most of them were mine.

The door slammed. Sweeney said, "Done," and grabbed the shotgun from the whiskey barrel. "Let's move. We don't want to be trying to find our way out of the bayou in the dark."

He didn't have to ask twice.

Sweeney poled off using the shotgun. The rowboat slipped back into the canal with a hiss, then he dropped the gun between us and picked up the oars. His biceps bulged as he tugged us through thick, gnarled reeds. I swatted a bug off my shirt and palpated my forearm, avoiding eye contact with Sweeney. On top of the scrapes, my skin was hot from a mass of insect bites.

When we made it out of the canal and into the river, Sweeney leaned forward, lifted the gun and speared into the water. The splash sounded explosive in the still air. Minutes later, alligators started to surface. They raised their eyes above the water-line like tiny periscopes. I kept my hands crossed carefully in my lap.

All of a sudden, Sweeney started to chatter as if we'd just concluded a fine brunch with close friends. "Beautiful, isn't it? Nothing like early evening in the bayou. See that over there? That's resurrection fern, the stuff dies off and if you didn't know better, you'd think that's it, rip the dead crap out, but just one rain and it revives like Jesus himself. And then there's rain trees. Don't see them in the swamp, but man, you ain't got nothing like it in the North. The flowers are gold, then pink, then red and when they drop, it feels like rain or spit, maybe." He laughed.

I cut him off. "Can we talk?"

"That's what we're doing."

"About what happened. NeVille doesn't seem capable of these murders."

"*Seem* is the operative word. Look, doll, I've seen him in his real colors. Sane, articulate and fit for murder. This was his game-self. Ryan told you to trust me, right? You think he'd let some crackpot be the prime investigator in his wife's murder?"

I'd been asking myself the same question. My fists clenched. "Do you have other suspects?"

He hesitated. I watched the way he slapped the oar against the water. I'd hit a nerve. "You want the truth?" he said at last. "If it ain't NeVille, then I gotta believe Tommy's pissing up a tree with no prey."

We were gliding with the current now. I rubbed my arms for warmth and waited for Sweeney to continue. Something was troubling him. "Tell you what," he said. "Meet me tonight at Dock of the Bay, it's way out on Bourbon, edge of the Quarter. You come by, and I'll show you the complete files. Not just the shock shots. You'll see for yourself. Take out NeVille and the train don't ride."

The last thing I wanted to do was spend more time with this jerk. Yet now that I'd come this far, I wanted to see Sweeney's notes. All these years, I assumed Ryan had kept me and Tony away from the investigation because he already had the best person on the case. But clearly, Ryan's elite investigator was anything but elite. I didn't trust him. I wasn't ready to leave this case in the hands of an incompetent, not when there was still a slim chance I could help Ryan finally close his wife's murder. There had to be another link besides NeVille. I agreed reluctantly to a ten o'clock meeting.

We continued on in silence. Pearl River was transformed by the setting sun. A great blue heron took flight in our wake. Deer rambled along the shore. I took a deep breath. I wanted to get back to K.T. and the real world. The thought made me remember the beeper I'd shut off earlier. My hand groped for it, but it was gone. Great.

"Miller."

I didn't respond, hoping he'd get the hint and shut up. He didn't.

"Look," he said, "about what I did back there... it was dead wrong. I kinda, well, there was a situation... Hell." He lifted his shirt and I braced for an attack. "See that." When I didn't move, he said, "Shit," and handed me his handgun, aiming the barrel at his belly. "Now, lean in here."

I did. He was showing me yet another scar, this one just below his ribs. It looked like a hieroglyphic of a snowflake.

"After Mary's death, Ryan and me got separated. The lieu felt I'd been interfering too much with their investigation. My new partner was a young gal. To make a long story short, she screwed up and I got nailed. What happened back there just triggered some bad shit for me. Sorry."

"Sure. Forget about it." Both of us knew my heart wasn't in my words, but it sufficed to bring about a truce.

We pulled up to the Royal Orleans at twenty minutes after seven. I hopped out and waved Sweeney off. The doormen hesitated as I limped into the elegant lobby. The knights in armor that graced the top of the staircase seemed to rise up in shock as I strode by, dead set on catching the elevator.

K.T. hadn't even left me a note. For an instant, I considered running straight to the restaurant. Then I got a good glimpse of myself in the mirror. I looked like an escapee from a grade-B movie. I stripped, removed my bandages and headed for the shower. The water stung my cuts, yet it felt good. I shifted the shower head so the pounding focused on my shoulders, then I closed my eyes. The murder photos flashed back. I shook my head and soaped up. My breasts were bruised. I stared at them, reliving the horror I'd felt when Sweeney had sicced NeVille on me. Maybe K.T. was right. Maybe it was time for me to get out of the business.

Soap worked its way into my eyes. I raised my face to the water, then quickly cupped the showerhead with my hand. I'd heard a sound in the other room. Shit. I blinked hard, the soap still burning. Cursing Hitchcock for a lifetime of *Psycho* redux, I tore a towel from the steel rack on the other end of bath enclosure.

K.T.'s voice came as a relief. For about five seconds. "What the hell is all this blood?" she shouted through the door. She must have seen my clothes and backpack. I peeked out as the bathroom door slammed open. "Are you okay?" she demanded.

Her skin was flushed. The veins in her neck pulsed visibly. I could tell that her emotions were swinging wildly from fury to fear to relief.

"I'm sorry, baby." I reached out a hand. "I wanted to call you, I really did, but things got... rough."

"Oh, damn you." She covered her eyes and shook her head. For a moment, I thought she was about to retreat, then she burst out, "You bastard! I can't lose you again, don't you know that? Damn." All of a sudden she was crying.

"Aw, K.T." I pushed aside the shower curtain, but before I could step out, she was inside with me, fully clothed.

"Damn you, damn you," she cried, pounding my shoulder with her fist.

My lips burrowed into her hair. "I'm sorry," I whispered. When her sobs had quieted, I murmured into her ear, "You do know you're supposed to be naked, don't you?"

Hands slapped my clavicle. She cursed me again. Meanwhile, I started stripping her, tossing the sopping clothes over the curtain rod. A twinkle returned to her eyes and all at once it was my turn to cry. We stood there, clinging to each other like estranged lovers united after too many years. Had only a few hours passed since we held each other like this? My mouth found hers and my kiss demanded response. K.T. pressed against me, her flesh at last exposed and against me. I clasped her waist, her buttocks, yet no matter how firmly I pulled her to me, my body needed more. I sank to my knees, her swollen belly pillowing my head. She eased back, lowering my head, gently tugging my hair. My tongue found her, drank her in. The quickening of her breath transported me. The world collapsed around us and all that mattered were my hands, her smell, the water pouring over us, her sounds, the pounding of her pulse against my mouth. Later we both sank into the tub, rocking against each other, calling each other's names over and over, an incantation.

After we had wrung out K.T.'s clothes and strung them on the dryer line, while we were toweling off, I noticed K.T.'s eyes shift to the bruises on my breasts. With a lift of her eyebrows she asked me if she'd caused them. I reassured her, then reluctantly told her about the day. She shook her head and walked out.

"If you want me to drop this, I will," I said, surprising myself.

She looked quizzically at me. "You can't be serious."

"I am." She watched me apply the fresh bandages.

"Oh great." She threw her arms up. "So now what do I do? Tell you to give up your work, let some other idiot try to save unknown lives, or just say, fine darling, go get yourself killed, I'm so proud."

"Those aren't the only choices, K.T."

The key to the mini-fridge stuck. K.T. bumped me out of the way and opened it with a flick of the wrist, then grabbed a carton of milk. She tore the container open from the wrong end.

I patted down the bandage, then reached over and grabbed another Yoo-Hoo, though the temptation to guzzle something stronger crossed my mind. New Orleans does that to me.

Apparently, K.T. considered the same thing. She

said, "God, what I wouldn't do for a beer," and grimaced as the milk went down. "Okay, Rob, tell me what you want me to do."

"I'm not sure. This morning, you made a crack about me making up for murdering my sister."

"It was a stupid, mean —"

"Yeah, it was, but you were right. It doesn't matter if I was a kid. Or maybe it's worse, 'cause every second of her death is hardwired into my brain. Every sound, every scent, every drop of blood. She haunts me and the only thing that's helped me make peace is this damn job. Is that really so horrible?"

"The thought of something happening to you is what I find horrible. Can't you at least take this time off, while we're here? I promise to spend more time with you than I have so far. Winnie will have to understand."

The plaintive tone made me ache. I reached for her, but she wasn't ready to be held again, not unless she got what she wanted from me, what I wanted to give but couldn't. "I wish it was that easy, K.T., I do. But this isn't just any murder. Rubin's killing is connected to Mary Ryan's murder."

Her head whipped in my direction, fear exploding in her eyes. "The man Tony calls the eggshell maniac? That one? Oh, Christ, I can't take this." I watched her flutter nervously around the room, stuffing her bag until it looked ready to pop.

"K.T., I'm playing back-up on this investigation. Theo Sweeney is the one with all the exposure."

Her eyes flared. She flung a finger in the direction of my bandages. "Yes, I can see that."

"I don't want to let Ryan down —"

"Hey, we both missed out on having fathers —"

"K.T. —" The warning in my voice made her jaw muscles jump. We stared at each other for at least ten full seconds before she broke off eye contact.

"Okay, okay. Enough." She flung her bag on the floor. "So do it. Investigate away." She fell back on the bed and kicked off her shoes. "Look, Robin, I'm really wiped. We'll talk more later, but right now I need to crash. I told Winnie earlier that I'd stick it out to closing tomorrow, but tonight I need to sleep. I was kind of hoping we could spend the time together. Guess I was wrong."

The guilt alarm pinged. "I'll get back as fast as I can," I said. "Believe me, Sweeney is not my idea of a fun night on the town." I pulled out a pair of black jeans and a black cut-sleeve T-shirt. Preparation for a butch night. When I was fully dressed, I plopped down next to her on the bed. "Honey, if you don't want me to go, I won't. Just say the word."

She rolled her eyes. "Oh, no, I am *not* falling into that trap. It's your call, Rob. If you need to do this, then go ahead. If you want to stay here with me, believe me, you are more than welcome."

"You're not making this easy."

"I don't intend to."

I should've stopped right there, crawled next to her and swept her into my arms. If I'd known what was coming, nothing could've driven me from her side. Instead, I said, "Well, if I do decide to go, you'll be okay, right? I mean, we'll be okay?"

"We're great, Robin," she said, a little coldly. She must have seen me bristle because she added quickly, "Hon, I'm not trying to be difficult. Earlier tonight, I talked to Winston about our fight. He's the one who insisted I come back here. As far as I was concerned, if you didn't care enough about me to be where you were supposed to be, when you were supposed to be, you weren't worth my worry. Of course, worry may have been the reason my crème brûlée was more brûlée than crème. Honestly, Rob, when you get involved in a case —" With a karate chop to the air, she cut off her words. "I promised myself not to do that. What I was going to say was that Winnie gave me one of his twelve-step lectures. At first, I wanted to toss a pound of flour at him, but after a while, he made sense. I can't control what you do, all I can do is tell you how I feel. I hate your job. I hate watching you get hurt. But I'm not going anywhere."

"You're too damned healthy."

"Tell me that when Babboo's not making me feel so sick." She edged back onto the bed. "My damn feet are swollen."

"Guess it's my turn for caretaking." I fluffed a pillow behind her, removed her socks and rubbed her feet. "By the way, the Eggs Sardou was great."

She blinked at me. "You had Eggs Sardou in the bayou?"

"No, silly, from room service. Remember?" One of the things I've learned about pregnancy is that it wreaks havoc on the memory bank. "You ordered the eggs after you left. Anything coming back yet?"

She looked me full in the face. "Honey, I was so angry this morning, the last thing I would've done was order you some fancy-ass brunch."

I averted my gaze, but it was too late.

"What is it?" she asked, although I could tell she knew exactly what I was thinking. "Couldn't it be a simple mistake?"

"Whoever ordered the meal gave this room number and my name."

"So what. How many hotels have you stayed in? Are you saying it can't be a screwup?"

Shimmying up next to her, I asked, "When you talked to the victim —"

"You mean Lisa Rubin?" she corrected me, her eyes flashing.

"Yes, Lisa. Did you notice who was standing nearby?"

"Are you joking? It was our opening night. Winston and I did the calculations today. We topped two-hundred-fifty customers by nine o'clock. We were surrounded by people."

"But you remember Lisa?" A unexpected twinge of jealousy snuck in.

"Yes. We talked for twenty minutes or so. She was there with a friend, a local food critic. Dreyer Carr. A chubby man in his forties. Gay as they come. She told me about her husband's death and said she couldn't believe he'd left her as executor. The break-up was pretty bad, I gathered."

"You guys got personal real fast. Impressive."

She picked up on my tone and flared her nostrils at me. "Okay, Robin. She was a little drunk and, well, I guess maybe she *was* trying to impress me."

"Why would she do that?"

A flutter of eyelashes came in response.

"Rubin was gay?"

"Bisexual."

"And she hit on you?"

"Robin, remember she was murdered last night? I think your interrogation is going off course."

I wiped my nose like a boxer. Off course, my ass. "Fine, fine." Aw, shoot. My mouth wouldn't stop. "You're telling me that during the thirty minutes or so when the two of us weren't hip-to-hip in that overgrown playground you call a restaurant, you decided to cruise?"

"Oh Lawd. From distance to domination in one run-on sentence. Honey, I needed *air*. She just happened to be outside smoking."

"Who started the conversation?"

"I did. Winston had pointed Dreyer out to me earlier. I was hardly pleased to see one of the town's better-known food critics *outside* the restaurant." She noticed my quick smile. "Baby all better now?" She lifted my hand and kissed the palm.

"Do you have his phone number?"

She stared at me, wide-eyed. "Now?"

"Please."

K.T. rolled off the side of the bed, rummaged through her purse and withdrew a business card. Her movements were stiff and exaggerated. I took the card with one hand and leaned in for a kiss. My lips found air.

"You better get going, Robin."

I glanced at my watch. "Guess you're right."

We stared at each other like gunfighters waiting for the first draw.

K.T. said, "You look like a cast member for *West Side Story*, or maybe *Grease*." Her index finger flexed. I grabbed it with mine.

"Then I must be ready to rumble." This time, I landed the kiss and said, "Love you."

"And I love you, too, Robin. So much it scares me." K.T. stared at me with her doe eyes.

I knew what she meant, but couldn't admit it right then. The show had to go on. And vulnerability was not in the script. "Get some sleep." I smooched her palm, winked and sauntered out.

As soon as I exited the lobby, the heat smacked me in the face, followed by a swarm of flying termites. I batted them off and headed up to Bourbon Street.

New Orleans ran in reverse time. At ten, the town was just starting to stretch its limbs. Strolling along the main drag was like listening to a schizophrenic spin the dial on a too-loud radio. Music crashed out of bars and restaurants in tidal waves of blues, zydeco and rock. The air stank of stale whiskey and overly sweet frozen drinks, which spilled over as drunken conventioneers weaved down Bourbon. Sticky puddles slushed under my feet as I bumped through a crowd of kids attempting some bizarre dance that consisted of severe jerking motions. I'd long ago decided that teenagers come to New Orleans to learn how to guzzle, walk and conjugate *fuck* at the same time.

The Dock of the Bay was at the far end of Bourbon, where the crowds thinned and turned rougher with every passing hour. Sweeney had once again taken me to the edge of my comfort zone.

The French doors of the bar were thrown open to the street and a line of red-vested waiters streamed outside, where they instantly strutted through a dance routine keyed into Otis Redding's classic hit. I was a full thirty minutes late. Trying to find Sweeney in the bar was a little less difficult than trying to retrieve a lost ring from the local junkyard. Bodies pressed together to form an impenetrable wall.

I elbowed my way through the front line and stopped cold. A bruiser of a man crashed by me, almost knocking me to my knees. I caught a glimpse of a tattoo on the back of his bristly scalp. Egghead. How appropriate.

"Take it easy, honey. Let's get you to a table. Hey, Bobby!" I was handed off from one prep school boy to another. Someone took a swipe at my derriere before it landed on a chair. What fun.

The pheromone level in the place was downright atomic. Men and women who couldn't get laid in any other state of the union had turned into sexual panthers in heat. The bar seethed with over-ripe heterosexuality. A few Midwestern John-Boys garbed in khakis and button-down shirts had stumbled on this hell-hole. They pumped their groins alongside emaciated women in their twenties, garbed in black leather, hair dyed Adams family black, noses pierced. Businessmen, drunk and horny, spat seductions at over-done colleagues with poofed hair. In less than five minutes, I counted five possible convention affairs. They seemed oblivious to the scowls the locals were throwing them.

I checked out the other end of the dance floor. A tall, paunchy guy with a striped Land's End shirt and pressed blue jeans grabbed his crotch like Michael Jackson and did a neck roll I'd only seen in the offices of chiropractors. His yowl reminded me of the sound my cats make at dinner time. Next to him was a peroxide blonde, clad in a too-tight devil-red dress with a plunging back. She licked her lips and started stripping another deranged businessman of his jacket and tie. I'd lay odds she was an elementary school teacher.

"Turns you on, doesn't it?"

I didn't bother answering. "How the hell did you find me in here?"

Sweeney rubbed his nose. "I caught your scent."

I sniffed my underarm. "Damn that deodorant."

He squeezed my knee. "Funny girl."

"Hands off, Sweeney."

"I understand your type tends to swing both ways."

"The only thing I'm likely to swing is my fist."

"True confessions. You ever been with a man?"

I scraped back my chair.

"Is that a no?"

"Why the cross examination, Sweeney?"

"I like to know what waters I'm swimming in."

"Still, deep and dangerous. I'd strongly suggest you keep your feet on soil."

"Ha. Firewater, pure firewater. Which reminds me . . ." He flagged down a waiter. "Whatcha drinking?"

"Dixie."

He placed the order and then slammed a briefcase on the table. "Down to business."

"Great place for it. Could you have picked someplace noisier?" I shouted into his left ear.

"Nope. This is it. Loud and ugly. You could kill someone in here and no one'd know it until broom time."

"Lovely thought." He wasn't wrong, though. The place smelled of sweat and rot. Papering the walls were dollar bills with names scrawled on them and yellowed business cards with lipstick prints. I noticed a roach crawling leisurely toward Sweeney. Dante's Inferno had nothing on the Dock of the Bay. I slid the files toward me.

"Start with the summary," Sweeney hollered.

I started by wiping his spit off my ear. Damn. He'd really nailed me. I stuck a hand in my back pocket. The tissue I expected to find there was gone. Instead my fingers closed on something hard.

"What you got there, Miller?"

My hand shook.

"Holy shit." His words, not mine.

I held it up to the candlelight. The enamel took on the color of ripe cantaloupe. Sure enough, the two of us were staring at a human tooth.

## Chapter 5

"Describe the guy that bumped you again."

"Damn it. I told you three times. Besides, it could've been one of the prep boys. Or anyone else, for that matter. These streets make New York look like Bedford Falls."

"But the tattoo. That can't be a coincidence."

"Oh, hell, Sweeney, *egghead* doesn't have to mean shit. Ninety percent of the jerks in this room qualify for that tattoo."

"You can't be this stupid. Come on, give me the tooth." He wiggled his fingers at me.

"And what do you plan to do with it?"

"Give it to my mama for Christmas. What do you think? I'll pass it on to the N.O.P.D. Maybe it's from Rubin. Better yet, maybe it's from one of the earlier victims. You too shook to read the files?"

I grunted no, flipped open the file folder and planted my elbows on the table. The bruiser who'd bumped me had skipped out at a pretty brisk pace. Sweeney thought the description matched a pal of NeVille's, though the tattoo detail didn't fit. I cupped my palms around my eyes. My heart was racing, but I wasn't about to let Sweeney know.

Reading the files didn't help. I spread out four photographs with handwritten Post-it notes stuck to the corners.

Eileen Anderson: 33 years old, Irish Catholic, certified social worker. Murdered in Cambridge, Massachusetts, on Friday, August 23, 1985.

Hope Williams: 22 years old, agnostic, African American, nursing student. Murdered in San Francisco, California, on Saturday, May 3, 1986.

Betty Galonardi: 47 years old, Italian Catholic, school teacher. Murdered in New York City on Sunday, June 12, 1988.

Andrea Allen: 59 years old, Christian right-to-lifer, housewife. Murdered in Chicago, Illinois, on Thursday, January 25, 1990.

All of the victims had been beaten and stabbed repeatedly.

"I left out Mary's photo and I don't have one of Rubin yet." Sweeney pushed a piece of paper toward me. "Now take a look at that. NeVille can be traced to each of those cities around the time of the murder, with one exception. The dyke in Massachusetts."

"Eileen Anderson was a lesbian?"

"Appears so. Why you interested? It somehow more important when a sister's killed?" His jaw muscle twitched.

"Sweeney, are we working together on this, or are you just getting kicks from plucking my nerves?"

"That's right. Fuck me. That's right." He laughed. "I'm used to working alone, so I can get mighty ornery. You keep me in place, girl. Ha." He was on his second scotch. I hoped I wouldn't be around when he got to three.

"Rubin may have been bisexual," I said.

"That so?" He started to make a comment, but I shot him a warning look. "The other vics were straight, so we don't got a pattern. Something wrong with your Dixie?"

"I'm just taking my time, which may not be a bad lead for you to follow."

"Hey, this here's my second drink. For a former alcoholic, this shit's like watered-down piss. Case you didn't notice, it was a bitch of a day."

Former alcoholic, my ass. I wondered if Ryan knew that Sweeney was drinking again. I fought off the temptation to knee him. "What's this page? I can't read your handwriting."

"Notes on some searches Ryan ran." He leaned over and pointed. "That's shorthand for the National Center for, what the hell is it? Oh yeah, the Analysis of Violent Crime. You know, the Quantico place, run by the FBI's Behavioral Sciences Unit, or BSU. This is VICAP —"

"The Violent Criminal Apprehension Program and Profiler."

A slap of boozy breath swept over me. "Ha. Nice. Show me your stuff. By the way, Ryan thinks the guy's escaping profiling the way Bundy did, who was far from a loser. You know about Bundy? He was a good student, dated women, had a good work history. Got away with murder for years. This guy may be smarter than Bundy. Look at these notes. The crimes differ in almost every aspect. No wonder the FBI won't even sneeze our way."

"You honestly think NeVille is smart enough to maneuver this."

"Fuck. Maybe not. I'm spinning. You know how many times I've run this crap? I read and read, interview some shit-heads, think I got something and it all falls apart. Then I come back to NeVille. Everything makes sense for about ten minutes. Look." He stabbed the notes. "He was in the right place at the right time when Mary bought it. He was back in town when Williams got it. A year later he moved to Chicago. Boom. Down goes Allen. Then he moves on to the Big Apple and the spinster gets blown. Now here we are with Rubin. Don't it stink to you?"

The coincidence was hard to explain. Or ignore. I downed the rest of my Dixie and signaled for another. Sleep was a long way off. Sweeney's files were all handwritten, with details Ryan had not shared with me earlier. None of it made sense. Once we really got down to business, Sweeney lost his antagonism and Louisiana swagger. There were times I felt as if we were trying to put together a single image from jigsaw pieces belonging to six discrete puzzles. The murdered women had differed in age, careers, lifestyles, religions, marital status, style of dress, hair, eye color and body types. Based on the crime scene photos, in some instances the killer's actions seemed consistent with the profile of an organized mind. In others, he had been clearly disorganized, once even leaving behind a very clear imprint made by a tennis shoe. In three of the six murders, items had been stolen from the victim, most notably their wedding rings. With the exception of Allen in Chicago, all had been sexually assaulted. Besides the proximity to hotels and discovery of eggshell remnants, the cases shared one other common thread. Bizarre, nonsensical artifacts had been found on or near the victims — a different one each time. A smoking pipe made from a tropical American tree called calabash, a new snake-skin wallet filled with packets of ground coffee, a bottle of pine needles and bark, a knotted red neckerchief and, the most strange, three slices of bull's testicles curled around ice in a glass masonry jar. At two in the morning, we both gave up.

"No wonder you're so ornery," I muttered as I slipped my notepad into my back pocket.

"Thanks for understanding. I gotta give you credit for hanging in. I haven't worked with a woman since San Francisco. You haven't been seeing my best side."

"You have one?"

"Give me time, hon. Believe me, it gets better.

C'mon, I'll walk you back to the hotel. You think I'm rough, wait until you see the element we got outside."

"I'll be fine." He leaned over and grabbed my hand. I said, "What?" impatiently and he squeezed hard.

"Listen to me. Ryan said you had good instincts. So far I ain't seen much to confirm that. Someone's watching you. Hard. Hard enough to follow your ass here. Maybe it's NeVille or one of his buddies, or maybe some criminal genius who's got us all tied up in his own sick game. All I know is that tooth's not from some goddamned good-natured fairy. I gotta think you just got a warning to stay out of this. Me, I got nothing to lose. But I don't think your hole's as black as mine."

"I'll watch my back. Don't worry."

I didn't like the way he laughed. "If we wasn't in public, I'd give you another show and tell. This one a knife cut across my back. Happened in Chicago when I was investigating Allen's death. I was taking a piss in a pub when the cut came. Next thing I know I wake up in Rush's emergency room. That time, only thing that saved me was an off-duty cop who'd beered up enough and needed to take a leak. Guy saw the perp's behind drop out the john window. Nothing more. That was my warning. I took it seriously, much as I take anything seriously these days."

"I'll sleep on it."

"Right." He shook his head and pulled out his wallet. The conversation had ended.

We paid up and staggered out. The air was still and heavy. Instantly, my body started to steam; sweat beads dripped from my chin. Between exhaustion, painkillers and more rounds of beer than I wanted to remember, my legs felt like Silly Putty.

"Whoa." I leaned on Sweeney for support and cursed myself instantly. He was a good detective but a pig nonetheless, and I wanted to avoid physical contact at all costs.

"Yeah, soon you'll be begging for it. Women."

"Ah, shit, Sweeney, you are predictable."

His laugh was good-natured for a change as he guided me into the surge of clammy human sludge outside the bar. We headed back toward the center of the Quarter. "Whatever you do," he said, "don't rat me out to Ryan. Confidentially, he told me he's got some strange paternal thing going with you. Only reason I was willing to bother with you. Though now, I gotta say, you're starting to intrigue me."

"Don't get too intrigued."

"I understand you got a lady friend with you. Pregnant, too. Now how'd you manage that?"

I jammed on the brakes. "The line gets drawn here, Sweeney. No teasing, no questions. My friend is off limits, you understand?"

We faced off in the middle of Bourbon Street. No one noticed. Why should they? Over Sweeney's shoulder, I noticed a male couple in a dimly lit alley. They appeared to be indulging in what looked like unsafe practices.

"So the female dick's in love. Huh." Sweeney had a peculiar facial expression, as if it struck him as odd that lesbians could actually be *in love*.

I sobered up real fast. "Go home, Sweeney. I'll take my chances with the other swine."

"Like I never heard that before."

He didn't follow me. I was relieved to be rid of

him, although I had no way of knowing how differently I'd feel in just a few hours. Maybe it was the time, or maybe the beers, but I was feeling pretty edgy. I was too tired to sleep and too wired to trust. At another time in my life, I would have headed for Oz, a sleezy gay bar, and picked up some trouble, but that option was long gone. I suppose I could've gone back to the hotel and woken up K.T., but I knew from experience that a pregnant woman is hard to rouse. Besides, I smelled like smoke and booze, a combination unlikely to enliven K.T.'s interest. Instead, I got myself some coffee, claimed a street corner and ogled the crowd. It took me a while to figure out why so many college-aged kids were pointing at me and giggling. I leaned back and looked up. A swing above my head carried a pair of shapely blow-up legs, complete with ruby-red high heels. The bar's name, Red Light Gals, and my posture made me wonder if I'd been tagged as a working girl. Not good. I changed locations immediately. That's when I saw Egghead.

He was with another man, shorter, sporting a crew cut. From the back, it looked like NeVille but I couldn't make a firm ID. They were sharing a one-liter bottle of cheap beer. Egghead glanced my way, appeared to make eye contact, then muttered something to his companion. An instant later, both men ambled into a side street. Now, I've done some stupid things in my life, but wandering after a suspected serial killer down a dark alley was not one I wanted to add to my repertoire. I figured I'd get to the corner and just watch where they went. Period. I've been wrong before.

I scrambled across the street, darted over to the

first doorway and stopped. I was less than twenty feet from Bourbon, but I could've been beamed straight to a bombed-out section of Beirut. Enter the twilight zone. The pounding music had transformed into a hard pulse that vibrated up my legs. The garish lights disappeared into thick, damp shadows. The swarming crowds evaporated. My breath was so loud, it filled my head. All the houses were boarded up, except one. A voodoo shop. Christ figures carved from wood, black candles, hand-made dolls, African fertility statues and buckling photographs of saints crowded the window display. There was no sign of Egghead or his buddy. No sound of footsteps. It took me sixty seconds to make a decision.

Chimes sounded as I opened the door to the shop. The place was ten by ten, no bigger. Other than me, the only occupant in the store was an elderly woman knitting with the intensity of a brain surgeon. One needle slipped to the floor and she fumbled trying to retrieve it. Clearly, her eyesight wasn't great. The needle had fallen right by her foot. I handed it to her, then pretended to check out a plaster Madonna draped in a shredded wool shawl. A dish of coins and dollar bills rested in her outstretched hand.

"You make an offering, she bring you good luck." The raspy, deep voice startled me. I turned around. The old woman pointed a long, knotted finger that appeared to be caked with clay. "Make an offering. The devils will stay away."

When she lifted her face toward me I saw that her eyes were opaque. Cataracts, probably. They could've been marbles.

"Maybe you want High John the Conqueror root?"
"I'm just looking."

"Yes," she said, nodding to herself. "You're bleeding." Again, the finger stretched.

I glanced down. A bandage on my hand had begun to weep. How the hell? I waved my hand at her. She didn't react. I made a face. Still no response. Then a frown, sharp and distinct, disfigured her face. "So much death," she rasped. "Don't point at a grave, your finger will rot. Please, ask the Madonna for sanctum." I headed for the exit. "The cost of disbelief so steep," she muttered as the door chirped behind me.

The street was empty. I took a deep swallow of the still, sultry air. Perspiration pooled under my arms, in the small of my back. I wiped my forehead with the back of my hand. My legs felt rubbery. Dehydration, I thought. The cost of too many beers and fierce humidity. It was time to go back to the hotel, shower, sleep, crawl into bed with my swelling girlfriend and abandon this nightmare. I took one step toward sanity when a shriek pierced the night. My head snapped to the right. Another howl, clearly female. This time it broke off suddenly, as if a hand had been clamped over someone's mouth. The shout appeared to have come from the opposite corner, away from Bourbon. I glanced toward the main drag. The drunken parade continued undisturbed. I swung the door open to the voodoo shop and shouted, "Call the police. Someone's being mugged down the block."

The old lady smiled and shook her head. "The damned Herriot place. Yes. Spirits are restless tonight. Old deaths. Old sorrows."

I cursed her superstitious mumbo-jumbo first and my rescue instincts second, then dashed up the block, breathless with fear. The screams had dissipated into a strange mewling, the heartbreaking cry of kittens suffocating in a paper bag. My heart was thumping hard and I'd broken out in a rolling sweat. Where the hell were the cries coming from? A woman's cry burst into the air, a shotgun pellet of sound that bounced off the buildings, clear for an excruciating instant: "Help me." Then silence.

I paused to catch my breath and sniffed. Smoke. The scent a match makes when it's blown out. I paced in frantic circles, scanning the buildings studded with wrought-iron that loomed around me, toothless grins on ancient, mocking faces. Suddenly my attention snapped to an abandoned structure at the far corner. A light flickered in the second-floor window. Nothing more. But it was enough.

I weighed my options. The only weapon I had with me was my knowledge of tae-kwon do. But retreat was not possible. I sprinted across the street and up a short flight of steps. The taste of stale beer percolated into my throat.

I swallowed hard, grimacing as I fingered the splintered plywood planks nailed across the entry. Someone had smashed through them, and judging from the sharp edges, the break-in had been too damn recent. Heat rushed across my cheeks. I pressed my hips between the planks and palmed the door. It swung open easily. In an instant, the stench of mildew swept over me. Yet the air stank of something else as well. It took a few seconds for the smell to register. Cloyingly sweet, the scent inflamed my sinuses. Incense. No doubt about it.

The darkness beyond the threshold was unrelenting. The first step was the hardest. Spider webs collapsed into my hair. I batted them out in a sudden panic. In the distance, a siren wailed. Good. Maybe the old lady had called the cops after all. I pulled back the door and wedged a piece of wood underneath. I wanted them to find me easily. Then I retraced my steps. Under my feet, the pine boards bowed and swayed. Through the gaping slats, I glimpsed water, black and glistening like oil, emitting a smell of sewage that made my stomach churn. Too late I realized I was about to vomit. I lurched toward the central staircase and heaved. So much for the element of surprise. My retching echoed through the building. I had to find cover fast. The building style was known as a five bay, with a central hall and rooms to either side. All the doors on this floor were planked over. I scurried away from the stairs, then yelped as my right foot crashed through the floor. A splinter the size of a cigarette protruded from my ankle. No time to remove it. Someone was coming down the stairs and coming fast. I hoisted my foot up from the hole and limped toward the front door. Suddenly, it slammed shut. I hadn't seen anyone move the wedge, hadn't heard anyone on this floor. None of that mattered compared to the sudden blindness I experienced. I spun around, my hands in front of me, waving wildly, searching for a wall, a door, a hint of direction. The footsteps had slowed, one careful thud after another on the stairs behind me. Each creak gave me hope. Maybe the staircase would collapse. I fell to my knees and crawled deeper into the shadows.

A clear, repulsive splat sounded. I glared at the staircase, but I couldn't make sense of the image. A silhouette of a man perhaps, but something was wrong. The figure was too wide in the middle. There was, oh God . . . he was holding a limp body in his arms.

I stood suddenly, ramming my forehead into a door knob. Shit. I threw my shoulders into the door with all my force and gasped as it disintegrated around me. Dark, wet air rushed toward me as I noticed dully that I was falling, my hands bracing for a floor that had disappeared a long time ago.

## Chapter 6

*Tuesday, May 4*

Water dripped on my forehead. One bead after another. It pooled and rolled into my eyes. I blinked, moved my head to one side and moaned. Where the hell was I? My hands closed on the sheets. K.T.? Wait. Not sheets, drop cloth. I rubbed my fingers over the rough, damp canvas. A warning bell went off in my head. This was not the Royal Orleans. My sense of smell kicked in and I jerked myself off the floor. Regret hit at the same exact moment as the nausea. I had moved too fast. Five minutes later, I was wiping my mouth and recapping my last conscious thought.

He had killed again.

So why was I still alive?

I scratched muck off the face of my watch and checked the time. It was five-forty. A pale lavender light slipped in from cracks in a distant wall. Dawn. In New Orleans, houses are typically built with a basement-like ground floor designed to withstand floods. This structure was no exception. I took in my surroundings. At some point someone had begun renovating this place. From the looks of it, the work had stopped suddenly. I was standing among a heap of drop cloths, mouse turds, mildewed plasterboard, rusted paint cans and, I noted with a smile, an ancient but usable ladder. My first piece of luck in twenty-four hours.

My next task was assessing the damage I'd done to my body. Things could've been worse. Several of the cuts I'd received in the bayou had begun to bleed. My left arm and shoulder seemed badly bruised. What really concerned me, though, was the sliver of wood piercing my ankle. Pus had already begun oozing from around the wood and the surrounding skin was hot to the touch. Gritting my teeth, I grabbed the edge of the splinter and, after counting to ten twice, yanked it out. Blood spurted from the wound. I found the cleanest corner of my T-shirt, ripped it off with my teeth, then tied it around the wound. A doctor visit had better be in my very near future.

I dragged the ladder over to where I'd fallen and raised it so that the top two rungs poked through the gap in the ceiling. I pounded it against the upper floorboards a few times, shielding my eyes from the dust and shards showering over me. Climbing the ladder was harder than I'd expected. Twice the ladder began to give way and I clung to the rungs as it clanged to a halt. When I reached the top, my body drenched in sweat, stinking of decay and mold, I broke into tears of relief.

I was resting about two or three feet from the door I'd crashed through. The frame appeared to be in good shape. I stretched out one arm, grabbed hold and hoisted myself past the threshold. The springy floor no longer bothered me. Resting my cheek on the pine planks, I drank in the sight of the door leading back out to the street. It was propped open, just as I'd done last night. The air rolling toward me seemed unbearably moist and clean. I took a deep breath, then choked. Wait. The door had slammed shut last night. I was sure of it. I rolled onto my backside and sat up. Dust motes swam in the filtered light.

I noted where my ankle had sunk through the floor and picked my way around it. The staircase seemed intact. Carefully, gingerly, I made my way up to the second-floor landing. Thick dust caked the railing and steps. No other footsteps were visible but my own. There were two open rooms, each with furniture draped in yellowed cloth. I spent a full twenty minutes investigating, but I found nothing. No bloodstains. No signs of a disturbance. Not even the candle I'd seen flickering from the street last night.

Enough. My leg was throbbing. I had to get to a doctor before the infection got worse. I hobbled downstairs and finally emerged onto Dauphine. No one was around. An image came back to me from a *Twilight Zone* episode I'd seen in which the sole survivor of a nuclear blast races desperately through an abandoned, lifeless city. I half-expected Rod Serling to narrate my lumbering trek back to Bourbon. A stray black cat batted a crushed can of Budweiser in my direction and I kicked it out of my way. The can, not the cat. If I'd had the strength, the cat would've come with me. I was that desperate for companionship.

The silence and heat made me dizzy. My lips were cracked and my hands shook. To anyone else's eyes, I probably looked like a junkie in need of a fix. The only fix I needed, however, was a taxi. There was no way I could make it back to the Royal Orleans on foot. I sat down on a curb. In the daylight, this end of the French Quarter looked even worse. The street was lined with bars, sex shops and dilapidated buildings that recalled New York tenements. There wasn't a single telephone booth. The most appealing sight was a Lucky Dog cart in the shape of a hot dog. On wheels. A smile flickered over my lips. Why the hell not, I muttered to myself. I shuffled over and tried to figure out if I could pick the chain lock. Sure, it was theft, but desperate times call for desperate measures. With a little ingenuity, the cart could serve as a mode of surrealistic transportation. I was rattling the chain, clearly on the brink of delirium, when someone slapped me hard on the butt.

"Hey, baby."

I spun around. By now, any human voice would've been a welcome shock. But this voice belonged to an elderly black woman with friendly eyes, the color of rich coffee beans. I practically cheered. "Hey, baby, back at you."

"I ain't been a baby since my mama died. Sadie's the name." She patted my hip. "Stand up straight, chile." The woman appeared to have cerebral palsy. Her words were slightly slurred, thick with a New Orleans accent. Her hands shook and her back twisted to one side. She flashed me a big smile. "Not of'n I meet someone who looks worse 'n me. Now whatcha doing with Jimmy's dog?"

I pointed at my bloody leg. "I needed a ride."

She laughed heartily. "Sho' thin', baby, but you ain't hijackin' Jimmy's dog. Lemme see dat. Whooee. Yo' ankle der looks to be K & B purple. Me, my skin always black and shiny sweet." Her laugh was full-hearted. "Where's ya goin', baby?"

Given the circumstances, I didn't think it wise to suggest the Royal Orleans. "I need a doctor."

"Any fool see dat, even me." She winked at me. "Oh, girl, you is in sweet luck. I got me a real peach. And he in love with Sadie, dat fer sure." She laughed at her own joke. "Whatcha call youself, pum'kin?"

I picked up on her playful tone. "It's a secret, but I'll share it with you —"

"Whoa, now, you ain't abou' to reveal yo basketname." It was a warning, not a question. "My momma did dat to the doctor wha delivered me, thas why I looks this way." She flared out her stained green-striped gabardine skirt and showed me her legs.

"Robin," I said quietly. "My name's Robin."

"Good t'ing. I don't wanna hear no basketname."

She hooked my arm around her neck and lurched forward with amazing strength. I didn't try to engage her in conversation. The effort of bracing me against her hip cost plenty. Her labored breath rattled in my ear.

"Let me walk a little," I said, but the first step I took without her landed me face down on the street. After my bout with pneumonia, the events of the previous day has apparently done more damage than I'd realized.

We made it to the doctor in twenty minutes. My first impression was to run and run fast. We were near Armstrong Park. For the last block or so, well-tended homes with brilliantly painted balustrades strung with gaudy Mardi Gras beads and massive ferns alternated with boarded-up buildings coated with layers of graffiti. The tourist trade hadn't so much as brushed past these streets and my white skin, the parts visible through the filth, marked me as an outsider.

Sadie sensed my anxiety and stroked my arm in a way that made me want to cry out loud. "You wit' me, baby girl. Dat all anyone wanna know." She struck the door three times and shouted her name.

After everything I'd been through, I was ready for anything. Ghosts, rattlesnakes, bleeding saints. At least I thought I was. What I wasn't ready for was the kind-faced gentleman in a starched white jacket and pleated slacks who opened the door. He took in my appearance with a quick, intelligent nod. The man topped six-three, had smooth chocolate-brown skin, snow-white hair and piercing green eyes. A stethoscope draped around his neck, he extended a dry, warm palm to me and cracked a grin. "Someone had a rough night. Come on in. Good to see you, Sadie. You look ravishing, as usual."

"Thank you, Dr. Do-much," Sadie sang after us. She stood outside the door. "I got me a busy day. Mrs. Do-Nuttin' gonna pay me to make groceries for her. Figger dat. Take care of da rabbit, she a sweet one. Sadie knows."

I barely had time to thank her before she disappeared.

"Well, alone at last," he said, chuckling. He lowered me to a wooden bench, removed my sneakers and puckered his lips. "I'll be right back."

The apartment had a very familiar layout. In Brooklyn, we'd call it a railroad flat. Here, in New Orleans, it was known as a shotgun. All the rooms were on one floor, lined up in a neat row. If you had good aim and a steady hand, you could shoot a bullet straight through the living room, bedroom, out the kitchen window and smack into a tree in the back yard. I watched the doctor disappear behind the first set of sliding doors. He had a spring in his step that belied the already oppressive heat. The man appeared ageless. He could have been sixty. Or forty. All I knew was that he had a gentle and sure touch. More importantly, he had a telephone.

I braced myself on the wall and hopped over to a large, well-polished mahogany desk. A framed certificate told me I was in the office of a Dr. Jacob T. Lerebon. I gave him silent thanks as I lifted the receiver. K.T. answered in the middle of the first ring.

"My God! I've been worried sick. It's her. Hold on, for heaven's sake." Someone was with her. My pulse quickened.

"You okay? Is someone there?"

"Oh, honey." She broke into unbridled sobs.

Damn it. I shouted her name into the phone. Suddenly, a deep voice broke in. I was ready to bolt out the door when recognition hit. "Sweeney, is everything okay?"

"Depends on how you look at it. This poor woman is near hysterics. What the hell happened to you?"

I gave him the short version. He cursed me out. "Five this morning, your girlfriend called Ryan, who in turn called me, dressing me down for letting your ass drift in the wind, like I was personally responsible for your dumb-ass moves. Pissed me off royally, thank you. You haven't earned yourself any fans today."

"Fuck you, too. Put K.T. back on the line."

"Before I do, you may be interested in knowing that the tooth you found in your pocket probably did belong to Lisa Rubin. Her left incisor had been carved out from her gums. Nice, huh? My cop buddy got mighty pissed off when I lied about finding the tooth on the scene. Didn't like the implication that the N.O.P.D was less than perfect, not that I blame him. By the way, you don't have to thank me for keeping your name out of it, I owed you that much for the shit I pulled yesterday. So now we're even."

"Just put K.T. on." I shifted the phone to my other ear and wiped my eyes with my thumb. The first word she said was my name. She sounded terrible. "I'm sorry, honey. I am," was my lame response.

"What happened to you?" Her voice was reduced to a soft whine.

"Too much to explain now. I stumbled into the wrong building and got bumped up a bit. I'm seeing a doctor right now. Nothing serious. I'll be back at the hotel within an hour."

"I won't be here."

Blood stopped flowing to my limbs. I started to tremble uncontrollably. "What do you mean you won't be there?"

"Too much to explain now," she replied, her voice dripping with sarcasm. " I'm glad you're okay." And with those words, she hung up.

I stared at the buzzing receiver.

"Trouble all around, huh?" The doctor had returned carrying a small satchel and a plastic-wrapped gown. "Well, I've been around long enough to know when not to ask questions. Can you make it over here?" He pressed a wiry arm against the door opposite me, revealing an examination room unlike any I'd ever seen. The entire back wall was filled with exotic plants and potted herbs. He chuckled at me. "Yes, I have my own home-grown pharmacy. Now, from your accent, I'd say you come from the East. Probably the Big Apple. So these won't work for you. For you, I bring out *civilized* medicine." His laugh rumbled in his chest. I knew he was having fun at my expense, but somehow I didn't mind.

I smiled. "My idea of civilized medicine, for your information, is chicken soup and Yoo-Hoos, so you better get cooking." Then I limped past him. The air inside was as aromatic as a garden and filled with sunlight. A wall of windows opened onto an alley that resembled a tropical jungle. Off to one side stood an enormous birdcage, its lone occupant a yellow parakeet who was chattering happily to its image in a oval mirror. The examination table had a terrycloth pillow at one end. I started to wonder if there was any way I could get this guy as my primary-care physician. He left me alone long enough to strip and change into a gown. When he came back, he cut off sprigs of rosemary and lavender, wrapped them in a cheesecloth then dipped them into a vat of steaming water. He laid the bundle on my chest.

"Take a deep breath, darling, while I check you out." Some time later he tapped me on the shoulder and I was startled to realize I'd fallen asleep.

"Wow. What'd you do to me?"

"Sweetheart, you were so tired no one had to do anything. You just fell asleep. By the way, you snore. I can give you something for your sinuses if you trust an old boogie man from the Quarter."

"Can you move to New York?"

His laugh bounced around the room like a beach ball. "Not on your life." He washed his hands in the sink, dried them off, then plucked two vials from a closet. "Antibiotics and my secret sinus medicine," he said, dropping the bottles into a paper bag with a magician's dramatic flair. "A present from me, 'cause you're a friend of Sadie's." His smile was sly. "And since we're such good friends, maybe you'll tell me what you were doing in the old Herriot place on Dauphine."

I sat up and stared at him. "How'd you know?"

"You'd be surprised at what I know." His expression became serious. "You also talk in your sleep. Pretty coherent unconscious you have."

The room suddenly felt cold. I said, "I heard someone scream for help. A woman." His nod was patient. I wondered how much I could tell him, how much he already knew. I bit the inside of my cheek, then added, "I'm a private detective."

"I gathered as much." He opened the door and stepped out of sight. "Go ahead and change. You'll find one of my wife's T-shirts inside the plastic bag on the table. I also grabbed a pair of my son's jeans from the rummage pile. They should fit." He spoke loudly, with authority.

I didn't hesitate to comply. My own clothes had disappeared.

He continued talking. "Some say the Herriot place is haunted. Forty-seven years ago, a pregnant woman was beaten to death by her husband after he discovered she was having an affair with his female cousin. Lots of locals have heard her crying for help. Especially on moonless nights."

"C'mon, doc, you can't believe in that nonsense." The clothes fit perfectly. My sneakers, however, did not. My foot was too swollen. I loosened the laces.

"Science is the art of analyzing what is knowable today, with today's technology. That's all. People used to dismiss witch doctors and medicine men as the mythology of misguided primitive people. Today, we know that much of their medicine was astoundingly appropriate, predating our own remedies. When you stop to think about it, life consists of interaction on all levels, from micro to macro. Religion, science and magic may just be different aspects of the same reality. " He fell silent. "I'm not sure what I believe, but I know that it's never wise to discount anything just because it can't be proven by intellect or old white men in sterile university labs. Are you dressed?"

I called him back inside.

"You'll need to change the bandages once a day," he said, taking hold of my hand with surprising tenderness. With his head inclined toward me and his voice low, he raised our hands so that the edges of our palms touched my forehead briefly. "My mother was renowned in this area as a queen of voodoo. Who knows how much of her ways were instinct, insight or magic? I lived with her all my life and I never knew. But she taught me one thing I never forgot. Evil is palpable, as palpable as this thorn." He tore off a stem from a plant with purple leaves the size of a baby's foot. I looked closely and saw a soft, woody bark but no thorn. He lifted one of my fingers and pressed it gently against the stem. A stinging sensation made my hand jerk away. Our eyes met. "And it can be as difficult to detect. Your senses must be sharp and your mind clear from distraction." I waited for him to say something more. He just stared at me patiently, then smiled. "Of course, she also told me that if you feed someone snake eggs, they'll die soon after, with little snakes hatched in the stomach. That one always plays in my head when I see someone in surgery. Okay, enough chatter. You have a lot of work to do. I better let you get started." Five minutes later he opened the door of a taxi for me and winked. "Shadows in New Orleans are very, very long. You'll have to learn to walk around them."

The slamming of the car door punctuated his

sentence. The last twenty-four hours were enough to convince me that the best course of action would be to pick up K.T. and head straight for the airport. And I might've done just that if K.T. had been at the hotel. But she was not and neither was there a note of explanation. I tried the restaurant and got a brusque, "Yes, she's here, but she can't talk." I wasn't up to arguing. Instead I showered and headed straight for bed. Sleep came easier than it should have.

The blare of music in the next room woke me at 4:12. Black Sabbath. Who still listened to Black Sabbath? I opened my eyes and stared at the ceiling. The room was dark and I was bathed in sweat. Nightmares had plagued my slumber, but only one image stayed with me. A bloody skeleton dancing at the foot of my bed, a fetus dangling from the bones of its hand. I reached for the phone and dialed the restaurant again. The song was the same. Yes, K.T. was there. No, she wasn't available. She was being interviewed by Fitzhugh Chamelle. Yes, she'd take a message. Click.

Okay, so I knew where I stood. Death Valley would've been more hospitable. Not that I deserved much better. I sat up and stretched. Once this case was resolved, I'd make it up to her, maybe take a leave from the agency. But first I had to reach some kind of closure on this murder. I started searching for my notepad, then panicked. It had been in the back pocket of my jeans, which I'd left at Dr. Lerebon's office. A phone call netted me a recorded message. I left my phone number, hung up and raided the fridge. I was chowing down on a Nestle's

Crunch bar when I noticed the Federal Express packages resting on top of the television set, one from Ryan, one from Jill. I ripped them open and settled down at the desk.

Ryan's files held the usual police dossiers. Most of the info was identical to Serra's. The packet from my agency, however, was three inches thick, with separate reports from four different free-lance agents, none of them older than twenty-four. Evan Alexander was my favorite. The kid had bleached blonde hair, soulful blue eyes, a delicate silver stud in one nostril, peach fuzz sprouting from a cleft chin and the sharpest, most creative mind I'd encountered in years. I hired him two months ago, much to the chagrin of my conservative partner. Since then, Tony had him on a steady payroll.

His report started with a note to me:

*Hey ya, boss lady, in the big, old sleazy ease. I got lost in this one. Some real strange vibes rang through me. I did the basics, even went over that checklist you gave me. You know, what distinguishes the victims? Where'd the murders take place? Did the vics wear the same kind of earrings or nail polish, attend the same school, use drugs? Is the killer organized or disorganized, missionary, visionary, lust- or thrill-motivated, a power fiend, or a subversive? Checked the standard profiler files, too. Written by some idiot crime savant in D.C. who waves his wet palms over some cold files and determines the killer was an only child, abused by a maternal aunt, never washes his hands after he craps and gets hard-ons for cops. Then I did my thing. You'll be proud of me, Mad Miller.*

Jill teases me that the kid and I have some sick mother-son thing going on. I'll never admit it to her, but she could be right. I read his file first.

## Chapter 7

Evan had compiled accounts of the six murders from newspapers I'd never heard about, publications with titles like *The People's Gazette*. He'd managed to contact three of the six lead investigators, interview a few family members of two victims, and assemble names and phone numbers of people I might want to contact for more information. All this in less than nine hours. That's my boy, I thought, smiling to myself.

The smile evaporated the next instant when I read that he'd floated NeVille's name by one of the investigators on Rubin's case. The New Orleans Police Department had dismissed his inquiries immediately and demanded to know my license number. I was annoyed by Evan's *faux pas*, not the NOPD's response. Rubin's homicide was an active investigation. On top of that, the victim was ex-wife to a dead cop. No outlander could touch this case, especially not a New Yorker. Ryan had made it crystal clear that the only shot we had at obtaining inside information came from Sweeney. What concerned me now was getting my name pulled into the official investigation. I'd have to keep a very low profile from this point on.

The news from Chicago was more disturbing. Evan noted that the so-called eggshell murder of Andrea Allen, 59, Christian right-to-lifer and housewife, had been solved more than two years ago. The murderer turned out to be the unemployed 32-year-old son who had moved back home a few months earlier. My stomach sank as I read through the summary. NeVille's presence in Chicago at the time of Allen's homicide now appeared entirely coincidental. What if the other cases were also unrelated incidents? I rubbed my hands over my face, suddenly tired again. I reread the page in front of me. Evan had highlighted one sentence: *Andrea Allen had not been raped or otherwise sexually assaulted.* All the other women had. I reminded myself that this case had been the weakest link from the beginning.

We were down to five murders, including Mary Ryan and Lisa Rubin. Maybe this was progress, after all. I put aside the rest of Evan's report and thumbed through the other three. Pretty monotonous stuff, except for a stack of papers that originated with Elmore Wilmington, a man I'd first encountered in a kidnapping case this past winter. An artist living confidently with a severe neurological disorder called Tourette's syndrome, Wilmington's latest obsession was something he'd dubbed "imagination mapping." I laughed out loud as I unfolded a sixteen by twenty sheet of drawing paper on which he'd drawn a series of concentric and overlapping circles in brilliant shades of his own hand-made pastels. With Evan and Elmore in our stable, our agency was certainly going where no private investigators had gone before. Tony doesn't fully approve of their unorthodox approaches, but they thrill me.

I pivoted the desk lamp to better illuminate the drawing. The concentric circles illustrated the sequence, time lapse and location of the murders. Amazingly, he'd delineated Allen's murder with a dotted line and the typically ambiguous marginal note, "Obscures picture. Send to background." The dates of four of the six murders were drawn in vermillion. Allen's was ochre, Betty Galonardi's green and circled in yellow. I bent closer to read Wilmington's note. "Per: NYPD Izzy McGinn, Galonardi murder corrected to June 13th. Final coroner report estimated death post-midnight."

Sweeney had already given me the corrected date, but seeing it on paper sucked away a few cobwebs. I steepled my hands and held my breath. A warning signal began to buzz at the back of my head. With Allen's case removed and Galonardi's date corrected, the connection hit me like a spitball on the forehead. Friday, August 3, 1984. Friday, August 23, 1985. Saturday, May 3, 1986. Monday, June 13, 1988. Monday, May 3, 1993. Every murder had been committed on a date containing the number three. A mystical number. So maybe our killer was religious. I fingered the page and shook my head at the sudden clarity. The first three murders had occurred within a year of each other. The fourth took place after a two-year lapse. Allen's occurred two years after that. With her homicide removed, the lapse between Galonardi's murder in New York City and Lisa Rubin's death jumped to five years. Had another murder taken place in the meantime that we didn't know about yet? Or had something occurred in New York that scared off the killer, forced him to take a sojourn from his bloody pastime?

Another break in the pattern emerged. The killer had taken a bi-coastal approach until now: San Francisco first, then Massachusetts, back to San Francisco, then New York and most recently, New Orleans. Why? I stood up, stretched, then blurted, "Shit." Rubin was from Berkeley. So the pattern held. Now all I had to do was figure out what the hell it all meant. Piece of cake.

Speaking of cake...

I checked my watch and my stomach grumbled in response. It was twenty past six and I hadn't had a real meal since yesterday. I dialed K.T.'s restaurant again. The response was pretty much the same. She was "indisposed." The idiot on the other end actually used that word. *Indisposed.* I'd have to deal with her later tonight, when we had time to talk and I had ample time to beg, justify and make amends. I threw some paperwork into a backpack and focused on my most pressing problem. Getting into a decent restaurant at prime time. Les Enfants was out until K.T. and I had some private time. Another option sprang to mind. I used to do travel writing and I still have a few solid connections around town, including one at The Red Bike, one of the hottest new restaurants in town. A quick phone conversation with the owner won me entry to a seven o'clock seating.

That settled, I made a quick call to New York and then dialed Tom Ryan. The first few minutes he spent shouting at me with the bravado of a pissed-off father impatient at his own fear.

"Are you done?" I asked.

"Not really. How are you, by the way?"

"Fine. Do you want to hear my news?"

"All I want to hear is that you and K.T. are booked on the next flight home."

"Ryan, I'm *fine*."

"That's not what Theo said. He wants you out of the picture. Called you a loose cannon. I understand you almost got him killed in the bayou. The bottom line, Miller, is if you or Theo got whacked, it'd be on my head and my neck ain't strong enough to hold up that kind of weight. Not anymore. I hired you and I'm firing you. That's the joy of being a bonafide cash client. Send me a bill, send your files to Theo."

"Theo's an asshole."

"Granted. But he's a damn good investigator."

"Would a damn good investigator fail to find out that one of the six eggshell murders was resolved more than two years ago?" I heard electricity hiss on the line. "Ryan, did you hear me?"

"No, I've been struck deaf and dumb by your brilliance. Which one?" He listened in silence until I started talking about the date patterns. When I added in the tidbit about the corrected date of Galonardi's murder, he spat out a string of curses, all directed at himself. "What kind of fucking moron am I? All that shit is obvious and it took some amateur to figure it out. I should retire from the force. Damn it."

"Am I rehired?"

"I don't know... can't believe Theo didn't catch this. Maybe he's got his nose pressed too hard against the window."

"Or maybe he's just too dense. Did you ever question whether he was the right guy for this job? And don't give me your old boy's club answer."

"No one's better, Robin. Seriously. Or so I thought. I mean... Christ. This investigation has been in his hands for years, what if I've screwed up again? Tony's been aching to pitch in and help, but Sweeney's such a hard-ass I thought... No, no, he wouldn't let me down. I know that. No one knows better than he does what Mary meant to me, what it means to lose a wife you adore —"

He sounded so hurt, I had to back off. "Well, maybe something else is going on with him." I hesitated. "The other night when we met, he had a couple of drinks."

"Shit." For a second or two he was quiet, then he said, "Sweeney does that now and then, thinks he can hold a few brews and not go off. I should've seen that coming. These past few months have been real hard on him. His mother, well, I guess I can call her that. She raised him. Isn't that what matters? Anyway, she passed away in November. The man spent the last five years watching her die. Bone cancer. No one thought she'd last six months. But Theo brought her up North and took care of her, read to her, bathed her, drove her to national parks, put a skylight over her bed so she could see the stars at night —"

"Sweeney did this? You got to be kidding. The man has the sensitivity of a rabid raccoon."

"You don't know him like I do, Robin. He's a good guy. I'm not going to condemn him for making one mistake. I'll talk to him about the drinking, get a sense of how far he's gone. Still, maybe I should keep you on this a little longer. You and your motley crew bring a new perspective." In his own way, Ryan was telling me he was worried about Sweeney's capabilities.

"Yeah, that's us. Motley Incorporated." My ankle had begun to throb. I lowered my sock and checked the bandage. The wound was oozing. "Did I tell you we charge extra for accepting insults?"

"Yeah, well, just make sure you submit an itemized bill. And, Miller, thanks. This is the first time in years I think it's possible we may get a real break."

"Don't get mushy on me, Tom."

"Piss off." He hung up with a smile in his voice. It's not too often I can do that for such a good friend. The satisfaction I felt almost made up for the hours I'd suffered with Sweeney. Almost.

My dinner reservation was less than ten minutes away. Not that it really mattered in New Orleans. Reservations just mean you have to wait less than an hour for a seat. I changed my bandages, donned a pair of khakis and a carelessly ironed white shirt, wrote K.T. a detailed and apologetic note, swallowed my medicine and finally started for the door. I was twenty minutes late, which meant I'd be right on time. The phone rang just as I was heading out. I scrambled for the receiver, praying it was K.T., realizing with a start how much I missed her, how worried I was that I'd screwed things up once more.

It was Dr. Lerebon. He'd found my notebook and offered to meet me at the Napoleon House, one of the few quiet bars in town, around eleven. One thing about New Orleans, insomniacs have plenty of company. Normally, I wouldn't have hesitated, but I was anxious about getting time with K.T. I negotiated with him and we finally agreed to meet at nine instead, which meant I had to high-tail it over to The Red Bike.

After a day spent alone in a dim hotel room, the cacophony of the streets was overwhelming. Strangers rushed by, caught me by the elbow, spun me around. Music seemed to cascade toward me from every direction. Kids too young to attend movies alone tap-danced for money, their eyes vacant, their movements mechanical, without joy. By the time I got to the restaurant, I was ready for a drink. I ordered a Dixie beer, Oysters Rockefeller, crawfish with remoulade sauce and a side of gumbo. The waiters, all men, were just as I remembered them from the last time. Dressed in all black, with deep Southern accents, they were indulgent to some diners and benignly neglectful of others. I got lucky. The man serving me liked the quantity of food I'd ordered. He slipped me extra pecan cheese twists and winked.

A cut by the Gypsy Kings was piped through the dining room. The music transported me to a quieter place. I leaned back, let the ceiling fans sweep the chill air over my face and sighed. I wanted desperately just to be another patron on vacation, instead of a detective picking through the fragments of six brutal murders. I dumped my files into the backpack and spooned a dish of Key lime pie that K.T. had once begrudgingly called the best in the universe. The admission had almost broke her heart. I smiled at the memory.

Less than forty-eight hours ago K.T. and I had lain on the hotel bed, wrapped around each other, bodies slick with sweat, hearts pounding, our eyes locked in shared dismay that our love-making remained so energetic and so assured. It had been like that from the beginning, with one exception. Remembering the first time we'd made love after I knew she was pregnant brought another smile to my face. K.T. had taken me home from the hospital and stayed there as I recovered from pneumonia. One unusually warm day in March, we sat in the back yard watching a flock of goldfinches devouring thistle from a feeder I'd just hung up. K.T. gestured for me to open my legs so she could nestle against me on the chaise lounge. Up until then, we had done little more than kiss, still deep in negotiations over the terms of phase two of our turbulent relationship. But the weight of K.T.'s slender back pressed along my body, her head resting between my breasts, my legs crossed over her thighs, became too much all at once. I started stroking the sides of her swollen breasts, wondering what they looked like now that she was pregnant, wondering how sensitive her nipples had become, how swollen her lips would be now that blood pounded through her with increasing force, how she'd respond to my mouth, my tongue.

Without knowing it, I groaned beneath her. We exchanged no words, each of us pretending to be engrossed in watching the birds. Quietly, she gyrated against me, so slight a movement I could barely tell if it was her or the wind rocking us. My breath quickened and I tightened in response, an exquisite discomfort demanding more from K.T. than this teasing pressure. I pressed my hands beneath her shirt, ran my fingers upward from her hips. Her waist had begun to disappear. Her breasts had grown so much that they fell gently to the sides. She arched slightly and I could see through her turtleneck that her nipples, so much more pronounced than before, had hardened. The changes in her body excited me.

I locked my ankles over hers, ran my hands over her breasts, heard her gasp. She pulled at my thighs and whispered, "Gentle." With excruciating tenderness I brushed a single fingertip over each erect nipple. She twisted her head to one side, the pulse in her neck synchronized to the soft pumping of her hips. Her hands rested on her abdomen, kneading herself. After another moment, she let out a burst of air. "Enough teasing, Robin."

I led her back up to my room, stripping as I climbed the stairs. K.T. remained clothed. She backed me into the room with feverish kisses, her hands under my panties, squeezing my butt. I tried to remove her turtleneck but she stopped me cold, with a look I'll never forget.

"I want this *slow*." She insisted that I sit on the bed, naked and impatient for her flesh, as she undressed. The button of her jeans took forever to unhook. She lingered over the zipper, grinding her hips until the pants finally, finally fell to the floor. The fabric of her turtleneck twisted and undulated over her skin, accentuating the shape of her breasts, the curve of her spine. When her body was finally exposed, a tremor ran through me. Her belly had begun to swell, her nipples had grown as dark as espresso beans. Since the last time we'd made love, months earlier, the muscular angles of her body had turned strangely alien and astoundingly alluring. I latched onto her hips, tossed her next to me on the bed and froze.

She's pregnant, I thought suddenly. Pregnant. A fetus is growing inside her body. Images from a *Nova* special on human development flickered before me.

Within a nanosecond, the energy between us altered. The moon had eclipsed the sun and all I could hear were the wolves approaching from the dark recesses of my mind. I tried to relight the fire by bending to lick her nipples. But once there, I was too afraid to suck.

K.T. laughed out loud, realizing immediately that something had changed. "I'm not that fragile," she said lightly.

"It's not you I'm worried about." I was poised above her, propped on my elbows like a wooden bridge swaying over churning waters. I was terrified I'd fall on her and crush the baby. What the hell was I supposed to do? My friend Beth had read that oral sex with a pregnant woman could be dangerous if air was blown into her vagina accidentally. Certainly penetration had to be safe. But we hadn't stopped to wash our hands since filling the bird feeder. What if I gave her a bacterial infection?

K.T. took charge. She slipped out from under me, pressed a palm against my back so that I fell against the mattress and straddled me.

"Check, ma'am?"

I started at the interruption. The waiter handed me the bill with a crooked, insider grin. I blinked hard and blushed. Back to reality. I glanced at my watch. It was time to meet Dr. Lerebon.

Getting my mind back on murder and mayhem was easier than it should have been. The door to The Red Bike opened up onto a quiet street just outside the Quarter. A faint mist had crept into the air. I picked up my pace and soon reentered the raucous steam bath of Bourbon Street. Some people think the French Quarter is romantic. I'm not one of them. I hesitated for a second before joining the surge of bodies. Think of it as merging into a five-lane highway in Los Angeles, with the on-ramp no longer than the length of a mad cow. My New York edge served me well. I elbowed through the drunks and veered onto a quieter side street.

The Napoleon House is located directly behind the Royal Orleans. I've always thought of it as an oasis, tonight more so than usual. My body was aching and any muscle not physically damaged was knotted by worry about K.T. Long a haven for artists and writers, Napoleon House is the only place in New Orleans with piped-in classical music. It even has a pay phone. As I entered, I rolled my head to one side and heard my neck click. The place was lit by brass hanging lamps with thirty-watt orange bulbs. Pipe smoke curled along the bar. On a night like this, the courtyard garden would be littered with flying termites. I waited for my eyes to adjust, then headed for one of the back tables positioned directly beneath a ceiling fan.

I recognized an aria from *La Boheme*: "Your tiny hand is frozen." One of K.T.'s favorites. I smiled.

Opera had never been in my repertoire of tunes to hum along with, but K.T. has changed that. For her, opera is pure passion, and after making love to *Lakmé* I'm inclined to agree.

A boy with acne and a Fifties-style goatee sauntered over to take my order. I asked for a Pimm's Cup, a house specialty made from Pimm's gin, lemonade and 7UP and checked out the bar. It hadn't changed since my last visit. The walls looked as if someone had prepped them for a paint job and then died before completing the assignment. They were covered with paintings and posters depicting Napoleon in various guises. One poster announced the imminent opening of the movie *Napoleon* at Radio City Music Hall, January 1981. At the table next to me sat a man wearing a beret and a T-shirt dotted with beer-drinking frogs.

I fanned out Evan's report file and scanned the A.P. news clippings. A number of them had been written by the same individual, F.B. Chamelle. Apparently a free-lance criminal reporter, he'd covered all of the murders. The name tickled my memory, but the click wouldn't come. I rummaged in my backpack for the clipping from Monday's *Times-Picayune*. Sure enough, the article had the same byline. I read through it again and then checked my watch. Dr. Lerebon was already ten minutes late and I didn't have time to spare. My drink came and went and Lerebon still hadn't showed. I knew I'd regret it but I ordered a second Pimm's Cup, then decided to make the most of Lerebon's delay.

I rose, pulled the business card from my wallet and picked up the pay phone. Dreyer Carr's answering machine clicked on. I identified myself and explained why I was calling. All of a sudden, a real voice broke in on the other end. If I hadn't known that the food critic was a member of the tribe, his intonation alone would've tagged him as gay. Either that or a charismatic leader of an evangelical congregation. His voice had a breathless, sing-song quality that mesmerized me instantly.

"Sorry, darling," he said, "but I was screening my calls. I am just so broken up about Lisa. Broken up, I tell you. Such a sweetheart of a girl. Skin like an angel. I just don't understand evil in the world, I really don't." He paused for breath. "Are you a for-real private investigator?" I had the sense that although he might be truly appalled by Rubin's death, he was also slightly thrilled by the drama.

"Yes, Mr. Carr. As I was saying, I'm conducting —"

"Call me Drey, please. 'Mr. Carr' makes me think of my father, which is something I try not to do, ever. Now, who's paying for your services, honey? Lee didn't have family in these parts, and her ex's folks are probably staging a perverse Mardi Gras celebration of their own right 'bout now. Her mama send you down here?"

"It's a little complicated to go into right now. Do you have time to answer a few questions?"

"A few or many. Right now I'm recovering from the downright nightmare of riches forced upon me by an overly solicitous chef at Mosca's. Honey, you ever feel inclined to consume a meal in which every course is laden with sauces derived from at least three varieties of dairy products, be sure to check it out, provided your stomach's younger and heartier than mine. Though I suppose I deserve it, eating the way I do, year after —"

"Mr. Carr —"

"Drey," he said, correcting me. "Sorry. Go ahead. I'll behave."

"Were you and Lisa good friends?"

"If you're asking if we were lovers —"

I laughed, surprising us both.

Dreyer Carr said, "I see," with a pleasant chuckle. "Lee and I met when she first moved here, a mere child she was at the time, and almost instantly smitten with Pete. I was the one who got her into the paper. At first, they put the poor girl on obit duty, an occupation equaled in dullness only by actuaries and toll takers. But she was a dynamo and soon managed to pry her way into the grimy oyster shell of the city section. Irritated the hell out of her colleagues, but as far as I was concerned she'd worked her way up to pearl status." I had the sense that Dreyer used this analogy before. "That's when the new mag up in San Francisco swept in and stole her from N'awlins."

I tried to sneak a question in while he paused for breath. "You mentioned something earlier about her ex-husband's family —"

"No secrets there. The Strampos clan despised Lee. For good reason, I suppose. About a year or so ago, she and Pete split, shortly after she conceived."

"Was it his child?"

"Oh, honey, yes. But she aborted right away."

For an instant, I pictured K.T. and the way she plastered my friend Beth's stethoscope on her abdomen and urged me to listen to the swoosh of blood through the placenta, her eyes wide with amazement.

"I take it Pete was not pleased."

"Not pleased? Girl, clearly you don't know Southern men. This was his progeny, his heir, his raison d'etre. He was going to be a bold old papa. Instead, Lee left him, took the editorial job at *Bay Insight*, terminated the pregnancy and fell in love with a wisp of a lesbian she met on the plane to San Francisco. You think this straight-laced, play-by-the-rules police officer just smiled and said, 'You go, girl'? Hardly. He was devastated. Smashed every lamp, sculpture and photograph in the house. Put his night stick through her computer monitor... Is that the Toreador song from *Carmen* I hear in the background? Oh, it sends shivers up and down my spine. Reminds me of an old boyfriend of mine. Magnificent man. Left me for a woman. Imagine."

I shifted the phone to my other ear, checked my watch, then surveyed the room. Lerebon still had not arrived. "Did he hit Lisa?"

"Oh, no. Not Pete. He toed the line way before straddling that precipice. Property was one thing, but he'd never, ever lay a finger on her. He eventually came around, too, told me once that he'd never stop loving Lee, despite everything. Around three months ago, he stopped by the paper and asked me to tell Lee that she could come home anytime. To tell the truth, I felt sad for him. Especially since Lee hardly even mentioned his name when we talked. Too thrilled by her new life."

"What about the family?"

"Do you know anything about Shreveport?"

"A little."

"Where are you on the liberal scale?"

"Excuse me?"

"All this talk about homosexuals make you nervous?"

"Oh . . . not at all. Believe me, we're on the same side."

"Thought that might be the case. Well, the Strampos are from the *other* side. Way other. AIDS is God's revenge on sodomites. Lesbians are perverting human nature. Abortion is a crime against the Lord. Nobody can dance like a Negro. A while back, Pete's mom and dad were arrested for protesting against an abortion clinic. Get the picture?"

"In technicolor," I said. Maybe Lisa Rubin's death was not linked to the eggshell murders after all.

"You think the family's capable of violence?"

"No doubt in my mind. But before you go storming out to the Strampos *maison* in your Birkenstock boots, I should tell you that they took off to a relative's place in Alabama right after Pete's funeral. They weren't expected back in town for at least two weeks."

I'd have to verify the information, so I asked Drey to spell their names for me. Then I gulped down the last of my drink. I signaled for another automatically. "Anything else you can tell me about the night of the murder?"

"Not really. We had dinner at Les Enfants, a fabulous new place owned by two fabulous chefs. The female partner's a sister, by the way. Sexy enough to make *my* head turn and, girl, my head just doesn't swing that way." A flush swept over my cheeks. I wasn't sure if its source was the compliment or the booze. "Lee was absolutely smitten. Would've nailed that woman right on the prep table if she'd had half the chance."

I cleared my throat, suddenly uncomfortable with Drey's repartee. "Did she talk to anyone else? Did anyone approach the two of you?"

"Not that I can remember. She left after me. I think she was hoping the bronze goddess, her term by the by, would seek her out later on. I kept telling her the woman didn't seem interested, well, at least not as interested as Lee would've liked. But she was determined."

A movement near the end of the bar caught my eye. The good doctor had arrived at the same time as my buzz. How fortunate for me. I waved and pointed my table out to him. Then I rushed to conclude my conversation with Dreyer Carr. "One last question. Did you ever hear of a writer F.B. Chamelle?"

"Crime section. Don't know anything about him though. I'll ask around tomorrow, if you want."

I said, "That'd be great. You can leave a message at the Royal Orleans if you learn anything. You've been a lot of help. I appreciate it."

"Anything for Lisa," he said. "Call back if you like. I'll be home. And now I'm off to search for my ancient *Carmen* tape and some raunchy memories. Good luck."

My fingers begin to tingle as I hung up the phone. Maybe it was time for me to switch back to my usual poison, Yoo-Hoo with a Twinkies chaser. I crossed the room and slid into a seat opposite Dr. Jacob Lerebon.

"Well, this was interesting reading," he said as he pushed my notebook across the table.

"How refreshing. An honest interloper."

He ignored my comment. "You have quite a messy job."

"I guess they could compare favorably with the gaping, pus-filled wounds you tend."

"I'd take my job over yours any day." He scratched his neck and focused on a spot beyond my shoulder. I glanced around. No one was there. I realized he was thinking. Something about his expression made me nervous.

"What is it?" I asked.

"*Lwa.*"

I thought he was asking for the loo, so I pointed out the bathrooms to him.

He snorted, waved away the beatnik-redux waiter and leaned in toward me. "The connection is obvious," he said, his word clipped and precise. As he rubbed his hands together I thought I could smell fresh herbs. Thyme. Rosemary. Dill.

"Dr. Lerebon, I have no idea what you are talking about."

"*Vodoun.* The murderer has some familiarity with it, I'm just not sure how much."

"Voodoo?" I asked, stunned to hear the word escape my lips. Another case of body-snatching, I almost muttered out loud. The kindly doctor of earlier today had been replaced with a narrow-eyed weirdo. I scratched back my chair, ready to make a swift exit. But even as I cocked an indulgent smile his way, bells started ringing in my head. Crime scene anomalies clicked in front of me. Cracked eggshells. A knotted red neckerchief. The slice of bull's testicles wrapped carefully around ice. I sat back down. "I'm listening."

A smirk returned to his face. "The urban rabbit is ready to learn. How much do you know about voodoo?"

"How much do you know about making *kreplach*?"

I was relieved to hear his laughter. "Fair enough." He swept my glass to one side and planted his elbows on the table. The glare from the bare orange bulbs made his emerald eyes appear on fire. "*Vodoun. Candomblé. Santería.*" My skin grew hot as he almost sang the words. "Forget everything you know, everything you've seen in movies. Tell me, is voodoo magic?"

I nodded.

"No, no." The table wobbled as he shifted positions suddenly. "Voodoo is a *religion*, a rich and encompassing religion. It originated in a region of Africa called Dahomey. Today the area is known as Benin."

My mouth was dry. I smacked my lips and asked, "Can we skip the history lesson?"

"You think history is unimportant?" He leaned back, crossed his arms over his chest and frowned.

"I think there's a murderer on the loose and time is very precious. While you may not appreciate my impatience, his next victim might."

"Okay, I understand. May I see the notebook again?"

With some reluctance I handed it over. He pocketed it instantly and stood up. A second later he headed for the pay phone. With his back turned toward me, he spoke quickly, without gestures. When he returned to the table, he said, "It appears we need to take a short trip." He took my hand like he was a schoolmaster and I a recalcitrant toddler, then he suggested I pay the bill.

I shook my hand free and slapped money on the table. His tough, authoritative tone made me think I should find a way to scratch an S.O.S. into the table top in case I never reappeared. Lerebon didn't give me time. He moved behind me and thrust me toward the door.

# Chapter 8

I scrambled toward the curb, aware that Lerebon's fingers circled my wrist with enough pressure to ensure that I followed but not enough to hurt. He flagged a taxi with a short staccato whistle and held me tight as the car screeched to a halt in front of us. I had to make a quick assessment: Was Dr. Lerebon dangerous? In New Orleans, I'd become Alice in Wonderland, my New York instincts disconnected, my understanding of language and culture insufficient for interpreting events. Lerebon opened the taxi door and pinned me with his piercing green eyes. Just beyond him tourists meandered along the street, laughing, dancing to music still audible from Bourbon Street.

My heart skipped a beat. The grim visage of a skeleton, eyes horribly alive, the mouth twisted in a bitter smile, suddenly entered my view. I blinked, reminded myself it was a person wearing a mask, a vestige no doubt from Mardi Gras revelries. I started to turn away, but stopped suddenly, unsure why. The muscular arms of the skeleton were bound by plastic Hawaiian leis in rainbow hues. All at once my attention snapped to the skeleton's T-shirt. *Les Enfants.* A silhouette of a boy and girl mounting a hobby horse. The logo for K.T.'s restaurant. The coincidence unnerved me. Without thinking, I jerked in his direction.

Lerebon yanked me backward and put his mouth to my ear. "I understand matters of life and death. This is about saving life. Get in the cab."

"What?" I gaped at him, then immediately glanced back to the street. The skeleton had disappeared. The crowd he'd been moving with ambled blithely toward the main drag, oblivious to anyone else's presence. Clearly, the skeleton had not been one of their party.

Lerebon touched the side of my face. "Please, just get in the cab." I forced my gaze back to him. He leaned inside the cab, exchanged words with the driver and then nodded. "You better sit in the front," he said to me.

My hotel was within running distance. I'd be insane to go anywhere except home.

Lerebon assumed his most reassuring physician-like tone. "Robin, I'm taking you to meet someone important. You need to do this. Now, please, don't make me explain anything else."

For all I knew, Lerebon could've arranged for this cab in advance. He could be another maniac in a city ripe with them. But for some reason, I trusted him just a little more than I trusted myself at the moment. Had the skeleton even been there? Was I drunker than I thought?

I glanced at the back seat as I slid in. A stack of yellowed, puckered newspapers were strewn over the seat next to Lerebon. "Not a real good place to save your papers," I muttered to the driver, needing a target for my rising anxiety.

"You don't want to see what's under that, miss. Believe me. I better warn you about something else as well. The a.c.'s broke, so you gotta settle for wind. And I promise lots of it." The driver spoke with a New Jersey accent. I took a closer look at him as we peeled away from the curb. He had large eyes, rough-shaven jowls and puckered lips. He reminded me of Louis Armstrong a few years past his prime.

Lerebon repeated the street address and the driver's eyes widened. He stared at the doctor through the rear-view mirror and then scratched the back of his neck like a dog just bitten by a five-pound flea. "Hooey. Don't take many tourists there. You from around here?"

"Born and raised," Lerebon answered.

Their small talk made my skin crawl. Something about Christmas in the oaks and fried oysters. Lerebon made some comment about locals avoiding the "high rise," and the driver out-and-out whooped. The joke escaped me. I turned on the radio to drown out their voices. The hissing speakers popped and whined, then zeroed in on Frank Sinatra. Old Blue Eyes crooning about old black magic. I wasn't in the mood. The other stations spat zydeco and rock at me. I clicked it off and leaned out the window like a family dog lapping up fresh air. The wind itself was balmy, briny and contained a hint of fried bread. Sweat cooled my skin. I remembered for a moment that there were parts of this city I enjoyed. None of them involved death.

After a few minutes of blissful silence, the driver slapped the steering wheel and grinned. "I coulda kicked you two out, but I know better than to worry about neighborhoods. It ain't the neighborhood that kills ya, it's being slow on the draw. Take that shooting," he said, nodding toward the back seat. "It happened in one of the better parts of town. There's blood on that seat," he said almost proudly.

I cursed to myself.

He went on to explain how he'd made a pickup in the Garden District. Two white kids. They made him pull over in an empty parking lot and shot him in the leg when he refused to hand over his fares. "They should've known not to mess with Chuckie. I whipped out my magnum and wasted the creep sitting right there." He patted the compartment separating us. "I killed one of them and paralyzed the other. Kids today think they can't die." He grunted. "They should've asked this old Navy man about death before pulling that shit on me. I could of told them." He patted my knee and I jerked sharply toward the door. "You sound like you're from back East," he said nonchalantly, as if we'd been chatting about the weather.

My stomach spurted acid into my mouth. "I am."

"Well, so am I, sister. And as soon as I can save enough, I'm moving back home. Plan to open a restaurant in Jersey City. I make great manicotti." My head was spinning. He pulled over to a corner and said, "This is it."

We were in a impoverished, residential part of town. The houses were small with yards barely a few feet deep. Most of the structures were run-down, with gaping windows, cracked shutters and cracked foundation walls. The one we'd pulled up to was an exception. It was freshly painted, the lawn immaculate except for a smattering of bruised bananas that had fallen from an astoundingly fecund tree which towered over the yard.

Lerebon handed two twenties to the driver and asked him to wait. I had a feeling Chuckie wasn't too keen about the idea, but he agreed anyway. I stomped outside, stumbled over tree roots that had exploded through the pavement, and demanded to know where we were in a voice that reminded me of Lois Lane in the arms of a supersonic Superman. Okay, maybe I was a little high-strung.

"Have you ever come down here for the Jazz Festival?" he asked, escorting me through an aluminum gate that clanged so loud I wondered if the neighbors had dived for cover. "We're not far from the fairgrounds," he explained. "And no, I wouldn't recommend your coming here alone. Ironic, though. A block or so away, it's yuppie town. Beautiful homes, organic food grocery stores. My aunt lives here. Please —" He gestured toward the front door with a flourish.

It swung open before I got there. The shotgun

welcome I'd half-expected didn't come. Instead, I stared at an attractive woman with hair as white as Dr. Lerebon's and almost as short. She was close to six feet, had skin smooth as pudding and dark penetrating eyes. She peered at me through tortoise-shell glasses, lowered her double chin and asked Lerebon if I was *the one*.

I wasn't sure how I felt about being *the one*. Through the doorway I could see a human skull sitting nonchalantly on top of a broad shelf, as if it were a planter filled with daisies. It was flanked by candles, a miniature cane chair criss-crossed with ropes, a gild-edged mirror and gourds. To the left of the doorway stood a fish tank large enough to hold a swarm of lobsters for a mid-size restaurant. Instead, it held two snakes, as thick in circumference as my forearm. A reel of B sci-fi flicks from the Fifties played in my head. Zombies. Shrunken heads. The woman invited me in, but my feet wouldn't carry me past the threshold.

She shot me a lightning-bolt of a smile, glanced back over her shoulder, then winked at me. "That's Marie altar. I haven't touched a thing since she died. Come on, hon, we don't have much time. I'm a nurse at Saint Jude's and my shift's coming up" She pulled me inside. "My name's Roxanne, by the way. I don't expect that Jake gave you that piece of information. He's a brilliant doctor, or as my sister used to say, the last of the great *dokté-fey*, which means leaf doctor or some such thing, but he tends to favor mystery a bit too much. For the record, I'm not the expert on voodoo that Jakey thinks I am, but I know a lot more than he does. My sister made sure of that. If I can help, I will."

My head was pounding. Since arriving in New Orleans, I'd poured more alcohol into my body than I had the previous six months. To my surprise, I found myself craving another drink. I rubbed my temples and asked, "Will someone please tell me what's going on?"

"Aunt Rox inherited my mother's *asson* and her understanding of the *lwa-Ginen*."

"Oh, for heaven's sake." She stopped short and wagged a finger at her nephew. "Next you'll have me talking in tongues. Don't make it sound so exotic. Your mama was the *manbo*. Me, I'm not much more than a librarian."

"Right. Tell the neighbors that."

"I do . . . not that they listen. They still miss Marie, angel that she was. Come on through here."

We marched through a long, dim hall lined with old photographs, none of which I had time to examine. Roxanne had the gait of a soldier anxious to charge. We ended in a dining room that had clearly seen a lot of action. The wooden floors were scuffed clear of varnish, the pine table bore knife marks and pools of candle wax, and the cane-seat of the chair in which I sat held a butt-friendly indent. I wiggled forward and waited for someone to talk.

"As I started to explain at the bar," Dr. Lerebon began in a ponderous tone, "Voodoo is an ancient religion in which animism and magic —"

His aunt broke in. "Lordy, if your mama could hear you." To me, she said, "Honey, can you pass me the notebook that so disturbed Jakey? Thanks."

I exchanged looks with Lerebon. He retrieved my notebook from his pocket and slid it across the table. The veins on the back of his hand bulged, thick as well-fed earthworms. I could almost read his heartbeat in their pulse. Lerebon was pumped.

While she read my notes, I asked Lerebon about the word he'd used earlier at the bar. He spelled it for me.

"I suppose I do resort to less than accessible terminology when discussing voodoo, but for me the language itself is magic. Especially when those words materialized on my mother's lips. She was an extraordinary woman. *Lwa* is a word we use to describe the spirits who mediate between humans and God."

"Close enough," Roxanne muttered, still reading my notes and nodding to herself.

A smile played over his lips. I could tell that he enjoyed being corrected by his aunt. "The *lwa* are present in trees, rivers, the flame of a candle, sometimes even the human body. There is nothing and no one beyond their reach. Some people mistakenly call them gods. They're not. Voodoo believes in a supreme being who uses the *lwa* as his intermediaries —"

"Jakey, you talk too much. Excuse me, Robin, are the dates of these murders correct?" Roxanne extended the notebook to me, her fingers tapping the page.

I stared at the page, then her, then back at the page, the hairs on the back of my neck rising. She had the earlier list of homicides, the one I'd gotten from Sweeney. "Why do you ask?"

"Something's wrong here. I expected the murders to have all been on a Friday, Saturday or Monday. This here woman was killed on a Thursday and this one on a Sunday." A pinkie slid along Allen's name and then circled Galonardi's. "Now, that doesn't make sense given the rest of what I'm reading."

"Which is?" Dr. Lerebon had moved behind his aunt. The two of them harumphed and nodded at the notebook while I sat opposite, my hands raking my hair in disbelief.

"Hey, remember me?"

They glanced over to me at the same time. Roxanne said, "If you expect me to start jerking my limbs and wailing out the name of the murderer, you've been watching too much television."

Impatient, I blurted, "Galonardi *was* murdered on a Monday. The date there is wrong. And Allen's murder has been closed."

"All right!" She slapped her hands together. "Now we're getting somewhere. Come on over here."

The three of us squeezed into a narrow hallway studded with bookcases. She dragged a thick volume down from the top shelf, thumbed through it and slapped the book over one forearm so hard the spine snapped.

"*Ogou Feray,*" she announced with satisfaction.

I stared down at a graphic symbol that resembled a man constructed from asterisks, bars, triangles and curlicues.

"This is called a *vèvè*, a symbolic drawing unique to a specific *lwa*," Lerebon explained, breathing hard over my shoulder.

"Oh, shush, Jake," Roxanne said. "What's important for you to know is that Ogou is a warrior and overseer of the fire realm. Red is the color associated with him. See this painting? The red scarf around his neck is a common fixture in drawings. He has many connections among the *lwa*, including sexual relations with Ezili, who represents love. This illustration on this page ... right here ... depicts her as a mulatto. A beautiful, alluring woman, known to be rather free with her affections. Are you Catholic?"

I said, "No," and reflected on my earlier conversation with Dreyer Carr about Pete Strampos' family. I wondered if traditional religion somehow factored into the murders.

"Good, then you shouldn't be too offended. In some circles, she is seen as the *Vodoun* counterpart to the Virgin Mary."

"Roxy —" Jacob sounded a warning note.

"Okay, darling boy, I'll get back to Ogou." She closed the book and pulled a small pamphlet from another shelf. "Offerings to him typically included the sacrifice of a bull, ram or a red rooster. He is often symbolized by trees, most commonly pine or calabash. The predominant symbol for Ogou, however, is a saber driven into the earth. An image with many violent connotations, especially among those who do not fully understand voodoo."

"Why are you telling me all this?" I asked, still puzzled.

"Ogou's special days —" She drew the words out, teasing us both. "His special days are Friday, Saturday and Monday. These killings match the pattern."

She attributed more significance to her pronouncement than I did. "With all due respect, couldn't the timing just be a coincidence? I'm more interested in finding out if there's anything in those books that connects Ogou to eggs or eggshells?"

"As far as I can tell, the eggshells are irrelevant. Maybe they're supposed to distract you. A decoy of sorts, or a private joke. To anyone not familiar with the attributes of *lwa*, the eggshells would appear to be the only shared characteristic among these killings.

But the rest of what he left behind at the crime scenes is far more telling. Whoever committed these murders is familiar with voodoo, I can guarantee that." We headed back into the dining room. "Read your own notes now that you have this new information."

She thrust the book back into my hands and planted her hands on her hips as I read.

> *Unexplained artifacts found on or near the victims included:*
>
> 1. *A knotted red neckerchief (Mary Ryan)*
> 2. *A pipe made from a tropical American tree called calabash (Eileen Anderson)*
> 3. *A bottle of pine needles and bark shavings (Hope Williams)*
> 4. *Three slices of bull's testicles wrapped around ice and placed in a sterilized glass mason jar (Betty Galonardi)*
> 5. *A new snake-skin wallet filled with packets of ground coffee (Andrea Allen)*
>
> *None identified for Lisa Rubin, as yet.*

Suddenly, the connection among the homicides appeared undeniable. My knees buckled. Lerebon caught me and lowered me into a chair. After nine years, we'd finally caught the scent of Mary Ryan's murderer.

Ten minutes later, I was sliding back into the passenger side of the taxi, biting my nails. NeVille was looking better and better to me as a suspect.

Perhaps his daft, inarticulate manner had been a con, another joke on the stupid investigators who'd missed the blatant clues left behind at each and every murder. A native of New Orleans, he certainly had ample opportunity to learn about voodoo. The only problem was, I hated to think that Sweeney had been right about anything.

"You're pretty quiet," Lerebon said, leaning over my shoulder from the back seat.

"Your aunt's given me a lot to think about." I needed more information on NeVille. Where he was born. What kind of family life he had. What exposure he might've had to voodoo while growing up. The list of basic investigative requirements clicked off in my head. Childhood traumas. Romantic disappointments. Psychiatric history. Criminal records. I'd been so ready to dismiss Sweeney's theories that I hadn't asked the right questions.

The doctor squeezed my shoulder. "You're exhausted. Now is not the time to think. Do you have any friends in the city?"

I had much better than that. I had K.T. And his words made me yearn for a night spent curled up in her arms. I angled my wrist so that the ambient light from the car next to us shone on my watch. It was close to eleven. At that time, two long days ago, I'd watched K.T. plop down on a stool at the prep table and lustily indulge in a glass of icy milk and an enormous plate of warm bread pudding. Given the tension between us since then, the odds were high I'd find her there tonight. I asked the driver to drop me off at Les Enfants. Lerebon and I shook hands formally. My emotions were stretched too thin for anything else and he appeared to recognize that. At another time, I'd thank him appropriately. For now, I needed K.T.

Despite the hour, the restaurant was bustling. Dinner had metamorphosed into liquor-laced coffees and butter-drenched desserts. One of Winston's specialities was a soup of coffee laced with vanilla ice cream, Bailey's and Amaretto. The scent wafted to me from the nearest table.

"How many?" I didn't recognize the maitre d' from the other night.

"Not tonight. Too full."

She didn't take no for an answer. "Well, luckily you have two stomachs, the one that says I'm full and the other that's reserved for dessert."

"No, thanks. I'm here to see K.T. Bellflower. Is she here still?"

Her solicitude kicked up a notch. "Why, I'm not sure. Why don't we go and see."

I thrust my arm out to stop her. "I know the way."

The restaurant was organized around an open kitchen, with a variety of prep stations. To get to the back, you had to pass a porthole near the wood-burning stove. Heidi, the Swedish giant with a flare for fish, was stoking the fire. She shouted, "Hot potato!" as I passed by, a plank of blackened salmon balanced precariously on a pizza paddle she thrust in my direction. The heat seared my cheek. I wondered if she was warning K.T. about my arrival.

I overestimated my importance. K.T. wasn't in clear sight and no one even glanced up at my unannounced entrance. They were too busy filling orders, cleaning and sneaking out for smokes. An order of boiled shrimp with gazpacho buzzed by my head. I dodged and turned the corner. Two waiters were picking through a basket laden with the remains of focaccia and jalapeño corn bread.

I slid over and asked, "Is K.T. around?"

One of them wiped his mouth and said, "Haven't seen her since that newspaper guy left here."

"When was that?"

"Around seven, I think. Maybe earlier. Could've been six. Things were hopping."

The other waiter chimed in. "My feet are burning up. I've never seen a place catch on like this before. You see the look on Winnie's face?"

Only good friends call Winston Hawkings by his nickname. I asked the waiter for his name.

"Bobby. I've worked with Winnie for years."

"Where can I find him?"

A frown puckered his eyebrows. "Geez, now that you mentioned it, I haven't seen Winnie for a few hours either." He yanked on the tails of his vest and shouted over my head, "Melinda, you see K.T. or Winston?"

The woman he called to was at the sink, scrubbing pans. She shut the faucet and wiped her hands on her apron. "What's that, Bobby?"

"K.T. or Winston around?"

She shook her head and strode over. "Winston ran out a few hours ago to see his lawyer. A problem about the liquor license. K.T. I haven't seen since that creepy black guy left here."

My flesh started to tingle. I wasn't sure why.

"What was creepy about him?" I asked.

"Don't know, exactly." She stared up at the ceiling as if expecting to find the answer etched in plaster. "I just got the heebie-jeebies from him."

Bobby laughed. "Fitzhugh Chamelle," he said, mockingly. "He looked like a comics-book villain, didn't he? I swear his hair was the color of Reggie's, you know, from the Archie comics."

Melinda shrugged. "You're showing your age, Bobby. Mine too. He did have that blue-black sheen like Reggie."

Blood fled from my limbs. *Blue-black hair.* That's how K.T. described the man who had followed her back from Café du Monde. "Can I use a phone?" The new urgency in my tone was hard to miss.

"Who are you anyway?" The second waiter interrupted.

I told him my name. Bobby and Melinda exchanged private glances. Clearly, they knew about our relationship. Melinda led me into an office and left me alone. I dialed our hotel room. On the fifth ring, the voice-mail service kicked in. My message was short: "If you get back to the room before me, don't leave until I get there."

All at once a fever swept over me. My hands shook as I walked back out into the kitchen. Where had K.T. gone? I leaned on the refrigerator handle, trying to catch my breath. Surely I was overreacting, my rising panic the cost of a long, grueling day. Measuring each step, I sought out Melinda. She was once again immersed in cleanup, this time loading the dishwasher with impressive efficiency.

"Do you have another minute?"

"Sure. Is it about K.T.?"

I swallowed first, watched the dishwasher liquid

rise to the fill line, then asked, "Can you tell me anything else about this Chamelle guy? What paper he writes for or —"

I cut off my own words. Bile erupted into my throat. The name snapped into place. F.B. Chamelle. The crime writer who had covered each and every one of the eggshell homicides. The name that Evan Alexander had highlighted in yellow. A wave of nausea swept over me and I darted toward the bathroom. I barely made it through the door before my guts repelled everything I'd consumed in the last five hours. Clinging to the bowl, my body jerking with each heave, my imagination painted horrors for me. The image of Mary Ryan's battered and bloody torso. Click. Lisa Rubin's twisted limbs, the gaping wounds crimson mouths screaming from her flesh. Click.

I sank to my knees, grasped the rim so hard my wrists started to throb. Please, God, please, God. Bouncing my forehead against the seat, prayers rushing through me with the speed of sobs. After a short eternity, I finally lifted my head and wiped my eyes. Then the real nightmare began. Gulping hard, I raised the lid of the toilet. A smudge of blood lined the rim. I shot to my feet and scanned the bathroom with widened eyes. Blood in the sink. Small droplets, but bloodstains nonetheless. On the floor, brown smears like so many others I've seen in recent years.

No. Not like others I've seen. Not like anything I've seen.

## Chapter 9

**Wednesday, May 5**

I couldn't remember how I made it back to the hotel. Did I run the whole way? No, that was impossible. My ankle still hurt too much. I must've called a taxi. The phone cord wound about my fingers, cutting off circulation. Somehow, it felt good.

"Robin, are you listening?"

My eyes tightened. Little stars burst in the darkness. This was a dream. I was dreaming. Why was someone screaming in my ear?

"Robin, I'm sending Sweeney over there right now. I called him on the other line. He should be there in fifteen, twenty minutes tops. Don't leave the hotel. Do you understand?"

Swimming. My arms weary from propelling me through the dark weight of the water. So hard to move. But I couldn't stay still. Another thrust and I'd explode into the light. K.T. would be there.

I opened my eyes. The room was still dark. Thomas Ryan still mumbled in my ear. K.T. was gone.

"Tom," I gasped. No other words would come. I said his name and started to weep again. I hated the sound. Hated the tightness in my chest, the inability to speak, to look around, to breathe.

"We don't know what happened yet, Rob. You have to hang on."

He was talking in slow motion. I stared at the phone and allowed myself to drift. My head was floating, but my body wouldn't follow.

"You sure no one in the restaurant cut themselves? You checked with everyone?"

Crimson. The color of fire engines, bicycles and tops. The color of my sister's dress the day I killed her.

"Tom, did I call the police? Did I tell you?" My memory bank felt clogged. I blinked hard. The room blurred.

"No, hon, you called me instead, and that's fine for now."

Right. The cops wouldn't take me seriously. Not in New Orleans. Not in any big city where a person isn't considered missing until his or her body washes up with the spring thaw.

"How's your breathing now? Steadier?"

"Sure, Ryan, I'm steady as a rock. Can you check out Chamelle for me?"

"I'll move mountains, Robin. Mountains. As soon as Sweeney gets there, I'll call in every chit I can. We'll find her."

K.T. I held the phone to my chest and rocked. Her copper hair, her green eyes, a spark of spring in them when she smiled. The softness of her skin. The rise of her belly. Her belly. At the memory, I gagged, dropped the phone and stumbled into the bathroom. Dry heaves racked my body. I had nothing left to give. Nothing.

I hadn't wanted the baby. Not really. The decision had been strictly hers, made long before I found my way back into her life. We weren't even sure what we'd do once it was here. Now they were both gone and I felt on the verge of going mad.

My mouth tasted like soured milk. I rinsed and spat repeatedly. When I returned to the room, Ryan's voice buzzed through the air like a trapped horsefly. I retrieved the phone. "Sorry. I can't stop barfing." The door of the refrigerator snapped open. I pushed aside the Yoo-Hoo and containers of skim milk and dug out three miniature bottles of booze. Vodka, gin and rum. I gulped one down.

"What are you doing now?" Ryan's voice held an edge.

"Guess."

His silence told me more than I wanted to know. He knew exactly what I was doing. And he disapproved. "This isn't you, Robin."

"What the hell is me, Tom? Tell me that. I murdered K.T. I murdered my sister Carol. What kind of woman is that?"

"You don't know what you're saying."

I twisted the cap off the gin. More than anything else, I wanted to pass out. The alcohol ran down my throat like a feather down a thigh. A seductive warmth drifted through me. So nice. My fingertips tingled.

"Fuck it. First, you blow me out of the sky by informing me that Sweeney's off the wagon, and now you're going to fall down and join him. Is that it? Are you telling me that everyone I put confidence in is going to screw me? If I mean anything to you, Robin, *anything*, you'll put the booze down right now. And I mean right now!"

Why was he shouting? I draped the phone wire over my shoulder and let the phone bounce gently against my back, like a tree branch in a stiff spring breeze. Better. Much better. I closed my eyes. No. Not better. The room spun as images of K.T.'s face, sliced and bloody, snapped into my brain.

I cried softly to myself as I tossed the last empty bottle in the ice bucket. Ryan's ravings hadn't stopped.

"K.T. may still be alive, and you're taking the chicken-ass path out. If ever you needed to be sober, it's now. Do you hear me? I did the same shit-face routine you're succumbing to now, and it blew me out of Mary's investigation. If I'd been thinking straight back then . . . Christ! K.T. is probably still alive, Robin, and you need to be alert."

He was right. I had to think clearly, even though it was the last thing I wanted to do. I sat down on the floor, pressing my back hard against the footboard. "I stopped drinking, okay? Now, ease off. My head's pounding."

I retraced my steps. Before coming upstairs, I'd searched the grounds of the hotel, climbed up and down the stairwells, checked the boiler room. Only then had I dared to return to the room where K.T. and I had made love, spooned in sleep, whispered and clenched hands, searched each other's mouths. Ryan was right. K.T. could still be alive. There hadn't been any signs of blood near the hotel or in our room. Plus, if Roxanne's theories were right, the bastard would only strike on Friday, Saturday or Monday. At least, he'd never deviated from that pattern. Maybe he'd snared K.T. in some private hell of his own, waiting. I had to hold on. I had to believe. At least for now.

Ryan's sigh was unmistakable. "Good, good," he muttered to himself. I could almost hear him gulping for air. This had to be hard for him, too. The madman who had taken K.T. from me had murdered his wife as well. Nine terrible years ago. He'd never fallen in love again. I rubbed my hands over my face as if I were scrubbing mud from my skin. This insanity had to end.

I filled Ryan in on my visit with Roxanne Lerebon, my voice a low monotone. I'd grown gratefully numb. When I finished explaining the voodoo connections, Ryan was clearly more surprised than I had been and far more disturbed. We assessed the details we had accumulated on the five homicides with the ease of criminal clinicians, emotions dulled and pulses steady. When the knock on the door came,

I didn't even jump. My progress was measured by the loss of appropriate response. Some career I'd chosen.

Sweeney looked as if he hadn't slept in days. A wiry beard had sprouted on his chin, setting off a scar along his chin I hadn't noticed previously. He stared at me hard, clearly gauging my mental state, then peered over my shoulder at the phone dangling from the arm of the desk chair. "That Ryan still? Good. Let him debrief me, you're in no shape."

While he talked to Ryan, I retreated to the bathroom again. I balanced myself on the tub's edge and dropped the rubber plug into the sink's drain. The rushing water drowned out most but not all of their conversation. It sounded like Sweeney was trying hard to convince Ryan that he wasn't a complete fuck-up. The last thing I needed to hear was Sweeney apologizing to his good friend for screwing up years of investigative work. I had my own screw-ups to worry about, and they were doozies. The terry- cloth wash towel was almost too hot to touch. I flopped it over my face and leaned my head back. At one point, I thought I heard Sweeney sob. I pressed my hands to my ears and waited for him to stop.

For a few seconds after he hung up all I could hear was the buzzing of the light fixture.

"Hey." Sweeney rapped on the closed bathroom door. "How you doing in there?"

"Use your imagination."

"Mind if I open —"

"Go ahead."

The door swung to the side. Sweeney stepped in and gingerly lowered himself onto the toilet, his big booted feet tracking sludge over the tiles. We both noticed K.T.'s bra hanging to dry over the towel rack at the same time. I reached over and tucked it into my pocket, gulping as I did so.

"Look," he said, "what can I say? Shit." He stuck a finger in the sink basin and made small swirling motions in the water like a schoolboy waiting to be chastised for messing up on the big test. I almost felt sorry for him. Almost. How many lives had his incompetence cost?

I stood up suddenly. "Sweeney, I'm not up to this right now."

"Can't blame you. You must think I'm an asshole, and me coming from here." I got the impression he was talking more to himself than to me. "That's what living in San Francisco did for me, made me forget my roots. I shoulda thought of asking some locals about the eggshell stuff, maybe then I'd've hit on something before this, but that voodoo stuff is mostly for black folk or swampers and, well, none of that ever crossed my mind. And that news about the Allen murder, its being closed and all that, hell, I got no excuse for that. I just didn't follow up. Shit happens. You have any idea how fucking rare it is for a cold case to get yanked out of deep freeze *years* after a vic's done in?" He glared at me hard. "Don't look at me like that, Miller. I fucked up, okay, I fucked up. I know for a fact I wasn't the only one. Think about how many people have touched this case at some point, me, Ryan, your partner —"

I pulled hard on the door but it slammed against his boots.

Without moving his feet so much as an inch,

Sweeney narrowed his eyes at me and drew his thumb along his upper lip where sweat beads had erupted. This guy hated apologizing to me, hated asking me to understand his ineptitude. I didn't avert my gaze. Let the asshole suffer.

He snorted like a hippo considering a charge, then grabbed the towel I'd dropped back in the sink and rubbed it over his own face. "Tough broad, I'll hand you that."

The intimacy of the setting suddenly disturbed me. I growled, "Let me out of here, Sweeney."

"Sure thing, but you gotta hear me first, and if you think this comes easy to me, you are dead wrong. I'm sorry, sorry for badmouthing you when it looks like maybe you're a better dick than I thought. Hell, you may be a better dick than me, and coming from a big-balled Southerner like me, that says a lot." The smile on his face had pain behind it. He was trying way too hard, and I didn't care a twit. I wanted out.

"Sweeney, move your legs. I got work to do."

"Okay, okay, here you go," he said, kicking the door open with his heel. It crashed against the towel bar with such force, the framed prints on the wall almost bounced off their hooks. I stepped by him without a second look.

He wouldn't back off. "All I'm saying is, you'd be making a big mistake if you think you can move this baby without me. I'll even let you call the next shot. Give me an assignment, Madam Dick. Come on, I mean it, what can I do to help?" he asked, following too closely on my heels.

I waved him away. The volatile pit bull had

turned into a big, sloppy Saint Bernard, over-eager for a rescue mission. No matter where I moved, he was half a step behind me. His new persona annoyed me as much as his last. "Back off!" I snapped finally.

Thick-fingered hands closed around my biceps. "Don't do this. I'm not a complete fuck-up. Your friend needs both of us. Tell me what to do. Anything."

The words erupted from me, flaming with sarcasm. "Find K.T." I bit my lip before the sob could crack loose.

"I plan to do just that."

"How? *How?*" A hint of hysteria crept into my voice. I couldn't lose control again. I took a deep breath and asked, "Can you get help from the local police force?"

"If anyone can, I'm the man. Those boys have my bucks to thank for some of their best drunks. What do you want to know?"

His comment wasn't real encouraging. Just what I needed, assistance from cops who counted favors by the number of drinks someone had bought them. Still, this was the best hand I had to play. But what if this moron was overstating his connections and information sources? I stood nose to nose with him and asked, "Were there any peculiar items found near Rubin's body? And don't assume I don't already know the answer."

"Yeah, hot shot," he said, nodding confidently. "A plaster cast statue of a ram ready to attack." The cocky edge had returned. "So what do I win for being right?"

"Nada." I walked away and rummaged in a

drawer for an antiacid. My stomach was a cauldron of fire. "The voodoo angle seems to hold up. The ram's another symbol of Ogou Feray."

"What'd you say?" He sounded confused. I spun around to face him and repeated myself. Sweeney's face had turned red. "You want to tell me what the fuck you're talking about, or you gonna keep spitting this mumbo-jumbo crap at me?"

I gave him a quick run-down.

"Shit." He yanked up his pants like a cowboy about to mount a bronco and strode by me toward the balcony doors. Staring through them, he said quietly, "So Ryan didn't give me the full scoop on the phone."

"I don't have time or interest in soothing your bruised ego, Sweeney," I said. "Do you know if the statue was used in the homicide?"

Still looking away from me, he said, "The perp probably used it to knock out Rubin. He left it standing between her legs, a friggin' victory flag. What else you want to know?" He turned back and plucked at the hairs of his eyebrows, waiting for my next question. The son of a bitch knew I was testing the extent of his knowledge, and he was relishing the chance to prove himself.

In the end, I had to admit that neither of us had a full deck of cards. To make this investigation fly, we'd have to work together, no matter how much we disliked each other. And I had no doubt that the distaste was mutual.

"Okay, Sweeney, you want an assignment?" I said. "Here's one. Get me everything you can on Fitzhugh

Chamelle, if he has a criminal record. Where he lives. What car he drives. How he might link up to NeVille." I scratched his name on the hotel pad.

"Why don't you fuckin' ask me for the asshole's high school album. Shit, Miller, it's the middle of the night."

I muttered under my breath.

"See," he said, "there you go again, looking down at me like I got shit on my shoes. You want honesty, right?"

I spun around. "You ready for true confessions, Sweeney? Is that it? Okay, tell me how you missed out on Chamelle? He covered every damn homicide you investigated, listed facts that no one should've known but the cops."

"Hey, I admit I'm not big on reading newspapers. So shoot me. Just 'cause I get my dose of daily dirt from the radio doesn't make me an idiot, and before you turn your nose up at me, remember I've been doing this alone. Solo. No staff, no flunkies, no computer shit." He flicked a nail against my laptop. "So Chamelle's another nut I forgot to screw. Let me get to him now, okay? I'll screw him so tight, his eyes'll pop."

I winced at the image. If K.T.'s life hadn't been at stake, I would've kicked this asshole out a long time ago. "We don't have a lot of time, and we sure as hell don't have time for your games."

"You need me and my games more than you think." He ground his teeth, clearly trying to rein himself in. "The one thing you can't get in this town but I can are police files, police info. My buddies on the force are all night owls. I'll make the calls right now." He reached for the phone, his eyes demanding assent.

My nod was nearly imperceptible. "But use the lobby phone. I need this line."

He dropped the phone back in the cradle and scrambled toward the door. "Fine, fine. Fuck the phone. I'll just haul my ass across the street, to command central. Just don't go anywhere without me."

"Sure, you and my American Express card."

"Miller, listen up," he said, his hand on the door knob. "I know you told Ryan about my drinking. He came down on me like a piano dropped from the top of the Sears Tower. For your info, I already put a call in to my sponsor. As of tonight, I'm working this thing sober." He pointed to the trash can where I'd tossed the liquor bottles. "I suggest you do the same."

The last thing I needed was a lecture from the likes of Sweeney. I turned my back on him. As soon as I heard the lock click, my breath came easier. I pulled over the chair and called Dreyer Carr. No one answered. After the second try, I gave up. Considering the hour, he may have turned off the phone ringer and volume. I left a message, again urging him to contact me if he found anything out about Chamelle. The next call was to my office. By now, it was after two in the morning. I left detailed instructions for Jill, then dialed my partner Tony Serra. Even diminished by AIDS, Tony was one of the most dedicated and insightful investigators I'd ever known. After half a second of grogginess, he zeroed in on my briefing with amazing speed.

"So this reporter looks like he could be the primo

perp. Let me do some follow-up from here in case that donkey Sweeney takes another tumble. I'm a little disappointed in Ryan. He usually sizes them up better than this, otherwise I never would've taken a chance on you way back when. I gotta tell you, from the way he's talked about Sweeney, I always assumed the guy could walk on water. I even tried to interest him in joining SIA."

I started to interrupt.

"Hold on, partner, this was *way* before you came on board. The guy never bothered to return my calls. I figured he was another HIV-phobic asshole, so I didn't push."

"Did you meet him when Betty Galonardi was murdered?"

"Hold on, let me think. The spinster schoolteacher, right? There was a rumor some librarian killed himself over her. I remember thinking maybe the dead guy's mom had killed Galonardi in revenge. Shit, did I meet Sweeney then? I should remember that, shouldn't I?" Tony's memory had begun deteriorating in recent weeks. The frustration in his voice disturbed me. "Come on, Serra, what was the year? 'Eighty-five?"

I supplied the answer his memory wouldn't surrender. " 'Eighty-eight."

"Okay, that's why I don't remember. I was in Paris that summer. By the time I returned, Sweeney was done and gone. That's right. I did some look-see when I got home, but the trail was stone-dead by then. Also —" He cut himself off. "You're not going to like what I gotta say."

I clenched my fists in anticipation. "Go ahead."

"Galonardi was a dyke, I mean, a lesbian." Shivers ran through my limbs as he spoke. "At least according to her next-door neighbor, an older guy who was kind of wacky himself. I never got absolute con- firmation, but the vic sure looked like a butch from her photos. Short hair, squared-off nails, man-tailored shirts. Back then, I hadn't had much exposure to these types, so —"

I burst in. "You blew it off? You blew the case off because she was gay?"

"Miller, don't make this personal."

"Okay, partner, I'll remember that the next time I decide the death of an Italian not important enough for me to investigate."

"I *did* investigate. Remember, I was doing this for Tommy, not some paying client I could give a shit about, but things were still pretty raw for me back then. I'd been kicked off the force and treated like a pariah by the guys I would've died defending, all 'cause I had the shit luck of contracting the 'gay disease.' I'm just being honest here. In 'eighty-eight, the only thing I felt towards homosexuals was anger. Pure and simple. I'm not saying I was right, I know I wasn't, I'm just saying I may not have done my best work back then."

I pressed my hand against the glass of the patio doors. Serra had changed a lot since we'd begun working together, but this was the first time either of us had ever broached the subject directly.

In not much more than a whisper, he added, "You know I don't feel that way anymore, don't you? Robin?"

"Okay, okay, fine." The hand holding the phone

shook uncontrollably. Fatigue and booze were getting the better of me. "I guess you never bothered telling Sweeney all this."

"Don't remember if I did or not. Sorry."

My notebook looked like it had been used as cat litter. The pages were stained and ripped. I flipped through them carefully. "So Lisa Rubin was bi, Galonardi and Anderson gay." My chest hurt as I phrased the next question. "Any chance Mary Ryan —"

"Oh, for crying out loud, she and Tommy were madly in love."

Counting to ten stopped the expletives from erupting from my mouth. "Tony." One, two, three. "Aren't you the one who told me friendship can muddy even the clearest water? All I'm asking is if it's possible —"

"Shit. Okay. Sure, it's possible. You want to be the one to pose that question to Ryan, because I sure as hell don't. The man is still in love with her. He still despises himself for driving her into that fleabag hotel. You want to add a new dimension to his nightmares?"

Tony had a point. "Maybe we can take another approach," I said. "Can you check Hope Williams' story? Let's see if the pattern holds up with her. In the meantime, I have more pressing concerns. Like how do I find K.T. Any suggestions?" So calm, I thought, listening to myself. Just another case. Just another case that would decide the course of the rest of my life. The pressure on my chest intensified. "Can you repeat that, Tony? I wasn't listening."

"You know me, Miller, I'm never quick to give false hope to anyone, so if I tell you my guts say we still got a chance to get her back alive, you better believe I mean it. And I do think there's time. Not much, but maybe it'll be enough. Seems to me, whoever the perp is, he's thumbing you right about now. I think you've tapped into something. Give me the run-down once again, this time with your eyes closed and your memory one-hundred percent engaged. As hard as it is, the best thing you can do for K.T. right now is turn off your emotions."

Tony's strategy had worked in the past for our clients. The end result for me, however, was more confusion. On the one hand, I had Barry NeVille, who seemed to have had opportunity for at least four out of five murders, but no obvious motive. Then there was the egghead who'd crashed into me at Dock of the Bay, shoved Rubin's tooth in my pocket, and later lured me in the direction of the supposedly haunted Herriott place on Dauphine. Was he working in collaboration with NeVille? And what did either of these men have to do with Chamelle? I pushed myself further back in time. If Chamelle was the same man who'd followed K.T., he could have been the one who ordered the Eggs Sardou sent up to my room. The killer appeared to have a bizarre sense of humor. From the evidence we had, he apparently took pleasure in teasing investigators, planting obscure clues, dumping red herrings by the caseload, all to demonstrate his superiority. The man was good. But we were gaining on him.

Sweeney shouted my name through the door. I took my time concluding the call with Tony, then let him in. He barreled past me, trailing the scent of fresh, strong coffee. For that sin alone, I could've decked him.

"Dammit. We're working on the same side, aren't we?" He was almost whining.

"Sure we are," I said. "Let's just say right now I got more faith in my own investigative abilities than yours. What did you find out?"

I heard him mutter a few choice curse words before he turned to face me. "Chamelle's got contacts on the force as well. My bud said he showed up on the scene just hours after the police did. No one knows how, or at least, no one's saying. He's a real loose bird, floats in and out without tossing a feather. I tried to get a number for him, but no luck. Geoffrey, my pal, says that this Fitzhugh is definitely a local, maybe even got some Cajun blood in him, vaguely remembers him asking for inside dope on any maggot with hoodoo vibes, but that's all he could tell me."

"You want to translate that?"

"Fitz has demonstrated interest in the crimes of the occult. Clear enough. He had no criminal record. No car registered in his name. Maybe you can find something on him in your magic compact digital thing."

I grunted but fired up my laptop anyway. Twice I had to shoo Sweeney away. He stared at the screen like a two-year-old discovering Disney.

"Shit," he exclaimed. "This stuff's insane. How many addresses are on that thing? Isn't this violating privacy? No one should have this much info but the feds."

Without answering, I switched CDs, then dialed into our online subscription research services. The bottom line was the same: Fitzhugh Chamelle did not show up in any phone or address directory. There were plenty of news stories filed by him, though. All grisly murders, the harrowing details described with exceptional clarity. Most of the homicides occurred in Louisiana and the surrounding states. The exceptions were the out-of-town murders I already knew about, and all of those stories ran two to three days after the victims had been found, which implied that Chamelle hadn't just been in the right place at the right time. He'd sought these stories out.

I slammed the lid of the laptop. Nothing made sense anymore. My brain started percolating conspiracy theories. Was a right-winged militia masterminding these murders? Was Chamelle the ring leader, or just a news reporter who'd latched onto the eggshell murders with unsettling zeal? And how the hell did NeVille fit into all this? Sweeney patted my shoulder and I swung around so fast, he stumbled back onto the bed.

"You gotta calm down, hon, or you gonna hurt someone, maybe yourself."

I glanced past him to the alarm clock. Daylight was not far away, and K.T. still hadn't been found.

He followed my gaze. "Never look at the time. That's how you get ulcers. I should know."

"You have ulcers?" The prospect struck me as ludicrous.

"Had. After my wife passed on. Breast cancer... she caught it late. You don't want to know about it."

I noticed he didn't mention her suicide.

"Maybe I understand more than you think I do about what it feels to lose someone you love. My wife —" Astoundingly, his voice broke. He wiped his nose like a boxer and strode into the bathroom. Just when I started to think maybe he was human, he returned and winked at me like we were long-lost buddies. My skin crawled. "Can we get back on track now, huh?" he asked. "You've had a shot at the electronic thing, so now why don't I prove to you what I'm made of. I'm gonna find your girlfriend, I swear. No one's better on the street than me. Even Ryan still believes that. Give me two hours."

I'd give him all the time in the world, as long as he'd leave me alone. I told him pretty much the same. He took it in good humor and left without much fanfare. Almost a minute later, I left the room myself. For two hours, I plodded through every inch of the Royal Orleans, then moved on to the two closest hotels. Finally, around six a.m., I stumbled back into my room.

The smell that hit me first was K.T.'s vanilla perfume, wafting through the louver panels of the closet door. My fingers squeezed into the gap between two slats and clung there as I steadied myself. I'd half-expected to find her there, in bed, waiting for me, confused by the terror etched into my face.

I couldn't fool myself any longer. There was a good chance that somewhere in this city K.T.'s body waited to be found. I collapsed onto the bed. Once again, I'd failed. Once again, I'd lost someone I loved. I pulled my hair back from my face hard, held my hands there against my temple, my pulse beating wildly. Something flickered in my peripheral vision. A light. The message light was on. I dove for the phone. A mechanical voice announced the number of messages in the queue. The first message took forever to begin. It was Sweeney. He'd traced K.T. Bellflower to a flight that had departed New Orleans the previous evening, bound for New York City. No seat on that flight had been assigned to Fitzhugh Chamelle, at least under that name.

The relief didn't even have time to set in before the second message began.

"It's K.T." Her voice was raspy, hoarse. I burst into tears of relief. "I'm sorry I didn't call before this. I couldn't, there was no time, I barely made the flight as it was and maybe, oh hell, maybe I wanted you to feel as alone and frightened as I did. Stupid, stupid. I need you now, oh God —" I strained to hear her. Announcements in the background drowned out her thin voice. Was she still in an airport? "I'm at Beth Israel Hospital, in New York." A long, terrifying pause. The sound of her breathing told me she was fighting back her own tears. My throat tightened. "The bleeding started at the restaurant and there was no one around I could talk to. Not you. Not even Winnie. So I called Dr. Wolf and she said to take the first flight home, which is exactly what I did. Ginny's with me now." Static on the line. I realized with a start that the muscle in my left thigh was twitching wildly. I rubbed it hard, waiting, dreading her next words.

"I'm miscarrying, Rob. I'm losing my baby. And I need you with me. Dammit —" The message ended abruptly with her sobs.

I took the next plane home.

# Chapter 10

The coffee tasted like melted plastic and cigarette ash. I spilled the entire Greek-motif cupful, still steaming, into the trash can, then stared at my reflection on the polished metal casing of the pay phone. My eyes were the color of watered-down tomato juice, a cowlick had sprouted where my part used to be, and my lips were chapped and bloody from where I'd chewed them during the long flight home. And I looked better than I felt.

I'd taken a taxi straight to the hospital. The madman hunched over the wheel had treated red traffic lights the same as yellow: pause then accelerate at space-shuttle speeds. The only good news was that he'd managed to get me to the hospital in record-breaking time. We'd screeched to a halt at the hospital entrance, narrowly missing an elderly woman with a walker. I'd stuffed dollars into his sweaty palm, exited and almost dislocated my shoulder hauling luggage out of the cavernous, foul-smelling trunk in the nanosecond that Mario Andretti gave me before soaring off to catch his next fare.

The institutionalized health-care stench pelted my senses the instant I moved through the revolving doors. A parrot-voiced clerk appeared to be paging the entire medical personnel in one long squawk. Trembling, I trudged through the long maze of musty corridor. K.T. didn't belong in this place, didn't belong in anyplace this sterile, this devoid of light and warmth. I thought of my lover, the way she smells when she comes home at night, her hands carrying a wealth of scent stolen from her kitchen: fresh-baked bread, sticky cinnamon rolls, caramelized onions, cloves. And in bed at night, her hair smells of lemon, her skin moist and perfumed with rosewater.

The elevator pinged and I'd found myself suddenly at the threshold to her room. My breath fluttered then caught in my chest like a butterfly pinned to the cold ground by a pebble of hail. K.T. lay curled on her side, sleeping in a narrow metal bed with white sheets, white blankets, all stamped *Property of Beth Israel Hospital.* A yellowed, torn curtain shielded her from the other patient and a television that flickered in silence, pumping the room with an icy gray light.

Sitting vigil at her bedside was K.T.'s sister, Virginia. She sat as close as she could, knees tucked beneath the bed, gripping the safety railing with both hands, her chin resting between them. Her eyelids fluttered with obvious exhaustion. I didn't need anyone to tell me that Ginny held the seat I should've occupied. I dropped the luggage in the corner and Ginny started. The look she speared in my direction was poison-tipped.

After dramatically referring to her wristwatch, she said, "Nice of you to come. Are you certain there isn't some pickpocket you need to chase after? Or perhaps some miscreant dog has violated the curb rules?" She cupped her ear. "Say, isn't that a car alarm sounding now? Perhaps you should check it out. We wouldn't want some honorable physician's car radio appropriated by wayward teenagers, would we?"

Ginny blows hot and cold about me, depending on circumstances. At that moment, searing Sahara winds stormed in my direction. Without fully realizing what I was doing, my hands swept over my cheeks. They felt like hot coals.

"She lost the baby two hours ago." Ginny's tone was dispassionate on purpose. I clutched my stomach and turned away. "They scheduled a D and C for late this afternoon," she said. "Think you can stick around that long?"

Until she'd spoken the words, part of me had clung to the illusion that the baby would be okay, that K.T. was somehow emotionally and physically strong enough to prevent herself from miscarrying. But the baby was gone. I was surprised at how sick I felt. Bile rose into my mouth. I swallowed hard, brushed my hand over K.T.'s hip, then faced Ginny.

She ignored my outstretched hand. "Well?" she asked, her eyebrows cocked at me, ready and more than willing to fire a new salvo of accusations at me. "I know this interferes with your schedule."

The Bellflowers are not known for their subtlety. I didn't respond to her jibe. For one, I deserved it. But I also had to believe that at least some of Ginny's hostility was a spillover from the tension in her marriage. Her husband, Larry, is a beat cop who shares some of my less desirable traits.

"Virginia, I'm sorry I wasn't here. I promise you and K.T. —" I looked toward my lover. She frowned in her sleep. "I promise you, from now on I'll be by her side."

Ginny arched an eyebrow. "Your promises mean so much to me. By the way, someone called from your office a little earlier. Emergency, of course." Her sting found its mark. I took it like a champ, apologized again, and retreated like a rabbit. The pay phone was just down the hall.

The damn on-hold music continued whining in my ear. What was taking Jill so long? I didn't want to be out of the room when K.T. woke up.

"Okay, sorry," Jill said at last. "Tony had all of these files locked up in his office. I've got everything in front of me now."

"Good. I know your load's pretty heavy right now, but any help you can throw me is great. You're going to have to coordinate with Theo Sweeney. Or maybe you can ask Wilmington to pitch in. I'd love to have old Elmore spitting random curse words at Sweeney. You can get Sweeney's number from Ryan, if the reptile has one. I just don't have the time —"

"Don't you dare apologize. If you did insist on

leading the investigation, I'd be furious with you. Now go over the instructions once more."

I kneaded the bridge of my nose, forcing myself to concentrate. So much still had to be done, and it had to be done fast, before the trail evaporated as it had after every other murder. Chamelle had to be located and grilled. I needed to know more about NeVille and see if there was a connection between him and Chamelle. The voodoo angle had to be explored thoroughly. We needed to check up on the Galonardi case and find out if there was a reason why the murderer went on a five-year hiatus. I ran down the mental list, deciding which tasks I could trust to Sweeney and which ones I wanted my own group to pursue. A few assignments I'd take on myself.

When I was done, Jill fell silent. "Robin, this is a tall order. We're running that undercover op at the Grand Central bar and we're already backed up on security checks."

"I don't want to hear this." I glanced down the hall toward K.T.'s room. Ginny had promised to signal me the instant K.T.'s eyes opened. "Just find a way to get this done. Call in other investigators. Lorelli's always desperate for work. If Tony objects, tell him I'll foot the expense myself. I really don't care. Just get this done, okay?"

"Rob, I know Thomas Ryan's important to you, but I just don't get this obsess —" She corrected herself mid-stream. "I mean, your focus on this particular case, at this particular time, confuses me." Jill was a smart woman. She was choosing her words carefully, mindful of my short fuse. "Sweeney's handled it up till now, why don't you just let him continue? If it's okay with Ryan, I don't know why it's not with you."

Despite her careful treading, she'd drawn a spark. My fuse blew. "You want to know the reason?" I blurted. "Because I don't want to let Ryan down, okay? Why is it so goddamn hard to believe that I could feel responsibility —"

The painful lump in my throat solidified, cutting off my breath. An image rose before me. My father sitting at the foot of his bed, weeping silently in a darkened room, weeks after I'd accidentally discharged a twenty-two into my sister Carol's chest. I'd crept up beside him and tried desperately to curl under his arms. In response, he locked his hands onto his elbows, rocking himself, praying in a language I'd never heard on his lips before. He never acknowledged my presence. I was three years old.

I gasped for air. Found myself leaning against the wall, crying.

Jill whispered into my ear, "Forget I mentioned it. Give K.T. a hug from John and me."

Nodding to myself, I dropped the phone back in its cradle. When I straightened up, I caught Ginny staring at me from down the hall. She wagged a finger at me.

K.T. was propped up on her elbows; her eyes were glassy, the skin beneath them puffy and raw-looking. As soon as she saw me, she started crying again. I dropped the bed railing and gathered her into my arms. Her belly still felt swollen. I bit my lip hard. "I'm sorry, honey," I said. The words were for her ears only. She shushed me, covered my mouth with hers.

Ginny cleared her throat loudly. Standing akimbo, in a tough-girl stance, she asked, "Sis, you want me to come back later?"

K.T. made a poor attempt at a smile and said, "If you don't mind. We need a little time." She stretched a palm toward her sister. I moved aside.

"Not at all," Ginny said. "Lurlene called earlier. Should I tell her it's okay to come by?"

K.T. glanced at me over her sister's shoulder. The thought of being trapped in a room with Ginny and K.T.'s best friend made my blood curdle. The image of rabid wolves descending on a lame doe flashed before me.

"Tell her I'll call tomorrow," K.T. said quietly. "Now, get some rest. And Gin, thanks for always being there." They stared at each other so intensely I felt embarrassed. Sibling relationships like theirs scare me. In my family, emotions are like crystal baubles you store on high shelves in curio cabinets, behind firmly latched doors, in rooms rarely frequented. Dare to touch them and they may shatter in your hand. In contrast, the Bellflowers flopped around in their emotions like hogs in good, ripe mud. The intimacy between them unnerved me. I moved away.

"Don't be too hard on Robin, despite what I said last night," K.T. murmured in an embarrassed tone she appeared to think I couldn't hear. "The tango takes two partners, remember? And believe me, sis, I've taken my share of missteps."

Ginny shot me a warning look over her shoulder, then muttered something back to her sister. They hugged tightly and a second later Ginny left the room. Nothing left to distract K.T. and me from each other. My skin sizzled. What now?

"Can you move this pillow?" K.T. asked, squirming into a sitting position.

I took the assignment gladly. Now that we were alone, I felt reluctant to make eye contact with K.T. The room felt unbearably hot. I opened another button on my denim shirt and rolled up my sleeves.

"Sit down, Robin."

I noticed that she was pointing to the chair and not patting the bed. K.T. wanted to have a *serious* talk. The urge to run tingled through me.

She cleared her throat, prelude to words I was sure I didn't want to hear.

"Hon," I said in a preemptive strike, "maybe this isn't the time for us to talk —"

K.T. widened her suddenly stony eyes. The warning in them did the trick. I leaned back in the chair, crossed my arms over my chest and braced myself for what was to come.

She puckered her lips, gazing at me with eyes that once again grew moist. After gulping hard, she finally asked, "Are you relieved?" Her skin flushed as the question escaped her lips. "I need to hear the truth. Are you relieved?"

Her words ripped through me like a bull's horns shredding a matador's cape. I'd expected her to nail me for not being by her side, for being too involved in my work, for ignoring her, for causing her so much stress and worry. But not this. Was I relieved? My chest tightened abruptly.

I started to utter something, but K.T. waved her index finger at me. "Think first, Robin."

"K.T., I know what this baby meant —"

"That's not what I'm asking you. I know you care about me, and I know you hurt for me. But what I want to know is, are you relieved?"

"I don't understand. What difference would it make?"

A sad smirk flickered over her face. "Sometimes you really are clueless," she said. "Just answer the question."

I rubbed my face hard. Was I relieved she'd lost the baby? From the beginning, I'd been a reluctant bystander. I'd fallen in love with K.T. way before she started trying to get pregnant. The relationship derailed before even the option of parenting had had time to surface between us. By the time a second chance at building a life with K.T. came along, the pregnancy was already underway, the terms I'd have to accept in order to have her back in my life. In truth, I hadn't thought much about the baby, about how it would change our lives, our relationship. We both agreed that K.T. had decided to travel the motherhood road solo. The full extent of my role in her life and eventually in the baby's life still had not been defined. And I liked it that way. What the hell did I know about parenting? I'd been raised in a house of silent recrimination, resentment and mourning. Taking care of myself had been challenge enough. For me, assuming the care and feeding of a lover was the emotional equivalent of scaling Mount Everest. Add in a child and you might as well ask me to man the first mission to Jupiter.

Our hands met. What *did* I feel about the miscarriage? I leaned forward, rested my cheek on her belly. It already felt less firm, the rush of blood I'd grown accustomed to feeling there seemed less pronounced. K.T. moved one hand to the back of my head, brushing my hair away from my face in long, slow motions. Over the last three months, I'd watched K.T.'s breasts swell and ripen in preparation for the baby. I'd seen the little tadpole embryo appear, ghost-like, on the sonogram, squinted in amazement at the almost imperceptible flicker of a seven-week-old pulse and last month heard for the first time the rhythmic swoosh of the baby's heartbeat in Dr. Wolf's office. All the time, I'd thought, this is K.T.'s baby. K.T.'s going to be a mother. K.T.'s carrying new life inside her body.

All at once, I began sobbing, clinging to K.T. as the realization hit me. I was anything but relieved. Somehow, without knowing it, I'd become attached to the pregnancy. Attached to the child K.T. had been carrying. "I'm sorry, K.T.," I managed to mutter between blowing my nose and sobbing. "I should've been there for you. Not just last night."

"It's okay, hon." She reached over, snatched a tissue from the night table and dabbed my nose. "We both made mistakes." Her smile was small. "Yours were bigger, of course."

We both jumped at the tap of knuckles on the door. Lunch was being served by a tall woman wearing a name tag that read, Peg Bernstein. The odor of steamed chicken and carrots wafted toward us. K.T. grimaced and waved away the cart. The thick-waisted orderly said, "Don't worry, you're not on the list," and moved around the curtain. "Hello, Mrs. Glazier, you awake enough to take some food?"

K.T. and I stared at the curtain.

"My husband didn't show again." The voice was

young and hoarse. "Bastard treated me like shit the whole pregnancy, drank himself sick with his friends, and then doesn't even show up to see how I'm doing."

"Tough going, hon. Let's move that tray closer." The orderly sounded as if she regretted her friendly overture.

"It's his fault, you know. That's what the doctor said. All the goddamn crying and stress he caused me did this. Why the fuck else would I miscarry after five months, huh?"

"Can't answer that one. Take care, now." Peg Bernstein and her lunch cart rattled by us without a second glance.

A new alarm sounded inside my head. "Do they know why this happened?" I asked in a whisper, suddenly hyper-conscious of our lack of privacy.

She shook her head. "No, not yet." Her tone was equally muted. "They have to run some tests. Dr. Wolf said most times, when these things happen, it's nature's —" There was a sudden intake of breath and then her voice broke. After a moment, she said, "I hate fucking statistics." K.T.'s hands fluttered to her belly. I caught her fingers in mine and kissed them, fearing she'd been about to stroke her stomach the way she had been all these months. "Maybe there's something wrong with me," she said. "After all, I'm thirty-seven. Do you know how fast my fertility is dropping?"

I rubbed her knuckles. "Maybe it's my fault. I put you through hell these last few days. I never should've taken on that investigation. If I hadn't —"

"You're not responsible, Robin."

"How do we know that? You were crazy with worry Monday night because of me."

"Worry doesn't cause miscarriages."

I glanced meaningfully at the curtain. K.T. mouthed the word, "No," and drew *loco*-circles by her temples.

My mind replayed the last few days. "Do you think I did something wrong when we made love? Was I, you know —"

"Ah, Robin, this is not helping." She squeezed my hand. "If we're looking for something to blame, let's blame my eggs, or my hormones, or the placement of the placenta. Right now, I just need to know you're not leaving me."

"Oh, God, K.T.," I said, "of course I'm not. This time you're stuck with me."

"What a nice threat." She flashed a half-smile, which collapsed instantly. "I wanted this baby so much."

"I know."

"It hurts," she whispered, as she drew her knees up to her chest. "I can't believe how much it hurts."

The time for words had gone. I crawled into bed beside her and rocked her until we both fell asleep.

Around four o'clock, they came to take K.T. into surgery. I could feel my chest tighten as I watched them wheel her into the elevator. Just before the doors closed, she fingered the sign language motion for "I love you." Strange how some moments crystallize in your memory, sparking through you like a lightning bolt, striking the darkest corners of your heart and mind whenever you dare to approach them. At that instant, I knew that I'd never loved anyone the way I love K.T., that I'd never felt as much fear and vulnerability. An inexplicable fury erupted in my gut, boiled through me like lava, made my skin flush, my belly knot.

I strode back into K.T.'s room, exited, returned. I stared at her empty bed for what seemed like hours, then I beat the pillows with my fists, tucked in the sheets with abrupt karate chops, folded the blanket into a tight, tight square. Clearly, nurse-maid puttering would not quiet the odd tingling in my scalp. Something had disturbed me deeply, something I couldn't yet name. My mind kept skipping back to Thomas Ryan, the guilt and shame he must've felt when his drinking and carousing finally drove Mary out of his life. The anguish he must've suffered when the medical examiner flipped back the sheet to display her bloodied, mangled corpse.

Not a random murder, but a murder of passion, of punishment.

Ogou Feray. Ezili.

*Click.*

I bolted for the phone. Jill answered almost immediately.

"I need you to check something out," I said.

"How's K.T.?" Her tone held a reprimand I didn't deserve.

"She's in surgery... and, for the record, I am *not* abandoning her."

A pause. "Sorry. Go ahead."

I told her what I'd just realized and went over the phone calls I needed her to make. She didn't argue. "Do you want me to fill in Ryan?"

"Leave Ryan out of it for now."

"Understood. How about Sweeney? Ryan said

Sweeney would check in with me at least twice a day. I expect his call in the next half-hour."

I hesitated. With all his incompetence, Sweeney still had an edge on me. His police connections and his first-hand knowledge of the other criminal investigations couldn't be discounted. "Quid pro quo," I muttered out loud.

"What?"

"Yeah, tell him what we have. But make sure you find out what he knows *first*. If he clams up, cut him off. Right now, I think there's a part of Sweeney that's more interested in one-upping me than in finding the killer."

"He sounds like a sweetheart. Can't wait." Her sigh was exaggerated. "I have some other info you might find interesting."

"Go ahead."

"Tony called up the cop who'd found Galonardi. Clyde Peltier. Guess where he was born?"

Her pronunciation gave away the answer. "New Orleans."

"Close enough. Saint Peter's Parish. Back in 'eighty-eight, Clyde was so green you could draw sap from him. That's a direct quote, by the way. Galonardi was his first homicide. According to Tony, the kid puked the instant he saw her. He didn't even have time to stop and aim, he did it right there, on the body. Must've pissed off the Chief of D's. Anyway, it turns out Clyde thought of voodoo the instant he saw that jar with the bull's testicles inside, but the other boys in blue chalked it off. He said one cop told him he'd better clear the swamp out of his brain if he wanted to have a career in N.Y.C. He decided to chomp down on what the vets on the force were

171

feeding him and keep his trap tight... that's another direct quote. Apparently Clyde Peltier likes his language colorful. Tony seemed to think he was straight up, but a little edgy about revisiting the investigation. Could be he was holding back." I heard her click away at the keyboard. "That's it. Tony said to give you his home number so you could follow up."

I pulled out a pen and scratch paper. "Did Tony ask him about Chamelle?"

Jill read off the digits, then said, "I don't think so. I got the impression it was a quick call." She started to add something, then stopped herself. I had a feeling she'd been about to comment on my partner's health. It was a topic that filled us both with dread. After a moment, she clucked her tongue and asked, "Do you suppose this can explain the gap in the murders? Maybe the killer learned that Clyde had picked up on the voodoo angle and decided he'd pushed his luck a little too far."

"Two problems with that, Jill." I lowered my voice as Mrs. Glazier, the other occupant in the room, shuffled into the bathroom. "One, how'd he find out what Clyde suspected when he mentioned it to so few people and it never became part of the official investigation? And two, the suspicions of a pissant rookie hardly seems enough to scare off a brutal serial killer who'd already gotten away with three murders."

"Maybe you're right about that, but consider this: Fitzhugh Chamelle has been able to get the inside scoop on every one of these homicides."

The toilet flushed. I cupped my hand around the

mouthpiece. "Have you had any luck in locating him?"

"Yes and no," Jill said.

The bathroom door squeaked. Mrs. Glazier took one glance at me and said, "Shit . . . I got better things to worry about than your conversations." She palmed a pack of cigarettes in her robe, turned on her heel and headed down the hall.

I love New York.

"Fitzhugh Chamelle is a pseudonym," Jill explained. "That's why you didn't find records for him. I asked John to call Dreyer Carr for me, plus a few of his newspaper buddies, and I'll hand it to that husband of mine, he came through in less than two hours. And to think I married him for his looks." She chuckled to herself. "Chamelle's real name is Fitzhugh Crock. John and I discussed the appropriateness of that surname for a news reporter." She waited for me to add a quip, but I wasn't in the mood. In a no-nonsense tone, she continued. "Chamelle's a freelance criminal writer with a pretty solid reputation. He has a regular stint with the *Times-Picayune*, contributes frequently to the San Francisco *Examiner*, and has had occasional bylines in most of the major dailies."

My eyebrows drew together. "John found this out with one call?"

"Two, plus the mining I did online."

"Any idea how long he's been connected to the *Examiner*?"

"No, but John's friend seemed to imply that Chamelle's an old-timer. I did get a physical description."

The sound of a guerney in the hallway made me jump. I said, "Hold on," and bolted to the door. The occupant of the adjoining room had returned. No sign of K.T., though. I checked my watch and picked up the phone from where I'd tossed it on the bed. "Sorry about that," I said, suddenly conscious of my racing pulse.

"No problem," Jill replied. She ran down the description of Chamelle. Point for point, he sounded identical to the man I'd seen tracking K.T. on Monday morning.

"What else do I have?" she mused to herself. "Okay, he's unmarried. No criminal record, no unusual financial situations. I checked myself. He owns a house in Metairie. I've called down there, but so far all I've gotten is his machine. You may want to try it yourself."

I didn't like the questions uncurling in my head. As Jill read off his phone number, I started to wonder why Sweeney's contacts on the New Orleans police force hadn't been able to dig up anything concrete on Chamelle. Unless they had and Sweeney was holding back on me. Maybe he wasn't as incompetent as I thought. Maybe he just didn't want me to get too far ahead of him. Fire ignited in my belly. The stakes were too great for such petty ego games, but if Sweeney wanted a fight, I'd give him one.

I told Jill to have Sweeney call me at the hospital, then I hung up and dialed Chamelle. The voice on the answering machine sounded all-American, the practiced, accent-free intonation of a network newscaster. My message was brusque, provocative: "I have some critical information concerning the eggshell murders... your specialty, I assume. It's time we talk." I left my name and office number. If Chamelle was on the up and up, his instincts as a reporter would compel him to call as soon as possible. If, on the other hand, he was a homicidal lunatic, my phone message was bound to flush him out. Either way, I'd just raised the ante. The question remained, who'd fold first?

I scrambled toward my briefcase to retrieve my laptop. I didn't have much time to spare before K.T. would be back. The phone wire was embedded in the base, with the hook-up jammed behind the bed. It took me a few minutes to maneuver, but I finally managed to hook up the laptop's modem. In a few seconds more, I was ready to surf. Chamelle was a prolific writer. In my first search, I pulled up 272 entries with his name highlighted. Evan Alexander had done an extraordinary job of extracting the newspaper files related to the so-called eggshell murders. But I was more interested in what Chamelle had written years before Mary Ryan's death. I narrowed the search parameters and watched the little hourglass blink with rising anxiety. If my hunch was wrong, I'd be back at square one.

"*No matches*" flashed on screen.

I changed the date and waited again. Again the search failed. My stomach juices boiled. One more try, I thought. This time I altered the name and crossed my fingers. An instant later, I got three hits. Fitzhugh Chamelle had begun his writing career under his real name, Crock. The first article I downloaded was a loosely written but insightful story about a series of sexual assaults aimed at "self-proclaimed" feminists. All of the attacks had taken place on university campuses in or near San Francisco. At the end, I found a short biographical note.

> *Fitzhugh Crock graduated summa cum laude from Stanford University. His sister, Sarah, was one of the women profiled in this piece. This is his first article for the* Examiner.

The date was 1973. A flush spread across my face. I poised my index finger over the enter key and held my breath.

"I can't believe this!" The bark came from the doorway. I recognized Ginny's angry tone instantly. I tapped the key and turned around. "You can't stop yourself, can you?" she snapped. Ginny had recently cut her hair to chin-length. It made the fire in her eyes more potent. She would've reduced a lesser woman to ash. I took the laser hit straight on and didn't flinch.

"K.T.'s still in surgery," I said. "What was I supposed to do? Sit here and bite my nails?"

"Gee, wouldn't that just be dreadful? What would happen if you actually allowed yourself to worry?" She marched into the room. "I can't believe how much alike you and Larry are. You're never one-hundred percent present —"

I cut her tirade short. "Enough, Ginny."

"Fine. Do you mind returning the phone to normal? I'm sure this strikes you as odd, but *our* family —" She stressed the word "our" for maximum effect. "*Our* family is very concerned about K.T., and I expect most of them will be calling in within the next hour or so."

She didn't wait for my response. Her head disappeared below the bed as she began struggling to reach the modular phone plug. She bumped against a metal leg and cursed.

Just before she pulled the line, I caught a glimpse of the article I'd just retrieved.

*"Barry NeVille Acquitted on Charge of Rape"*

The byline was Fitzhugh Crock.

## Chapter 11

I cupped an ice chip in my palm and slipped it between K.T.'s lips. The surgery was minor, but the impact of the last twenty-four hours was anything but. K.T. looked pale and drawn, her eyes reduced to puffy slits. She squeezed my hand and turned away. "I feel so empty," she murmured.

I responded with the inanity, "I know," and moved my chair closer. The hospital's visiting hours had ended much earlier, but so far I'd managed to avoid eviction. My own stay in a hospital was recent enough for me to know that the hardest moments came late at night, when the silence of the hallways became oppressive, the staccato coughs of strangers in unseen rooms an assault to the senses. The narrow confines of the hospital bed had trapped me in a spider's web of vivid nightmares that did not distinguish between sleep and waking.

"Can you shut the light?" K.T. asked, still not facing me.

I reached up and hit the switch. "Go ahead and try to sleep. I'll be right here."

"You should go home... there's nothing you can do here."

"You're wrong," I said, stroking her hand.

A small sob escaped from her lips, but she swallowed it quickly. In the dim light, I could barely see her nod, but it was more than enough for me. K.T. needed me by her side. I kissed her neck and cradled her in my arms.

Ginny had left shortly after five o'clock, and soon after her brother, T.B., had shown up. In typical form, Ginny had made it clear that her departure was made possible only because another *family* member had arrived on the scene. Lucky for me, that family member actually likes me. T.B.'s a medical examiner for the city of New York, and we've worked together on a few cases. Over time, we've developed a real affection for each other, which helps to offset Ginny's brooding reservation. As soon as he arrived, he buried me in his arms, comforting me on the loss he assumed K.T. and I shared. I was surprised at how good his hug felt, how willing I was to accept his sympathy.

T.B.'s a bit of an eccentric, with an odd fixation on Italian-Americans. His dining room table consists of a matinee poster of *The Godfather* sealed in lucite and mounted on a marble base. He has a slow Southern drawl and looks more like Ron Howard than he does either of his sisters.

He crossed over to K.T.'s bedside in what was clearly meant to be an Al Pacino swagger and said, "I'm gonna make you an offer you can't refuse. Give your big bro a smile, or —" The way he'd mugged for her had netted the first sincere grin from K.T. in the past twenty-four hours. He'd stayed until ten, when his beeper sounded. Despite my fondness for him, I was relieved when he left.

K.T. shivered against me. I got up and pulled the blanket up over her shoulders. Without speaking, she placed her hand on top of mine and curled into a tight fetal position. A steady creaking of the bed frame punctuated the small rocking motion she'd begun to make. Glancing through the doorway, I could just make out the time on the wall clock. Eleven-fifty. We were in for a long, long night.

Earlier, while T.B. still huddled by K.T.'s side, I'd managed to slip out to the pay phone and contact Jill. She informed me that Sweeney had been trying to contact me at the hospital for a few hours with no luck. She'd given me a number where I could reach him between six and seven. I'd called right away. As I listened to K.T.'s breathing grow steadier, I replayed our conversation.

The first thing he'd said was, "So she lost the baby." It wasn't a question or an expression of sympathy. Just a statement of simple fact. Yet I'd sensed a strange uneasiness in Sweeney, an uncertainty of how to proceed. I didn't make the conversation easier.

"How far along was she?" he asked.

"Three months." My voice was cold, the sound of rock hitting thick metal.

"Could they tell the sex?"

Pressure built up behind my eyes. *The sex.* "It was a girl," I said, each word tight and precise. Her name would've been Charlotte, after K.T.'s grandmother. I hadn't known that until less than an hour ago.

"What happened?"

"Cause undetermined," I said, mimicking the tone of the physician who had stepped in for Dr. Wolf. Undetermined. "Most likely some chromosomal defect."

"I see," he said, then after another moment, "So I'm assuming you're off the case."

"You're assuming wrong," I snapped. "My agency's on it, under my direction. We've made too much progress to stop now."

He coughed in my ear. "What kind of progress?" For a while I'd been hearing street sounds in the background. All of a sudden, there was rhythmic clip-clop echoing through the phone.

"Where the hell are you?"

"A bar near Jackson Square. Damn horse nearly ran my table over."

"Don't you ever go home?"

"Home is where my ass is. Right now it's here. You didn't answer my question. What progress?"

I was too tired to play cat-and-mouse. I gave him the full update on Fitzhugh Chamelle, including the article on NeVille, then waited for the information to set in. "By the way, did you know that Lisa Rubin left her husband and then had an abortion? Or that the Strampos family is super right-wing? There's even a chance the two of us are way off base and this is a much simpler homicide than we're making it out. You had to hear at least some of this from the NOPD." My tone mingled equal parts of accusation and snottiness. Sweeney brought out my best side.

He didn't respond.

"Sweeney, you keep holding out on me and I'll cut you off so fast your nose will bleed. I've accomplished more in the past few days than you have in the past goddamn nine *years*. You want to run parallel investigations, that's fine with me." I saved the sucker punch for last. "Right now, Ryan's confidence is riding with my team."

"You're a bitch, Miller," he shouted in my ear. "A stone-hearted bitch. You got a girlfriend there bleeding out a new life and you're worried about who's fuckin' running ahead on this investigation. When my wife lost our baby, I was a fuckin' wreck. Cried like a girl. Had to drink myself into oblivion just to stay alive those first few weeks. Christ! Is this what you dykes are like?"

"Fuck you, Sweeney. My grief is none of your business."

"Fuck you back. You wanna know what I know? Fine. You are dead on. I *am* holding some of my ammo in reserve, but you got it all ass-backwards. I ain't trying to beat you at some fuckin' head game ... I'm trying to keep you from playing with guns you don't know how to fire and you're too damn juvie to be toting in the first place. I've been protecting your ass, 'cause Ryan doesn't want his damn pseudo-daughter to bloody herself again."

His statement stung me like flesh on dry ice. His choice of words couldn't have been accidental. Ryan must've told him how my sister died, and how the family had reacted. I gulped, steadied myself on the wall.

The battery continued. "Okay, you and your *team* found out some stuff. Big, hairy deal. I got all that data nailed last night, plus some. You think my connections got smaller balls than yours? The Strampos family angle is colder than a witch's tit. Lisa was a shit to her old man, but the family didn't rub her out, even if she deserved it. Good try, though." His voice dripped with sarcasm. "Now try this on ... Did you know some people suspected that NeVille was behind an attack on Chamelle's sister, Sarah? No, I didn't think so. Or how about this? Sarah Crock is still up in San Francisco, running an occult store called Tea Leaves where her friggin' brother Fitz is a frequent visitor. Don't bother calling her, she's out of town for two weeks. Oh, yeah and I forgot ... a buddy fetched me pix of Fitz from the newspaper morgue. I passed it by staff at the Royal Orleans. Seems he'd asked a couple of folks there about you and your girlfriend. K.T. Bellflower, right? You never did tell me her name. I hear her new restaurant's doing pretty good. How's that for detecting, huh?"

I glanced around, searching for a water fountain. My mouth was desert-dry. Swallowing became difficult.

"Nothing to say, Miller?" he taunted.

"How's this?" I said. "Back in 'eighty-eight, the first officer on the scene made the link between the murders and voodoo emblems. Clyde Peltier ... name ring a bell? It was his *first* year on the job."

Not a home run, but at least I hit a ground ball. Sweeney sucked in his breath with a hiss. "Where'd you dig up that piece of trash?"

"My partner spoke to him."

"He's going by what a kid remembers from a crime that went down five years ago?"

"It was his first homicide. Not an event you easily forget. Do you remember him?"

"Shit. You're talking about one moron in the course of years of investigative work. Who the hell remembers? Maybe, maybe not. If I did, he never mentioned the voodoo crap to me, I'll tell you that much. He saying otherwise? 'Cause if he is, let me at him —"

"Calm down, Sweeney."

"I just don't want him making it out that I had a fuckin' red flag shoved up my nose and didn't know it."

"I'll give him the message."

"You seeing this asshole?"

"Maybe. I've been playing with some ideas I'd like to bounce off someone who's familiar with voodoo."

"Try me."

"Another time. So where do you stand now on Chamelle?"

"Me and some brothers played this thing out all afternoon. The way we see it, Chamelle could be setting up NeVille nice and slow for a one-way ticket to the chair. But there's no official dope on this angle, so I gotta keep playing it out on my own."

"Sounds pretty far-fetched to me. Say NeVille did attack Sarah Crock and say it was a traumatic event for her. I'll grant you that Chamelle may have been pretty pissed off that NeVille's been free and clear all these years, but you're saying the guy then proceeded to rape, maim and murder four other women just to tie up NeVille. Come on, Sweeney."

"Hey, don't get me wrong. I'm not saying Fitz's clock is ticking one second at a time. The bastard's obsessed with murder, for crissakes. You can't argue with that. Could be NeVille was the match that burned down old Fitz's wick. Or here's another take... maybe old Fitz and NeVille are a team. Fitz sure as hell wouldn't be the last guy to have stuck it to a family member. 'Specially not with folk from down here." He guffawed at his own lame joke. "You got a better motive?"

"I'm working on it."

He didn't like my answer. "Hey, I'm being up front with you. There's not a card that's face down on my table."

"Let's just say I'm taking a less traditional approach to this whole thing. The killer's using voodoo emblems for a reason. I want to know what that is."

Someone asked Sweeney if he wanted another drink. My eyebrows gathered.

"Yeah, another Coke. Lots of lemon," he answered, then he came back on without skipping a beat. "You're dead wrong. I bet if I laid out a sugar trail, you'd be the kind to bend on over and lick your way right into my big old trap. Voodoo's a red herring. Follow it till you choke. Me, I'm gonna head out for another visit to NeVille's camp first thing tomorrow. Your being there the other day kinda distracted me. Then I'm gonna track down Fitz and have a chat with the man. By the way, you have anyone besides me on the scene?"

Cornered and bagged. Sweeney had me and he knew it.

"What do you want, Sweeney?"

"Cooperation. Don't you think *Daddy* would want that?"

Anger steamed through me. The man knew how to push my buttons. "Up yours."

He laughed heartily. "Okay. Get back to your lesbian friend. I'll call you at home tomorrow. It must be nice having a nurse *and* a shrink live downstairs from you. One thing I don't know is how long you-all have owned that brownstone together."

How the hell did he know so much about me and my housemates? For that matter, how could he be so sure K.T. and I planned to go back to my house tomorrow?

"See, puppy girl, I'm a better detective than you think," he had said before hanging up.


K.T. moaned and I immediately lifted my head from where it had been resting on her hip. Still asleep, she began muttering disconnected phrases. The only word I made out clearly was *Charlotte*. It was twelve-fifteen. K.T.'s nightmares had begun.


*Thursday, May 6*

I kicked the door shut behind me and dropped our bags. Geeja and Mallomar raced to greet me. Their meows echoed in the hallway. I swept Geeja up in my arms and kissed her trim, cocoa-brown belly.

Her motor clicked on instantly. From nowhere, my eyes brimmed with tears. Meanwhile, something thudded onto my sneaker. I glanced down. Mallomar had draped herself over my foot and was throwing me one of her more insistent smoker-cat mewls.

"Okay, okay," I said. "Your turn's coming."

K.T. glared up at the staircase and said, "Think you can carry me, too?"

"Are you hurting?"

"A little. Maybe I'll just lie down on the couch down here for a while. I don't feel like going upstairs just yet."

"No problem." I parted the French doors to the living room to let her inside. "Let me feed the cats, then I'll fix us something."

"I'm not hungry."

Not a good sign. K.T.'s appetite is one of the things I love most about her. She consumes food and life with a zest that astounds and thrills me. But now she stood in the center of my living room, listless, gazing at the shuttered windows.

"Honey?" I walked over to her, touched the small of her back. "You okay?"

After an instant of hesitation, she shook her head. "I feel dead inside." Her eyes filled with her fear. "I don't feel anything, Robin. Nothing."

"The hormones —"

"*No.* I'm not talking about hormones. I mean *me.*" She pounded her chest. "My heart," she practically whispered. "I don't feel sad, or angry, or lonely, or —" Abruptly, she broke off eye contact.

"It's okay to say it, K.T."

In a voice I could barely hear, she said, "I feel disconnected from everything. My body, the miscarriage, work —" I braced myself for what was coming. "Even you."

Alarm zapped through me. The tables had turned. I know too well what it's like to shut down emotions to prevent myself from a complete melt-down. But I'd never seen K.T. retreat like this. I stroked my cheek with the heel of my palm to calm a nerve that had suddenly tightened along my jaw. Before I could respond, there was a tap on the wall behind me.

"Hey, it's me." I turned around. Beth stood in the hallway, her hand still poised on the outside door. "You forgot to lock up behind you. Hope you don't mind..." Her gaze swept from me to K.T.'s back. The expression in her eyes turned serious. "Jill called me yesterday to tell me what happened. How are you two doing?"

"Not so good," I muttered.

K.T. didn't answer. Instead she folded herself into the far corner of the couch.

Beth said, "I'm sorry. This must be hell for you. Did the doctor go over the stats with you —"

"Don't," K.T. said abruptly. "Don't." A bitter smirk flickered over her lips. "I really don't want to hear it."

My skin felt cold. Beth glanced at me. I warned her off with a blink of my eyes. She nodded, then kneeled down to rub Geeja behind the ear. "The cats really missed you this trip. Every time I came up, they slammed by my ankles, little linebackers, looking for their real mom." At the last word, she looked up nervously at K.T. She shouldn't have worried. K.T. had zoned us out. To me, Beth said, "Geeja was so upset, she got that little bald spot over her left ear. And Mallomar couldn't bring herself to eat for two whole days. You know how serious that is. Look, another week or so and she'd be absolutely svelte."

Beth herself appeared to have lost some weight in the past week and a half. The bracelet on her wrist hung loosely, the rings on her fingers seemed on the verge of falling off. Even when she was tucked into a tight squat, her jeans bagged around her thighs. She followed me into the kitchen, the cats zig-zagging around our feet. I pulled out a can of food.

"They had tuna last night," Beth said.

I smiled at her. Dark circles dulled the normal spark in my friend's eyes. She bit her bottom lip, averted her gaze. All at once, I realized Beth was trying to get up the nerve to tell me something.

"What is it, Beth?"

"Oh, damn, you don't need this right now."

I snapped off the lid of the can so fast, juice splashed onto my shirt. Beth wet a sponge and started scrubbing at the spot. I could feel her fingers trembling against me.

"You and Dinah —" I said, pressure building in my temples.

A quick nod, lips tight, chin quivering. In a minute, she'd be sobbing. I covered her hand with mine and lowered her onto a stool by the breakfast bar.

"She's met someone," Beth whispered.

I cocked my head at her, unsure I'd heard her right. Ever since Beth and Dinah had adopted their daughter, Carol, more than a year ago they'd been going through rough times. Most of the arguments they'd had since then stemmed from the sudden tension of balancing a long-term relationship with sudden parenthood. But the stress in their relationship also stemmed in part from my role in their lives. In recent years, Dinah and I had become horribly estranged while my old connection to Beth deepened.

I sat down opposite Beth, dazed by her news. Dinah was one of the most self-righteous prigs I knew. In my wilder days, she had delineated with painstaking honesty every misstep, every marginally immoral decision I'd ever made. She once accused me of treating relationships with the same consume-and-trash attititude I held toward junk food.

"Six and a half years," Beth said, more to herself than me. "She didn't even wait for the seven-year itch." She made a weak attempt at a smile, her eyes brimming with tears.

"How long —"

"About seven months after we adopted Carol. Around the same time all that craziness was going on with you, K.T., and Lurlene. So I guess it's been around nine months altogether. God! What an asshole I've been."

Nine months? It didn't seem possible. Just before I left for New Orleans, we all had dinner together. I watched them snuggle up to each other on the couch, tickling their daughter, gazing at each other over her head with obvious joy. "But you two spend so much time together. How'd she even find —"

Beth didn't wait for me to finish. "They met at a weekend conference. She's a therapist, too. Ironic, huh?" She wiped her eyes and said, "Her name's Petunia, for God's sake. How could Dinah fall in love with a woman named after a stupid flower? And, get this, she smokes like a damn chimney. I met her once, Dinah brought her home for dinner, then the two of them spent most of the time in her office. I didn't think twice about it. She'd also said that affairs were obscene, a chicken-hearted approach to relationship problems. Oh, shit."

"Ah, Beth, honey." I hugged her.

For a few minutes, she shook her head against me, as if she couldn't believe her own words, then she pounded my back, half-crying, half-laughing against my shoulder. "Can you believe it? After all the times she nailed you for fooling around with unfit women?" I waited for her to find a tissue in her pocket and blow her nose. "*Petunia* lives in Boston, which is why Dinah has had such an urgent need these past few months for professional development courses at some horrid, make-believe institute up there."

"When did you find this all out?"

"Two nights ago. Without telling me, she'd cancelled her afternoon clients and met Pet — that's what she calls her, can you barf? She met Pet at the airport. Apparently, she'd given Dinah an ultimatum. Break up with me, or it was all over. So, Dinah showed up around midnight, while my heart was in my mouth with so much fear that something had happened to her, and tells me, sorry, it's over. I almost fainted, I was so stunned. All the time we've been working things out, she's been saying, it's Carol, I can't handle being a mom, this isn't what I expected. So I've been bending over backwards to give her more time, take on more of the child-care arrangements myself. I'm an idiot, right?"

"Hardly."

"You know, when we adopted Carol, so many people told me about other couples who broke up after becoming parents. Dinah and I joked about it, made fun of those dipstick lesbians who hadn't fully anticipated the amount of work it takes to raise a kid. I tell you, Rob, these last two days, I feel like I'm going crazy. I can't make sense out of the last six and a half years of my life. Was it all bullshit?"

"Look, I witnessed those years. They were not bullshit, no matter what's happening now. Come on," I said, lifting her chin with my finger. "Carol needs you. I need you. You'll get through this. I promise you."

She threw her arms around my neck and held on. "I've missed you so much."

I rubbed her back, saw K.T. staring at me over the counter. I wondered how much she heard. "I'm going upstairs for a nap," she said quietly.

Beth and I spent the next few hours talking. Dinah intended to move to Boston and open a practice with Petunia. Her goal was to terminate her ongoing clients and get out of the house as fast as possible, perhaps as soon as July. She planned to ask me to buy out her share of the brownstone. The way Beth portrayed it, I sensed that Dinah expected me to put up an argument. In fact, the arrangement would work fine with me, since I earned enough from property rentals and book royalties to need an additional tax write-off. I gave Beth a written figure to pass on to Dinah, then assured her repeatedly that not only could she continue living downstairs, I expected her to. The most disturbing news I learned was that Dinah had firmly stated she did *not* want to have any further contact with Beth or Carol. Her rationale? Carol was young enough to recover from early parental separation, which in the long run would be less detrimental than continued parental conflict. Or some such nonsense. Legally, Dinah wasn't obligated to pay child support.

Around one o'clock, Beth left to pick up Carol from the day-care center. I called my accountant, told him about the buy-out, then checked in with my office. We'd made little additional progress since last night. At some point, I went upstairs to look in on K.T. She was asleep on my bed, one cat sharing her pillow and the other curled on her hip. I left them alone and went back down to make something for lunch. The phone rang as I was snatching my toast from the oven tray.

"Miller, we got trouble. Big trouble."

I sat down and said, "Go ahead, Sweeney, shoot."

Less than forty-eight hours later, those words would echo in my head.

# Chapter 12

Sweeney's next words hit like a scud missile. "NeVille's dead."

"*What?*"

"I got out to the bayou first thing this a.m. Found him hanging from a rope tied to the old, metallic car fender he'd rigged like a drainpipe. Heat'd made him swell up like one of those blowfish. Know the kind I mean? Guess who was with him? That asshole with the egghead tattoo, the one that slipped you the tooth. And he had another one, right in his pocket. Along with three C notes."

A thrill ran through me. "Did you get him?"

"Didn't have to. NeVille got him. Shotgun blast through the head. Greasy brain bits all over the place. Shit, you should've seen my arms. 'Squitoes, flies, gnats, every other friggin' insect life swarmed right over me. Even the gators got curious."

I dumped my sandwich in the trash. My appetite had disappeared. "Sounds like a murder-suicide," I said. The prospect made me uneasy. Just as we'd crested the highest loop on a wild roller coaster, someone had jammed on the brakes. We weren't crashing the way we should, though. Instead, we were suspended in air, the rules of gravity be damned. Something wasn't right.

"Looked like one, too," Sweeney said. "There was a stool kicked over right under NeVille's heels. Rope burns 'cross his right palm, like he tugged on the rope a while before finally letting go. Place was pretty messed up, too, like he'd beaten the crap out of the other guy before doing his own high kick. We got an I.D. on old egghead, by the way. Name on record is Jimmy Lee Troy, a kissing cousin of NeVille's, as dim-witted as NeVille liked to make himself out to be. Apparently, they got pretty buddybuddy after NeVille moved back down here. Troy done time for petty shit — boosting a car, assaulting a bartender dumb enough to try to stop a drunk from drinking, and one B and E. The detectives got it all figured out, nice and sweet. Let's see if you can guess the tune of this song."

"Jimmy Troy got squirmy on Rubin's homicide, so NeVille offed him."

"Bingo. Here's why I ain't on the force no more. Most cops got no imagination. The official line is,

Troy falls in with his cousin and gets suckered into going along on the homicide. Only Troy don't know how black his cousin is. He thinks all they're gonna do is dick around with her some. But then NeVille does his thing and Troy freaks. Maybe he starts sweating about going back to the house, this time for good. No con who's done time wants to be a lifer. So NeVille and him argue, even get down to knuckles. Then, boom, in the heat of the argument he blows Troy away. Now, here comes the good part, the man suddenly develops a conscience. After all, it's one thing slicing and dicing a chick, and quite another to excavate the face of your cousin with a shotgun right on your own doorstep." I winced at the image. "Oh yeah, NeVille bought himself a brand new baby yesterday. Twelve gauge. In his own friggin' name, for crissakes. Then, man, this one blew me away... they found a nice, shiny crucifix clutched in NeVille's left hand. Like he was praying for salvation. NeVille got religion. As far as everyone's concerned down here, case is closed. Open and shut. Send the fat lady home."

I heard K.T. moving around upstairs. "So what's the problem?"

"Too fuckin' convenient," he said. "I did some dicking on my own and I found out that the tattoo on Troy, it was stenciled in on Monday afternoon. Some dive in the Quarter. Less than twelve hours before Rubin got taken down. When the woman told him how much it'd be, he said, no problem, I'm not footing the bill. I'm gonna make money off this, that's what he said."

"You think someone was setting him up?"

"Hello? At least you're listening. You tell me what asshole's gonna get the word 'egghead' inked on his butt-bald scalp hours before collaborating on a crime in which an egg is cracked on the back of the vic's head, in almost the identical spot. Boys down here take that as confirming circumstantial evidence. Even my best pal down here thought NeVille had Troy marked as a way to prime his pump. What do you think?"

"The story's got merit."

"Okay, I'll give you that, but I still think someone was jerking his chain, making out like this homicide thing was all a big game. Maybe Troy didn't even know about the killing. But with that tattoo on his head, he'd be numero uno in the suspect department, don't you think?"

"What about the tooth?"

"What about it? It don't prove squat."

Footsteps sounded on the stairs. K.T. was finally coming back down. I lowered my voice. "Do you know where Troy was when the other killings occurred?"

"In the joint. Each and every time. He don't figure in this, I'm telling you."

"So you think NeVille set him up?"

"I did for maybe half a sec, but then I got a whiff of his puffed-up corpse, and my engine started to purr. NeVille's just another pawn. We're talking a master here. You're not gonna like this, sistor."

For some reason, I thought of Ryan. A shudder ran through me. "Go ahead, Sweeney."

K.T. came around the corner bearing the disheveled appearance of someone who'd just woken up. Her cheek held tracks imprinted by the weave of the blanket. She mouthed, "How much longer?" and I shrugged in response.

Sweeney said, "I paid a visit to Fitzhugh Chamelle's place out in Metairie. You ever been there?"

"Stop dragging this out."

The refrigerator gurgled as K.T. held the door open, staring at the contents. They weren't pretty. After one and a half weeks, whatever had once been barely edible was now fit for science. I could smell the sour milk from across the kitchen. She grunted and moved on to a cabinet. A box of graham crackers fell onto the counter.

"You New Yorkers sure are impatient," Sweeney said. "Okay, here's the skinny. Chamelle's flown the coop. I found dishes in the sink, but no suitcase in the house. Half of the master closet was empty." He took a dramatic breath. "I did find the car, though. In long-term parking at the airport."

My stomach tightened. I cupped my hand around the phone's mouthpiece and edged into the living room. "What're you saying, Sweeney?"

"Read the tea leaves."

"You think he's coming to New York City?" I asked with more sarcasm than I felt. "Why not Vegas? Or Mexico?"

"The last message on his answering machine was yours, Miller."

I glanced back toward the kitchen. K.T. stared at me from the pass-through. She hadn't missed a beat. The blood drained from her face. I strode over, shook my head, trying to reassure her, but she shied away from me. She emptied the tea kettle, filled it, emptied it again. When she finally placed it on the burner, her shoulders slumped. I kissed the back of her neck and exited. This time, I went and stood by the windows.

"I don't buy it, Sweeney. If he's about to go on a spree, why'd he pack so much?"

"Maybe you're his final act," he said ominously. Sweeney seemed to be enjoying himself too much. For some reason, the sick amusement he took in scaring me eased my nerves.

"Enough melodrama," I snapped. "Did you find anything incriminating in his house? Bloody artifacts? The knife he used to kill Rubin? You do recall the concept of evidence, Sweeney, don't you?"

"Yeah and he had fuckin' skulls under his pillow. This man's a pro, Miller."

"Must be why he so ably evaded your notice all these years. And by the way, how does the NOPD feel about your breaking and entering, which is a crime even in the Big Easy, I presume?"

He muttered a curse under his breath. The more irritated he became, the stronger I felt. "Easy for you to get on a high horse," he said. "You're not the one getting your hands dirty. Yeah, I broke into his place. And no, we're not dealing with a minor leaguer here. You should've seen his files on the eggshell murders. Methodical. Every single one labeled, indexed, cross-referenced. And volumes on voodoo. I'll put a case of Cuban cigars on this one. Chamelle's *it*."

As much as I wanted to disagree, my guts said Sweeney was right. Everything we knew pointed back to Chamelle. "So now what?" I asked wearily.

"Stay out of it, that's what. So far, Chamelle's killings have clicked according to his own perverse logic. The women got nailed for some reason we still don't understand, but we do know he's staying true to some brilliantly complex scheme. NeVille and Troy were the first real deviations. That is not a good sign. It means his fire's already high and, Miller, tomorrow's Friday."

One of the special days of Ogou Feray. A day on which the killer has struck twice before. At least it wasn't the thirteenth. I hung up from Sweeney and twisted the phone wire around my finger. The prospect of Chamelle tracking me to New York made me queasy. Especially with K.T. in the house. I glanced over to the kitchen. From the smells emanating from that direction, I gathered that she'd managed to find something to eat in the disaster area I called a kitchen. I sniffed. Eggs. Given the circumstances, the last culinary odor I wanted to curl around my head. I ducked through the French doors and clambered upstairs.

A while back, my partner Tony at long last convinced me to buy a handgun and take shooting lessons. The day I returned home with the gun triggered three weeks of insomnia. Then we finally headed out to the range. Bleary-eyed, sick to my stomach, I'd gritted my teeth while Tony put me through the paces. Each time I'd fired, my heart pounded so hard I could hear the pulse in my head. As my finger sank against the trigger in slow motion, my sister's face swelled up in my memory, the moment of her death replayed with exquisitely painful detail. The next time went only marginally better. But eventually, I'd slept again. Eventually, I'd fired the gun, the only reverberation in my limbs the kickback from the gun. The therapist I'd been seeing at the time had saluted my announcement with a stale cup of coffee. I'd used the gun once since then. To protect someone I loved. I'd do the same again, without blinking.

The gun was locked away in the bottom drawer of my desk. I pulled out the key and withdrew the slick leather case. The chamois cloth fell to the floor as I hefted the gun. I always forgot how surprisingly light the twenty-two was. A weapon that could rip through a heart and end a life should be too heavy for anyone to lift. Especially a three-year-old. I slipped the gun into my waistband and changed into an oversized polo shirt.

K.T. was poised at the kitchen counter, raising a forkful of egg to her mouth. She stopped when she saw me. We stared at each other for an instant before she asked coldly, "Would you like to tell me what that call was about?"

I glanced down at my ankle. The bandage hadn't been changed since yesterday. "Not really," I said. "I'd rather talk about us."

Her eyes widened. K.T. was the one who always raised relationship issues. On most days, given the choice between bungee-jumping from the Hoover dam and discussing emotions, I would've gladly taken the leap. But dire times called for dire actions. A heart-to-heart talk was nasty business, only a little less daunting than staring a killer in the eye. I figured if I could survive the latter, I could handle K.T. Still I had a hard time swallowing as I hopped onto the stool next to her. The gun pressed hard against my belly. A spasm of dread ripped through me.

"Do you want to break up with me?" I asked, boldly blunt.

K.T. choked. The fork clanged to the plate. I patted her on the back, but she shrugged me off. "I don't need the goddamn Hemlich maneuver, Robin. Jesus! Where'd that come from?"

"What you said earlier. What Ginny said in the hospital. I know I'm not easy to be with. My work is scary and dangerous. My psyche is not exactly aligned harmonically. I know my faults, K.T. The list is too long to run down. And I know you. You're an incredible, passionate woman and —" I took a deep breath. A damn brick rested on my chest. "The last thing I want to do is see you settle. You may not believe this, but —" Again, the pressure intensified. I felt like I was diving without an oxygen tank. "I've never loved anyone . . . damn." My eyes filled and I turned away. I didn't want to feel this much. I didn't want to need her so much.

I felt her hand on my knee. With an exaggerated Southern accent, she said, "Are you breaking up with me, or proposing?" Her tone was teasing. A little snort of disbelief escaped from me. How ironic. K.T. was resorting to humor to defuse the moment, a tactic I'd turned to a thousand times in the past.

"K.T., I'm serious. If you want to bolt, do so now."

Her features hardened. "You're serious." She shoved the plate aside and scraped her stool closer to mine. "Do you want me to leave? Is that it?"

Geeja appeared suddenly and leapt onto my lap. The cat had an uncanny sense of timing. I rubbed her under the neck and smiled sadly. Without raising my eyes, I said, "I want you to do whatever you need to do. But if you are going to leave, for heaven's sake, do it now."

She sucked in her breath abruptly. "You're scared."

I didn't correct her.

"Of what? Is this still about parenting? Is that it? Are you freaked out about being with me when I start up again?" She pushed herself to her feet and started pacing, talking more to herself than to me. "Of course. This time, you couldn't pretend to be a third party. Neither of us could. You'd have to be a real partner, not an innocent victim of my maternal urge —"

I stood abruptly and seized her gently but firmly by the shoulders. "K.T., stop. This is not about having a baby."

Her gaze drilled into mine. The disbelief in her eyes was almost palpable. A tremor exploded in my belly. "You want the cold, hard truth? I'm sorry you lost the baby, but ever since you did I've had this inexplicable noise in my head. Parenting is absolute insanity. Look what it's done to Beth and Dinah —"

"So that's it —"

"No! No, that's not it." I tried to control my voice. "I don't know why I feel this — it's like some alien has possessed my mind — but I keep thinking... Oh boy." My next words made me shake my head in astonishment. "Maybe this was fate. So that you and I *could* do this together. So that I could be a real parent with you." My eyes brimmed. "So the baby could be *ours*."

K.T.'s lips parted and the hard glaze that had coated her eyes these past few hours cracked like a sheet of caramelized sugar. They turned warm and liquid. "Oh, Robin, if I could believe that —"

I laughed through my tears. "Believe it. If there's one thing I wouldn't lie about, it's this." My hands dropped. "But that's why I need to know. You haven't been real pleased with me lately, not that I blame you, so —"

She stepped into me, shushed me with her lips. The taste of her mouth was intoxicating. I pressed her against me, kissed her with an urgency that shook me to my toes. All of a sudden, she jumped backward. I cursed myself. She'd felt the gun.

Moment of truth. I raised my shirt, revealing the butt of the gun. "This is a part of my life, K.T.," I said, raising my chin. "I don't enjoy my work, but I am proud of it. You're right, I can't save the world, I can't make up for killing my sister, but I can help make a small difference to a handful of people who are suffering grief you cannot even begin to imagine. At times, I can even bring peace to people who've lost their loved ones to unthinkable crimes. I want to do that for Ryan."

A delicate fingertip reached for the gun. She touched the metal and shivered. Then, all at once, she tugged it from my pants and slipped it into the knife drawer. "Let's go upstairs, Robin."

She quieted my question with a butterfly flutter of her fingertip along my lips, then led me up to the bedroom. K.T. insisted on undressing me slowly, gazing at me intensely all the time, pausing to lick the side of my neck, a shoulder blade, the mound of my breast along the line of the bra. Her touch was at once tentative and insistent. When I tried to touch her, she shook her head and gathered my hands by the wrists and held them tight against my belly. Then she finished stripping me, the only sound in the room the sigh and intake of our breathing.

## *Friday, May 7*

I don't remember for how many hours she made love to me, only that at the end, my body was limp, my legs quivering. We'd curled against each other, her mouth buried in my hair, and wept. Sleep, when it came, was a dark, still night without stars or demons. The respite lasted until shortly before dawn.

The phone jolted us apart. My arm instantly sprang across her body. "Hello." My heart raced.

Silence on the other end alerted me to trouble. I crawled over K.T. and sat up on the edge of the bed. "Who is this?"

"You should learn to mind your business." The voice was muffled, disguised.

"Chamelle?" I demanded.

A taut laugh. It echoed inside my head. "Things could get nasty." There was something strange about the voice. I struggled to identify what was wrong. "Do you know who I am?" the caller asked teasingly.

K.T. was sitting bolt upright, the sheets tucked

tightly under her arms. Terror gleamed in her eyes. I mouthed, "Get dressed now," then reached for my pants and said, "I have an idea."

"Do you know why I kill?" Curiosity and disdain curdled the voice.

My hands shook so hard, I couldn't find the tag of the zipper. "Why don't you tell me?"

"I don't kill at random. I'm not a butcher. For each death, there's a reason, an action of and for the gods, who watch and exact payment. Enough said. Know my warning's real. Tonight someone in your house will die —" My gaze snapped to K.T., who was frantically buttoning her blouse. "Tomorrow, if you don't heed this call, you will follow."

"I swear, if you hurt anyone I love —"

"Are you about to threaten me? Don't. And if you think the police can help you, think again. If you contact them, I will know, and you will have signed your own death sentence. " Another laugh, this one louder. And then I realized what had disturbed me about the voice. The sound was stereophonic, coming not only from the phone, but also trailing in through the open door of my bedroom.

The killer was in my home.

## Chapter 13

The first thing I thought was, the gun is downstairs. I almost laughed. Then I noticed K.T. huddled in the corner, hugging herself, waiting for me to say or do something. One look at her eyes and I knew she'd located the voice at the same instant I had.

I hit the plunger on the phone, but the killer had kept the line open. As long as he hung on, I couldn't dial out. I slammed the phone onto the bed and grabbed K.T. by the elbow. There was a rattle downstairs, as if drawers were being opened and closed in rapid succession. A thud sounded on the stairs and we both started. All of a sudden, Mallomar darted into the room and slithered under the bed. At almost the same moment, my black cat Geeja leapt from the dresser, her body growing like a blowfish on a line. She tore between my legs and darted for the steps before I could grab her.

I closed the door, bumped the dresser against the door with my hip and told K.T. to open the window. She stood there, her brow drawn with fear and confusion, clearly uncertain of what to do. I didn't blame her. The fire escape fronted the building and we were four stories up. Whoever was downstairs would expect us to take the single and most obvious escape route available. It was the last thing I intended to do. I forced myself to be calm.

"Okay, baby, we're going out the window. There's a drainpipe off to the left and the corner's constructed with stepped brownstones. I want you to go first. As soon as you get close to the yard, jump and scream at the top of your lungs. The picnic table is in the far left corner, remember?" She was squeezing my hand so hard, I winced. "Honey, please, go!"

She rested one hand on the sill, the other on her belly. I knew she must still be sore, but she glanced at me only once and as soon as I nodded, she swung out the window. I reached out and pressed my palm to the pipe. A fine rain had begun to fall, making the pipe slick. K.T. was struggling to retain her grip. Resting my full weight on my hands, I leaned out the window as far as possible to monitor her progress, listening with dread to the clang of K.T.'s hands slapping along the metal. I darted to the bed, ripped off the bedding and pillows, then tossed them to the ground below her. I prayed the pipe would hold for her, that the killer wouldn't think we'd take this way out. And then the image of Carol sprang to my mind. Bile spurted into my throat. We weren't the only ones at risk.

A faint creak sounded behind me. He was on the stairs now. I couldn't wait anymore. I hoisted myself through the window, poised to swing over to the corner. I wanted K.T. to get closer to the ground before I added my weight to the pipe, but I was aching to latch onto the pipe. She was perched about fifteen feet from the yard when the window below me squeaked, sweeping open with force. I glanced down, shocked.

Beth stuck out her head, saw K.T. and blurted, "Oh, my God!"

I shouted, "Get everyone out of the house now! Now!" Beth's attention snapped up toward me, then back to K.T. "Beth," I warned in a tone she had to remember from the last time I'd plunged her into my nightmare world. "Now!" She disappeared and K.T. leapt off the drainpipe. I watched her arms flail and then she hit the ground, her feet sliding out from under her. She lay there, curled like an S, still and unmoving.

A knock came on the door. Almost polite. The rap of a room service attendant, not a homicidal maniac. I heard my name whispered in an insane muffle and I howled wildly as I vaulted for the drainpipe. The stress of K.T.'s descent had weakened the joints. A metallic pop rang in my ear and I half fell, half slid down the pipe, my feet scrambling for a foothold. I was two-thirds down when the pipe ripped out of the foundation. I fell in slow motion, time enough to hear the crash in my bedroom, to hear the sounds of

Beth, Dinah and Carol scrambling through the back door. Then the world flickered and disappeared.

My fingers curled into grass wet with dew. I groaned and shifted my weight to one side. Something pinned my feet in place and I kicked them free. The linens I'd thrown had somehow tangled around my ankles. The smell of disturbed earth wormed into my nostrils and made me sneeze. I blinked, saw nothing but green mist, then blinked again. Slowly, my eyes focused. I was still in my back yard. Almost instantly, I patted myself down, expecting the warm stickiness of blood. My clothes were damp, but I found no wounds. After another minute, I propped myself up onto my elbows. No one else was near me. Not even K.T.'s prone body. My chest tightened.

Spinning onto my bruised knees, I surveyed the yard, searched the grass for footprints, then whirled around. The door leading to the second floor of Carol and Dinah's apartment had slammed shut suddenly. Had he dragged K.T. inside? The thought coursed through me like wildfire. I ran toward the shed, crashed inside and grabbed the first weapon I found. A hacksaw I'd used to trim the metal fence surrounding the yard. Wielding it in my hand like a bayonet, I tiptoed up the metal stairs, then turned the knob as slowly as possible. It was still unlocked. I sidled through the narrow doorway and gulped for air. To my ears, my ragged breath whined like the engines on a plane positioned for take-off.

A cold, gray sunlight poured into the small room Beth used as a study. Nowhere to hide in here, except the closet on the far wall. With a sinking gut, I noticed the door was slightly ajar. I edged it open with the point of the saw. Empty. A burst of relief ripped air from my lungs. With my eyes fixed on the doorway, I backed up and tried the desk phone. Dead silence. The killer must've cut the wires in the basement. For an instant, the prospect of searching not only the four floors of the brownstone, but also the musty shadows of the basement, overwhelmed me. Then I thought of K.T. and gritted my teeth.

I two-handed the saw and tiptoed into the hall. To the left was Dinah and Beth's bedroom. Or at least it had been. I glanced inside. The bed was unmade on one side. Tortoise-like, I crept through the apartment, noting dully that someone had slept on the couch I'd given Dinah years ago. Nothing had been disturbed. Except for the gallery of photographs that had lined the living room wall. All of them had been removed, leaving ghostly squares on the wall, places where a shared life had once been celebrated. This defacement was not the killer's work. I exited the apartment into the shared entry hall, sniffed something vile and base in the air. A grim realization stung me. The killer had returned to my home.

The stairs creaked under my feet. From above, I heard the patter of feet, as light as rain on the window, then a shriek pierced the air. Damning caution, I flew up the steps, ready to spear the saw at my assailant. The door thundered as I barreled through, taking in at a glance the smear of blood on the kitchen counter. I surveyed the room frantically. Mallomar was curled in a ball under the rocking chair, trembling violently, a willow on the edge of a tornado. Storming into the kitchen, a knot stone-hard in my throat, I retrieved the gun from the drawer where K.T. had placed it earlier. Before we made love. Before the world turned darker than shadows. A bloody knife rested in the kitchen sink.

I tossed aside the hacksaw, hefted the gun with grim satisfaction and headed for the stairs to my bedroom. The rush of blood to my head made sweat pearl up on my forehead. My pace was steady now, my purpose clear. This time I'd kill not just to protect myself. I'd kill for revenge.

The blood trail dotted the wood floor, guided me to the horror that I knew lay ahead. With each step, my mouth tightened, my finger tense against the trigger. Not grief, but fury controlled me. I reached the landing, took a deep breath, then kicked open the bedroom door. The sight curdled my stomach juices. With a strange sense of distance, I felt myself wobble, then slide to the floor, a wail unfurling in my belly and speeding through my body with the force of lava spewed from an erupting volcano. The gun thudded to the floor.

Geeja's body rested on my bed, her sleek coffee-brown torso sliced into two neat halves, her organs spilling madly onto the pillow where I'd slept moments ago.

Vomit burbled from my lips and then I let the howl explode. I remained there, rocking on my knees, for what seemed an eternity. Then with wracking sobs I stood and approached the bed. The killer had long gone. I knew that now. This was his warning to me, his statement of black art. The note next to her butchered corpse was a note just nine bitter words long.

*Next time, K.T. No cops. Your investigation ends here.*

I wrapped Geeja's remains in the stained mattress cover, her blood seeping along my forearms, tears blinding me. I held the crimson bundle against my chest, curled into myself and bawled. No more, I urged myself. At least not now. With one foot, I dragged toward the lamb's-wool tent in which Geeja liked to sleep and wedged the load inside. Suddenly, I was gasping desperately for air. I reeled toward the window and heaved again. Finally, finally, the spasms stopped. A faint cry carried toward me on the wind.

Across the way, in the adjoining yard, I spotted K.T., Dinah, Beth and Carol huddled inside my neighbor's ancient metal shed. The eye contact I made with K.T. even at this distance sent sparks through me. I spun on my heel and boomed down the stairs, dashing through my friends' apartment. The air in the back yard now felt like moist silk, a shroud of grief that whirled around me, suffocating yet welcome. I ran across to the picnic table, climbed on top and hurled myself over the fence. K.T. was running toward me before I landed.

For a while, the tears would not stop. We seesawed against each other, lost in a mad dance of grief and relief. My howls scared Carol and soon her high-pitched cry echoed mine. Beth separated us abruptly and began to furiously examine the length of my body, the triage nurse in her determined to establish whether or not I'd been hurt. The only coherent sound I managed to make was a name. *Geeja.* K.T. grabbed my hand in instant understanding. Beth covered her mouth. But the reaction that sank in deepest was Dinah's. She stood off to one side, holding Carol limply in her arms, her eyes glaring at me. Nearly twelve years ago, Dinah had been with me when a six-week-old gangly Geeja had loped across a dairy farm and flung her long-legged body against my feet, her contented mewl leaving me no option but to adopt her at once. A grumble rolled through my chest. The disgust written now on Dinah's face sealed off any chance we might have had of continuing a friendship.

I closed my eyes and continued to weep.

In a daze, I heard Dinah hand off Carol to Beth, with an abrupt, "I'm moving to Boston immediately. We'll settle the financial stuff over the phone."

As it turned out, the neighbors weren't home so we had to climb back into our yard. Dinah stormed ahead and disappeared before the rest of us made it inside. I collapsed into the desk chair and could go no further. Beth wanted to call the police, but I almost tackled her when she offered to go outside to use the pay phone. "No police," I shouted. Not at least until I'd had time to think and plot out my next step. If the killer's plan had been to scare me off, he'd taken the wrong tactic entirely. There was no way I'd go on knowing this madman was free, watching, waiting, stroking his sick, cruel ego.

The road to peace was paved with his blood and I had no illusions about the sacrifices his capture might require from me. But I would not risk K.T. or Beth or Carol. My pulse slowed.

"Stay here until I get back," I said.

K.T. rushed to my side and demanded to know where I was going. Beth brushed a hand along K.T.'s arm. My friend and I exchanged glances. After our experience with a kidnapper last year, Beth had a keen understanding of what was going on for me. In a hushed tone, she said, "We have to trust her. Believe me."

The trip up to my apartment plunged me back into the nightmare. With grim determination, I sponged off the counter, then mopped my way up the stairs. I gagged briefly in the doorway, then set about methodically cleaning the room until the only remaining signs of disturbance were the bloodied mattress and the scarlet bundle cradled in the cat's tent. Sunlight glinted off the barrel of my twenty-two. I tucked it back into my waistband, grabbed a change of clothes, then tucked Geeja's remains under one arm and returned to Beth's apartment.

K.T. and Beth stood by Carol's crib, whispering. The two of them turned puzzled faces toward me as I entered.

"I want you three to spend the next few days out of town. I don't want to know where." I handed over my checkbook and bank card. "Use this for payment." Another sob broke from me. "My password's June-seven." The day I adopted Geeja.

"Dinah took the car," Beth said.

"You have my car keys. Take it."

Beth's gaze settled on the bloody rags in my arms. She crossed to me with purpose. "All right, Rob," she said simply, "but first let me bury her." I averted my eyes as she left the room.

K.T. stayed behind to watch Carol. As soon as Beth shuffled out, I kissed K.T. deeply, then strode into the bathroom, showered and changed my bandages. When I returned, I heard the shovel's blade slice into the ground. I looked out the open bedroom window and bit my lip and curled my fingers into fists. K.T. had one hand on the railing of the crib, her attention focused on Carol as she slept soundly, her steady breath hissing softly. She glanced up at me. "Robin, why aren't we calling the police?"

"The killer appears to have been able to obtain privileged information from the police in previous homicides. Frankly, I want him to think he succeeded in scaring me off his trail."

Avoiding my eyes, she said in a small voice, "But he hasn't."

I didn't answer at once. Then I said, "No, K.T."

She pinched the bridge of her nose and nodded. "Beth sure knows you well. We'll leave as soon as she's done." Her moss-green eyes fixed on me. "How will I know you're okay?"

"I'll leave a message with Jill every day. Use a pay phone to call in." I walked up behind her and folded my arms around her waist. I could smell our love-making still on her skin. "You'll be safe as long as you're not with me."

"Do you think that's all I'm worried about?" She turned around sharply. "My God, how do you think I'll feel if something happens..." Her voice trailed off and she lowered her eyes. When Beth came in, the two of us were lost in a kiss I never wanted to end. I heard my friend clear her throat. She was ready for escape. I pulled away from K.T. and smiled bitterly.

A few minutes later, I was alone again. But not for long. I locked up and jogged the seven blocks to SIA's office. At eight a.m., the only one I expected to find in the office was Jill. But this morning she had company. Tony Serra, my partner, and Thomas Ryan, my reluctant client and skeptical friend, formed a small knot near the coffeemaker in the new reception area. All three of them started when the door slammed behind me.

Tony and Tom eyeballed me with the identical quizzical expression. It was like staring at Before and After shots of the same man. They were the same height, shared the same gnarled facial characteristics. Picture a boxer who's lost more matches than his bruised brain can remember. Puffy eyes, bent nose, cracked upper lip, thick, wiry necks. But where Ryan was beefy, with love handles a doting mother would love, Tony had grown rail-thin. Two months ago, he had had an allergic reaction to a new medicine, one of those miracle pills that's helping so many AIDS patients. But not Tony. I hadn't seen my partner face-to-face in almost a month and he'd shrunken further. I knew that he'd taken to wearing pants tailored for teenage boys. But in the past few weeks, his hair had fallen out almost completely, leaving him with a thready halo around the crown. At the moment it was slick with sweat. Ryan, on the other hand, looked better than I'd ever seen him. His wavy silver-gray locks rippled back from his ears, with a few white strands brushed down over his tanned forehead. All three of them shifted uncomfortably as I approached.

"What is he doing here?" I demanded to know, pointing to Ryan unceremoniously.

"Hi back at ya," he said with a sniff.

"Ryan..." I wasn't in the mood for games.

"Okay, Miller," he said. "Truth is, I didn't like the way things were going." At the same instant, his penetrating gaze sank to my waist. "You're carrying." The man was uncanny.

Suddenly I was the center of attention. All of it unwanted.

Tony sidled over and patted me down. "You haven't carried since —"

I cut him off. "Someone broke into my house and butchered Geeja."

Jill gasped. Tony's lips tightened into thin anchovy-like slivers, but Ryan didn't blink. My heart thudded. The veteran detective from San Francisco wasn't surprised.

"You knew he'd come after me?" I asked, a flush of anger and shock rising up from my neck.

Ryan turned away and opened the cabinet behind him. No one spoke as he retrieved a fresh mug and poured me a cup of coffee. The burbling liquid punctuated our silence. "Here," he said at last. "Drink this and calm down." I took the mug, heard my stomach gurgle in response. "I didn't *know* anything," he said, "but my guts told me to get out East on the Q.T. The C of Ds wasn't too pleased with me taking a sudden leave, but I've had the job up to here." Ryan slapped the bottom of his chin for emphasis. I glanced over his shoulder, caught an uneasy look in Jill's eyes. She shifted her focus to her fingernails. Not a good sign.

Tony said, "What happened at the house?"

I gave them the full story, watching their reactions with interest. Jill started to cry and excused herself. That left me alone with the bruiser boys. Tony leaned against the wall and did his best to keep from wheezing, but I could still pick up the distinct whistle of each breath. He'd grown incredibly weak. I sat down in one of the leather chairs he'd bought for the waiting room. Sure enough, he followed suit immediately. Ryan remained on his feet, one hand shoved deep into his pristine jeans, the other paw curled around a mug. He said, "You're backing off now, right?"

Tony started to cough, turned it into an exaggerated laugh. "Ryan, this is Miller. Do you really think she's going to let this jerk yank her chain and walk away? Shit, even I know she's not capable of retreat under fire." He steepled his hands by his mouth. " 'The land cannot be cleansed of the blood that is shed therein, but by the blood of him that shed it.' Numbers, thirty-five, thirty-three."

Normally, Tony's habit of quoting scripture rendered me capable of hurling potted plants through closed windows. But this time, I gritted my teeth and nodded woodenly.

Ryan raised an eyebrow, slurped a mouthful of coffee, then smacked his lips and said to Tony, "Maybe I should rethink your offer."

My head swiveled toward my partner. Tony threw me a sideways look, then said, "We'll discuss this later, Tom."

"The hell you will," I blurted.

"Miller doesn't know?" Ryan asked, as if I'd disappeared into thin air like the Cheshire cat.

"What don't I know?" The question was directed at Tony, but Ryan was the one who answered.

"Tony made me a partnership offer. I could quit the job, take my pension —"

I clanked my mug down on the glass table. "You did this without talking to me first?"

Tony stretched his neck to one side until it

popped. "You've been out of pocket, Robin." Then he leveled his gaze at me. I knew what was coming before he opened his mouth. "Dr. Wall says the countdown's begun. I don't have much time. You're good, but you're not the best. What you got is capital and a few years of serious experience. Ryan's got decades. SIA needs him."

Before I could respond Jill scrambled into the room, waving a notepad filled with her frenzied handwriting. "I just hung up from Evan," she announced breathlessly. "The kid is incredible."

Tony leaned toward me and murmured, "We'll finish this later."

"He's been calling family members and friends of the earlier victims for the past few days, probing, schmoozing, prying, praying with them, anything he could do to get them to talk," Jill said. "Listen to this. Eileen Anderson, she was the one killed up in Cambridge." The date clicked off in my head: August 23, 1985. The first woman murdered after Mary Ryan. "Her partner, Mariola, is still living in the same house in South Boston and just recently adopted a baby from China. Evan said she was thrilled someone was still looking into this."

A snort erupted from Tony. "Get to the meat."

"At the time of the murder, she and Eileen had been together seven years. Mariola said she felt like the cops thought she was the suspect, especially since there'd been anal penetration and no sperm. Then they started tailing her brother. When they came up empty there, they worked a couple of other weak leads, then finally dumped the case in the inactive file."

"Nothing new so far," Ryan said.

"Okay, here's where it gets interesting," she said. "At eighteen, Eileen married a neighbor she grew up with. Matthew McCarthy. She was pregnant at the time."

Ryan folded himself into the third leather chair with a high-pitched squeak. A pallor began spreading under his tan.

I leaned forward. "Did they have the baby?"

"Nope. The child died in utero, result of a car accident." She paused for effect. "Eileen Anderson had been on the way to meet her first female lover, which wasn't Mariola. McCarthy, by the way, is in the Air Force. So we've got another man in uniform."

My scalp sizzled. Echoes of Lisa Rubin's story. And Mary Ryan's. I stole a glance at Ryan. He riveted his eyes on his scuffed buckskins and cracked the knuckles of his left hand nervously. Tony scratched his chin and glared at me. He said, "Tommy, you want to check out for a while?"

"Nah. I'm fine." Ryan spoke to his shoes. "Go ahead, Jill."

"Next murder." She scanned her notes and clucked with amazement. "God, Rob, I can't believe you were right."

Tony barked, "Right about what?"

"Hope Williams," I said, prompting Jill to continue.

She squinted at me, nodded, then said, "At first glance, this seems unlike every other case. Hope was twenty-two, younger than any other victim and the only African American. On top of that, she was happily married to the same man for three years."

"Murder happened a year after Anderson," Ryan interrupted in a strained monotone. "Back on my turf. Williams was at the Sheraton attending a nursing conference. She lived maybe five, six miles from me." He looked me full in the face. "Her husband was not uniformed."

Jill said, "He was a programmer."

"Yeah. A nice kid," Ryan said. "The dee's on the investigation concluded she'd been another random killing. No one bought my take on the parallels to Mary's murder. She'd been raped, beaten up real bad and dropped with a bag of trash in another guest's bathroom. The eggshells meant shit to the peach-fuzzed kids they'd pulled from Homicide. I remember one guy, Anthony Haskell was the creep's name, he said to me, 'They found cherry pits in the trash too, Ryan. What you make of that?' And then he and his pals had a good chuckle on my skin."

Tony asked, "So what'd Evan find out. Williams was sneaking out for a rendezvous with the local butch queen?"

Jill and I looked daggers at Tony. He huffed, stood up and headed for the coffee. Jill glowered at his back. "She was straight, Tony."

I heard Ryan exhale loudly.

"Evan had a hard time tracking down people who'd talk about her," Jill went on, her tone tinged with annoyance.

Tony brushed his fingers over the coffee pot, appeared to reconsider his need for another cup and went to the cupboard instead. His watch beeped. Time for another pill.

"Her former husband hung up on him," Jill said. "Her parents are dead. Finally, he used the crisscross and pulled the name of a neighbor who'd lived across the street from where she grew up. The woman there was very friendly and spoke highly of Hope. Remembered how polite and refined she'd been even as a teenager. She said that Hope's boyfriend was the same way. Then she made some comment about how she'd always thought those two sweet kids would marry one day."

Ryan scratched his collarbone, a look of disgust flickering over his face. "So," he said. "We're talking about another childhood sweetheart, right?"

"Right," Jill said. "Turns out Williams dated this boy Bobby Oliveras from age thirteen to age nineteen. Then Bobby's best friend moved in on Hope. They were married four months later. No kids. Bobby moved out to Ohio. He's with the Cleveland Fire Department."

"Okay," Ryan said. "So we're up to Betty Galonardi. You can't tell me this falls into the same pattern. She was forty-seven, a spinster."

"Actually, she was gay too," Tony said reluctantly. I watched him pick out three pills from the case I'd given him for Christmas. "That makes three of the five vics dykes."

"We don't know Betty Galonardi was gay," Jill snapped. "You should've done more than settle for rumors. If Robin hadn't pointed Evan in the right direction —"

"Jill, it's okay," I said. "I can fight my own battles."

Tony and I made eye contact. He looked so sickly I couldn't stand to see him chastised for events so long in the past.

"Evan wasn't too successful on Galonardi. He talked to colleagues of hers at the school where she worked, but Betty didn't have many friends there. He heard much of what we already have in the files. She was a highly intellectual, reclusive woman. At some point, a librarian who'd struck up a friendship with Betty killed himself."

My mouth went dry. Another piece clicked into place. I listened carefully to Jill's next words. "Everyone assumed it was about unrequited love, but there's no hard evidence to support that theory. Personally, it sounds to me like the type of romantic gossip that permeates the education world, especially among high school teachers. You should ask K.T.'s sister about that, Rob."

"I don't have to," I said. Virginia often grumbled about the tawdry fairy tales circulating among her co-workers. Usually, there was an element of truth to the gossip. A motive snapped into place for me.

"The one interesting note we have here," Jill said, "comes from the super at her building. Alberto Cora. We already know Betty was throwing NeVille some odd jobs. Apparently, missing out on the opportunity to pick up some additional dollars pissed Alberto off so badly, it still burns him. He told Evan he'd confronted Betty about it. She said she'd done it at the request of a 'friend' she'd been seeing. The super remembered thinking it was bullshit, because — and I'm quoting Evan's notes here, Tony — 'All the guys in the building knew she was a dyke. It didn't matter who hit on her, she always said no.' Clearly, incontrovertible evidence," she concluded in a voice dripping with sarcasm. I almost grinned. Jill's social conscience had begun to outface mine.

Ryan jerked out of his seat and paced in a tight circle. We all stared at him, puzzled. He was muttering under his breath. All at once, he halted, dragged a hand heavily through his hair. "Did this Alberto talk to the cops?"

Jill practically chirped. "Sure did. He remembered a young man with a funny accent. "

I knew exactly who she meant. Clyde Peltier.

# Chapter 14

The four of us spent the next half-hour divvying up assignments. I laid out my take on the killer's motive. No one objected, though Ryan fell quiet and remained that way. The bear of a cop I'd met in San Francisco years ago would've normally stomped all over our case review. Instead, he sat back, listened and nodded with a remote interest like a member of the board who'd rather be out golfing. The only time he spoke was when I said we needed to get in touch with Sweeney. He'd hawked uncomfortably, then informed me that Sweeney had flown into town this morning at his request.

I cocked an eyebrow and said, "Thanks for the vote of confidence. Mind telling me where's he staying?"

"A dive in midtown," Ryan said evasively. "I'm meeting with him later on. If none of you mind, I think I should be the one to tell him what your crew dug up." He shoved papers into a worn satchel. "Meanwhile I better check in myself. I took the redeye in, then drove straight to Brooklyn. If I don't get a few zees, I'll be worthless."

As soon as he left, I asked Tony what he'd made of Ryan's odd mood.

"Who knows? This thing's driven him for years. Maybe he's got the jitters about being this close to shutting it down. I've seen other detectives react almost exactly the same way. One guy had this open case that kept him awake at nights for ten solid years. The day we nailed the perp, he up and retired. Said he'd lost the fire."

I had a different theory, one I wasn't ready to share yet.

"I'd like to pay Clyde Peltier another visit," I said. "Think you can arrange it for me?"

Tony said, "Sure," and headed into his office.

The phone rang a few minutes later. Jill lurched for it automatically. I didn't budge. Photographs, Evan's files and my own paperwork had buried my lap. Four of the five victims had abandoned childhood sweethearts who eventually entered uniformed professions. My gaze fell on an illustration that Roxanne Lerebon had loaned me. Ogou Feray, the powerful warrior who'd coupled with the *lwa* Ezili, an archetype in which two extreme aspects of femininity converged: the Madonna and the whore. The killer had to be someone who'd suffered his own jilted love. I scratched out a note: *Sic Evan on Chamelle's romantic history.*

Jill waved a hand at me. "It's Sweeney. You want to talk to him?"

In response, I blew her a ripe raspberry, then gathered up my files against my chest and waddled over. She shoved the phone against my ear and I pointed my chin at the note I'd just written. Jill slipped it out, nodded and retreated to her office.

"Hey, there," I said, looking for a place to dump my bundle. "I understand you and Ryan are part of a conspiracy to keep me in the dark. Too bad you guys didn't know that my team's the only one with a working searchlight." At a loss, I tossed the papers back onto the chair.

"What are you talking about?" His tone was vinegary. Maybe New York City didn't agree with him. I smiled at the thought.

"Ryan will fill you in later."

"Uh-uh. That's why I'm calling. I want to meet with you first."

My antennae hissed. "Why?"

"In person, Miller. Where can we meet?"

"Hold on." I asked Jill to find out if Tony had arranged for me to meet Peltier. She returned a second later with the information. Eleven-fifteen, at the pizzeria near the Carroll Street train station in Brooklyn. I knew the place well. They made the slices too thick and the sauce was runny. To make up for it, I'd have to get a chocolate Italian ice. Darn. I told Sweeney about the meeting and arranged to meet him at the same spot, one hour later. He yammered at me a few minutes more, clearly pissed off that I hadn't given him the full dope.

After I hung up, Jill took me aside. "Tony's taking a nap."

I shot a look at his closed office door. My partner had waged a valiant battle with his disease, but the white flag was slinking up the pole. "Okay," I said. "The two of us can handle this. How's the rest of our caseload?"

She scowled briefly. "One client fired us yesterday afternoon. Samson Ink. Real Data called me at home last night complaining about our lack of responsiveness. The others seem okay. We hired seven more undercover agents to float through Gemini's employment office. I've subcontracted out some work to Luce Lorelli and Hanson Associates."

I had a new appreciation for the urgency behind Tony's offer to Ryan. My watch read nine-forty. Time enough for me to log in some of the make-nice calls Tony excelled at and I usually bungled. My office door yawed open. The first thing I noticed was the picture John Zimmerman had taken of me and Geeja in my back yard last Halloween. I flopped onto the couch. I never did get around to making those calls.

At ten-thirty, I peeled myself off the sofa, whisked through the reception area and lobbed a half-felt wink at Jill as I headed out for my appointment. Beth and K.T. had taken my car, so I was at the mercy of the Metropolitan Transit Authority. On the way to the Seventh Avenue station, I patted myself down to make sure the handle of my gun didn't make my shirt bulge. The last thing I needed was for some punk to snatch my twenty-two.

It was a bizarre sensation to feel the warm metal of the handgun against my flesh as I strolled along the avenue in my neighborhood where on any given day I dropped off dry cleaning, bought groceries, sipped café latte, downed scones and bumped into vendors, friends and strangers I'd known for years. I passed the newsstand and descended into the station. My ankle had begun to heal, but I could feel it throbbing as my feet hit each step. A burst of ammonia greeted me at the first landing. Welcome to the bowels of Brooklyn, I thought. I heard the rumble of the train and bolted for the turnstile. The singular ding of a New York subway car told me the doors were about to close. I poured on the steam and slipped through the opening sideways.

Carroll Street was just three stops away. I didn't even have time to read the latest installment in the banner-strip on Rafael and Desirée. Would she abort or continue her unplanned pregnancy? Maybe on the way home I'd find out.

I was twenty minutes early, so I *had* to order a slice. A fresh pie had just emerged from the oven, but I insisted on my pizza being reheated anyway. The Al Pacino look-alike on the other side of the counter eyed me conspiratorially. "You like your pizza to snap," he said, nodding with confidence. Finally, someone who understood me.

My friend served me at an outside table. I heard the crust crack as I folded the slice in half and took a bite. It was better than I'd remembered. There was nothing left but crust when I crossed back to the counter. "Is this place under new management?" I asked.

The young man smiled. "My father," he said, chin high. He wiped a hand on his sauce-stained apron and extended it to me. "Sanguino, Junior. You like the pizza?"

"Here's my answer. Heat up another one."

He smiled broadly and tossed a slice into the oven.

"Does Officer Peltier eat here often?" I asked casually.

Sanguino beamed. "You know Clyde?" he asked. "Absolutely. He's a good man. Some of his friends come in, they make an order and then they stand there, hands in their pockets, waiting for someone to say, on the house. My father, he does it all the same. Me, I say, put the money on the counter. Officer Peltier's not like that. He even tips." He gestured over my shoulder. "Here he comes now."

I spun around. Sure enough, a cop strode through the open door, one hand poised awkwardly over his holster as if he wasn't sure whether he'd need to draw his gun or adjust his pants. The only people in the place were me and Sanguino. Peltier gave me the once-over, which gave me time to do the same. He was five-nine, at most, with prematurely gray hair, chipmunk cheeks, thin lips, bright steel-blue eyes and a hangdog expression. His body was surprisingly slight. Narrow shoulders, narrow hips. I checked out his hands. They were almost delicate. I couldn't imagine this guy on the streets of New York.

He looked a little edgy so I walked up to him,

introduced myself, then added quickly, "I'm carrying a gun for protection only. I'll be happy to show you my P.I. and gun licenses before we sit down."

He nodded, tapped his foot rapidly while I flipped through my wallet and pulled out the necessary papers. I handed them over, but he appeared to skim rather than read them. Sweat beaded up along the tops of his eyebrows. It was a gorgeous spring day, seventy-five degrees, with a stiff breeze rolling along the streets. I had on a long-sleeve dungaree shirt and a jean jacket and I was perfectly comfortable. Peltier was nervous.

I offered to buy him a slice, but he declined with a sniff. Sanguino slid my second order to me, then Peltier and I retreated to the patio.

"Did Tony explain the situation to you?" I asked.

"Frankly, no. I was pretty sure we had covered everything the other day." Peltier had retained a bit of the Cajun accent.

"Well, I have a few other questions about Galonardi."

He dropped his eyes to his hands. "Cold case," he muttered.

"Too bad no one listened to you about the voodoo angle. It was quick thinking," I said, oddly compelled to stroke his ego.

He shrugged. "It was Cajun thinking. Back then, I still had the swamp between my ears. My mama was always telling me tales about Congo dances and gris-gris. When my partner hooted at me, I don't know, I figured it were better to shush up. I didn't want the guys to think I was some scaramouch." He snickered to himself. "That's what my daddy used to call me. I'm not even sure what it means, but I knew it was real bad. Roger, that was my partner, he was a lot like him. Tough, but darned sharp. He retired last year." Peltier had to be in his late twenties, but he seemed about sixteen years old despite the gray hair.

"Can I ask you to go over what happened once again?"

He looked askance at me. "Your partner wouldn't tell me what this is all about. I don't get why you two are hunting down a squirrel who got no meat on his bones. Why so much interest in Galonardi?"

Tony believes that a good investigator never gives out information, he only takes it in. I decided to violate his rule. "We think the killer has struck again. This time in New Orleans." Peltier frowned sharply as I described Lisa Rubin's murder.

"Could be related," was all he said when I was done.

"Did you have any other leads back then that could help us now?" I asked.

"Just the wanga stuff... you know, hoodoo rites. And you-all already picked up on that." Peltier might be a good cop, but he was a lousy liar. He shrugged three or four times while he spoke, his eyes never once meeting mine.

I tried a different tack. "Did you know Galonardi was a lesbian?"

A flicker in his eyes, then the lids descended in a slow blink. "That's what some said."

"You didn't buy it?"

He hemmed a bit. "That's just flubdub. Galonardi was a big-boned lady with short hair. So was my mama. After my daddy passed on, she wouldn't look at another man no matter what wares he tried to sell her. Some of the neighbor folks thought she'd gone queer. But she hadn't. She just liked living alone."

I lowered my eyes to the slice in my hand and zeroed in on Peltier's conscience. "Too bad you couldn't nail the perp back then. It could've saved this poor woman down in New Orleans." I tore off a piece of pizza. "By the way, Galonardi's super made some comment about her having a special friend."

Peltier squirmed in his seat. "You're not from internal affairs, are you?"

The pizza was cold and my interview hot. I dropped the slice and leaned over the table. "None of this goes back to the job. I promise you."

"Shit." He whistled through his teeth. I could almost see the decision shimmy over his face. Peltier was ready to talk. "We dicked up that investigation but good. First, I was too weak-kneed to stand up for what I knew in my gut. You tell me that a jar of bull's testicles don't scream hoodoo. Hell, I *knew* it. Then all the boys were snickering about Galonardi being some bulldyke so what'd it matter, like there was a darned scorecard we could use to prioritize whose homicide we'd take serious. I spoke to the super, some Hispanic guy —"

"Alberto Cora."

"That's it." He stabbed a finger at me excitedly. "So he tells me about Galonardi talking about this friend and it sticks out like a Northerner ordering pee-can pie in Dixie. Where'd this friend come from? How come no one else seen him? Then Cora says this man had him an accent like mine. *Ding.*" I thought of Chamelle. "Now, I'd met this man who reminded me of a ragamuffin I knew when I was growing up ... Name escapes me now, but he was from back home and had done scut work for Galonardi —"

"Was his name Barry NeVille?"

His lips curled. "Barry sounds right. Don't recall the last name. He tried to play like he was retarded, but I knew his kind. After a while, I got him off the game, talking man to man. We sat down and jawed the fat for close to an hour and the only thing I knew for sure was his cool went up like dried moss in a campfire the minute I mentioned Galonardi's friend. He made some comment about his 'protector,' and then he scampered like a scared-ass mouse." He looked at my plate. "You eating that crust?"

I pushed the plate toward him. His hunger had suddenly returned.

"So I tell Roger we ought to track this turkey down and he just laughed, told me that I had a lot to learn about women if I thought this dyke had herself a real boyfriend. That was when Rog heard about this lunatic up in the Bronx who'd been boasting about raping old women. The lead seemed awfully well-timed, but I was a juvie so I went along." Peltier scratched at a cuticle and grimaced. "Rog beat this boy up bad and I stood there, dumb silent. Kid ended up confessing to the murder, so I thought maybe, you know, what the hell experience did I have?" He bit a fingernail, looked at me for understanding. I smiled back. "Turned out this nut wasn't even in the vicinity at the time of the murder.

I wanted to go back and pursue the earlier tack, but Roger told me to let it alone." He hesitated. "Don't get me wrong here. Rog was a great cop. I never seen him go that route again."

"Did you ever come across the name Fitzhugh Chamelle?"

"You razzing me?"

He must have seen the puzzlement in my eyes. "No, I guess you're not," he said. "Sure I heard of him. Fitz got himself a regular byline in the *Times-Picayune*, best paper in the country, in my opinion. No offense, but it beats the New York papers hands down. I was the one who called him up to New York back in 'eighty-eight. You had to read his articles, right? Man, did Roger ever chew me out about that one."

Peltier was an absolute gold mine. My partner must have been worse off than I realized if he could leave so much of this cache untapped.

"Fitz covered the Galonardi case real good," Peltier said. "He buddied up with my lieu. Ever since, he's called maybe twice a year to see if we got anything new for him. He was the only one back then who expressed a modicum of interest in my theories, but then again he was from New Orleans. When it didn't pan out, he'd wink at me and make it out like we was the only ones in New York City. I liked him."

"Any chance he was Galonardi's friend?"

"Nah. He was a might peculiar though. Told me he'd been chasing murders with hoodoo shades ever since his sister got raped in Berkeley with a stuffed snake carcass. He had particular interest in this...

what'd you say his name was? Barry —" He snapped his fingers. "Troy! That's it."

So NeVille had borrowed his cousin's last name.

Peltier went on. "Barry Troy. Hate when I forgot stuff like that. Anyway, Fitz told me he'd be chasing him all over the country, waiting for him to make the wrong move. He was practically begging me to nail the guy for Galonardi's murder, but I had to tell him the truth. I didn't make Troy as the perp."

A woman with a stroller craned her head at us as she strolled by. Peltier glanced at his watch suddenly and stood up. "Look, I got to get back on the beat. I'm glad I put this on the table." He smiled sheepishly. "Now it's your game."

"One last question."

"Shoot."

I swallowed hard. "Did you tell any of this to a private detective who was looking into Galonardi's murder?"

The muscles of his jaw tightened. "Yeah. He was the biggest asshole of them all. Swee-ney." He stretched the name out with distaste, the way a five-year-old might say *spinach*. My estimation of Peltier rose steeply. "He made me feel this small." He pinched two fingers together. "Him and Roger hit it off and the next thing I know both of them are calling *me* a bayou rat, like Sweeney was much better. I'll tell you what really ticked him off . . . I made some comment about his medal."

I swept a hand to my own neck, suddenly remembering the brass medal Sweeney wore around his neck. A stabbing pain shot through my head as the image gelled.

"Here this jerk's making fun of me 'cause I'm reading hoodoo in a bottle of bull's testicles and meanwhile he's walking around with a *vévé* around his neck."

Saliva evaporated from my mouth. I gaped at Peltier.

*Ogou Feray.*

In less than ten minutes, we'd be face to face.

# Chapter 15

I asked Peltier to wait around while I went inside to make a phone call to my office. No one had answered so I scurried back to the patio, but by then Peltier had disappeared. I rushed back into the pizzeria and asked Sanguino where he'd gone.

"His thing went off," he said, pantomiming talking on a radio. "A domestic disturbance on Second Place."

Shit. I darted back outside, checked the four corners for any sign of Sweeney. According to the plan we'd made earlier, he should arrive any minute.

He had rented a car, but I had no idea what kind. I scanned every parked car I passed. The last thing I wanted to do now was encounter him while I was on my own. I retraced my steps to the train station, glancing repeatedly over my shoulder. I was grateful for the weight of the gun and shifted it so I could more readily draw if I needed to.

How the hell had I missed the clues? I swore to myself out loud. In rapid succession, I replayed every moment we'd spent together. The emblem of Ogou Feray emblazoned on the medal he wore. The gothic drama he'd staged for me in the bayou, probably assuming I'd be stupid enough to buy NeVille as the killer, or chicken enough to be scared off by his rough-house tactics. And then there was Rubin's tooth. Most likely Sweeney himself placed it in my pocket. No doubt that bit of evidence never did end up with the NOPD. Who knew if he'd been in contact with the local authorities at all?

Damn, damn, damn! Scenes erupted in my brain, each one triggering another bitter realization. The off-handed comment Sweeney had made on the drive out to the bayou about Galonardi being the *last* murder, long before I had any idea that the Andrea Allen case had been solved two years previously. His slip on the date of Galonardi's murder. He'd had it right all along. Why shouldn't he, since he was the one who'd schemed and carried out each one of them? Then there was the convenient appearance of NeVille and his tattooed cousin on Bourbon Street, so near to where Sweeney and I'd just met. And the fiasco in the supposedly haunted house. All along, he'd been toying with me, testing my resolve, eating away at my nerve. Ryan was right after all. The killer had been playing a game. A game with deadly stakes. What my friend hadn't known was that we'd both been pawns from the start.

My mind retrieved the ghastly image of the decimated body of my cat, the cat I'd curled up with during long bouts of insomnia. Her bowels spilled on the bed where I slept. Tears sprang to my eyes. I wanted Sweeney dead.

The subway station air was cool and damp, but sweat crawled along my midriff. I slammed the token into the turnstile and tramped down the stairs to the platform. My eyes blinked to adjust to the dim, sulfur-tinged light, then I headed for the rear of the station that would let me off near the exit closest to my office. The sound of my footsteps echoed dully. I paused, took a deep breath. A trace of cheap cologne hung in the air, which made me think that I must've just missed the train. I watched an elderly man pass by and climb the stairs with difficulty. That's when it struck me that no one else was around. I started moving back to the center of the platform.

*Clack.*

In an instant my fingers curled around the butt of the gun. The sound had come from in front, but no one was visible. If it was Sweeney, he was good.

Suddenly I heard my name whispered. Playfully ominous. The same voice I'd heard on the phone this morning. He must've tailed me since the pizzeria, but I hadn't detected him. And I couldn't find him now. Sweeping my gaze from left to right slowly, I slunk around a steel pillar. There were too many places to hide. The trash dumpster was dead center of the platform, about fifteen feet from me. The staircases lay beyond that.

That's when it hit me. Instinctually I knew that this madman had carefully positioned himself between me and the exits. There was no way out for me. Unless a train came and came fast.

All at once, Sweeney reared up next to the dumpster, stretched his arms out to his sides and tilted his head back, a perverse echo of Christ on the cross. I pulled out my gun, snapped off the safety and took a bead on him. The Jennings twenty-two wasn't the best weapon at this distance, but it'd at least buy me time.

Sweeney shouted, "The moment has come. Shoot, my friend. Shoot and feel the glory of righteous vengeance." He'd assumed an entirely different accent. The clipped English of a Tulane graduate.

"What the hell is wrong with you?" I yelped, wincing at the panic in my voice, the thud of my heartbeat against my chest. My memory skidded back to the first time I'd driven with him, the crime scene photos he'd tossed in my lap. Every bloody tableau this man had brilliantly engraved in my brain.

"Like you, I'm the specter of justice. Come on, Miller, you must understand. Every case you take, you're avenging your sister's death."

I snarled, "I murdered her myself, Sweeney," then my voice broke and my knees felt ready to cave. He knew too much, knew how to unsettle me. I had to stay cool, focused.

He curled his lips. "So you seek vengeance against yourself and I seek it elsewhere. The difference is small, really."

Where the hell was a train? I strained for the slightest hint of a distant rumble. Nothing. Stall for time, I warned myself. Probe for his Achilles' heel.

Instantly, I thought of Ryan. "Why'd you slaughter your best friend's wife? Explain that." Would anyone hear me if I shouted? Could I even manage to make that much sound? My throat was so constricted, I was gasping for air.

"Mary, the Madonna. Yes. She was the second one. And the best." His arms fell to his sides. "She broke my friend's heart, left him when he needed her most. I went to plead his case and she scorned me. Like I was scum. As you thought. So easy to make you women believe the best or worst of me, whatever I want, whenever I want. I tried to teach that to Barry, but he wasn't a natural performer. He had to work *so* hard. Poor kid didn't know I was setting him up as my alibi all those years. You were better than I ever expected, by the way. Forced my hand. Made me kill my poor puppet and his dumb cousin. Chamelle's dead, too. But no one will ever find him. After you're gone, they'll assume you were his next and last victim. Before he retired to Argentina."

He patted his breast pocket. "Tickets and passport pre-arranged, under Chamelle's name. See how prepared I am?" He laughed and took a step in my direction. "But you wanted to know about Mary Ryan. I don't blame you. We always want to know *why*, don't we? And I want you to, Robin. You deserve that much for playing the game so well. When I went to see Mary at her hotel that night, she told me she was determined to divorce Ryan. You don't know him like I do, the way he was back then. He was a giant and she fuckin' toppled him, squeezed his balls till he squeaked like a girl." For an instant, he sounded like the pig I knew. He'd noticed the break himself. With a jerk of his chin, he said, "So sharp, Robin. So sharp. I knew only two other women as sharp as you. My wife, Celeste, and sweet, stoney Betty Galonardi."

"And you killed Betty." We were dancing backward. Each step he took, I matched with one that moved me farther away. A few more feet and I'd be flat against the wall.

"I cleansed them."

My hands were trembling. I forced myself to stop moving and focus on keeping a steady aim. Then his words sank in. "Mary was the *second* victim?"

A full smirk beamed at me. "Ryan is so good at confidences. If he'd told you about my wife, how she'd left me, you would've understood so much more, so much sooner. Celeste was my Ezili, like Mary was Ryan's. And like Mary, she betrayed me. Left me for someone else." Now he cocked his head and sneered at me. "A woman."

No wonder Ryan had looked so uneasy this morning. He must've realized how closely Sweeney matched the profile we'd mapped out of the killer. So where the hell was he now?

Sweeney swaggered toward me. "Then Celeste was stricken with breast cancer. That's when I first realized how committed God was to me and my life. How he wanted to work justice *through* me. Yes, Robin. Ogou Feray. It was so easy to make people believe she took her own life. But her death was not satisfying. Too impersonal. Do you know how she died?"

I shook my head.

He appeared to gloat. "She threw herself in front of a train. And now fate closes the circle here."

We both heard the murmur of faint voices upstairs at the same time. Someone was talking to the clerk in the token booth at the far end of the station.

"Last chance, Miller. Shoot!" he commanded.

"Forget it, Sweeney." The faint hum of a conversation just one flight away emboldened me. I said, "Lower yourself to the ground. Now!" Good, I thought. My voice sounded far less tremulous.

"Surrender is not a possibility, Miller," he said, his voice as cold as stone in winter. He glanced over his shoulder toward the stairs and shouted forcefully, "Fire in the tunnel! Get out now!" Then he pulled off his bomber jacket, plucked out a Bic lighter and set it aflame.

I hollered, but whoever was upstairs was too busy scrambling for assistance to hear me. "As much as I've enjoyed this cat-and-mouse game, it's over now. One of us will go down today." With unearthly speed, he whipped a thirty-eight semi-automatic from his shoulder holster and assumed a two-handed position. I barely had time to cock my gun. The bumbling detective I'd grown to despise was gone. I finally understood why Ryan had called Sweeney the best in the field. Without thinking, my finger sank hard against the trigger.

Click. Again I pulled and again the hammer hit nothing.

"I was in your house. Remember?" He dug into his pocket and withdrew a palmful of bullets, which he dropped one by one to the platform. "Your gun is worthless."

The game continued.

My gun clanged to the ground as I vaulted onto the tracks and ran faster than I ever had. The sudden darkness of the tunnel blinded me. I stumbled forward, one foot almost catching on the thick wooden ties. The third rail gleamed where passing trains had etched a line through the coal-black dross. An electric eel, I thought, ready to strike me if I veered the wrong way.

There was an archway off to my right. I flung myself into the recess, sucking in air like a fish. Sweeney's approaching footsteps were relaxed, rhythmic. Soot rushed into my nostrils as a slight breeze billowed around my ankles. I moved out, my eyes at last able to pick out shapes. Including the twelve-inch shadows slithering along the wall. Sweeney was less than ten feet away with his gun at half-mast.

I rushed headlong into the tunnel, staying in the center gutter between rails. Sweeney picked up speed behind me. The first bullet whizzed by my head. He wasn't aiming to kill. Not yet. He still underestimated my nerve, assumed he could scare me into submission. I had to use his disdain to my advantage. I traversed the tracks, making it harder for him to keep a steady aim.

Sweeney chortled. "Miller, slow down and I'll fill you in on the rest of details. You don't want to die before all your questions get answered, do you? Like who sent you that rich breakfast in New Orleans. And who had his nose up your pussy girl's crack? K.T.'s the name, right? Now there's a morsel worth devouring."

He was goading me, trying to snake under my skin, using the sick tactics he'd honed all week long. But under the bravado I detected something else. Desperation. With a tingle in my limbs, I knew he didn't want this hunt to go fast. This was the last game he intended to play and he wanted to make it memorable. The spectacle of the tooth he'd carved out from Lisa Rubin's jaw jolted into mind. I pledged to hurl myself onto the third rail before I let him butcher me.

My legs felt heavy and my ankle wound stung, but I kept my pace steady. The welcome sound of frenzied voices exploded back in the station. They must be investigating the fire. Maybe they'd see the bullets, the gun I'd tossed away. I howled like a wolf and kept hurtling deeper into the tunnel. The next station after Carroll was Smith and Ninth, an open-air section of elevated track. If I could stay ahead of him, I had a chance. But at the same instant the thought struck me, the opportunity evaporated.

The tunnel swerved suddenly to the left and I lost my footing. I pitched forward, smacking my chin hard against the track. For a few seconds I was stunned, but it was all the time Sweeney needed. Next thing I knew he was over me with the thirty-eight angled at my stomach.

"Get up, Miller." His eyes sparkled.

This was a killer unlike any I'd ever encountered. The man was absolutely evil. Malevolence rose from his skin like the stench of rot from a carcass. I shrank away from him.

"Now the fun starts," he said. "You wanna see the essence of Ogou, the warrior. Take a look." I followed the direction of his eyes. His pants tugged around his erection. "This is how it begins," he said patiently, an instructor to a challenged student. He rubbed the handle of his gun against his penis and moaned lightly. "This is my fire. The bolt of lightning." He smiled sadly at me. "For a while, I worried about whether or not you needed cleansing. You never abandoned a man. You never crushed a soldier's heart. All the others did, you understand that now. Being a lesbian's not enough to warrant my wrath. And then I got it. You reminded me of Betty." He puckered his lips, as if remembering her. "A strong woman. I wanted to make her my partner. She was pure, at forty-seven. Never with a man or a woman. But she rejected me."

The voices deep behind us started to fade. Knowing how minds work in the bruised Big Apple, they probably assumed the fire had been the work of juveniles out for an afternoon kick. My stomach knotted. I had no doubts about Sweeney's intentions, and now rescue seemed a more distant possibility. I rested my cheek against the cold, dank floor, my focus snapping suddenly toward the rat that glared at me from a few inches away. I jerked backward.

An explosion sounded near my head. Sweeney had put a bullet through the rat's belly. I covered my ears and rolled onto my side.

"See. You're all mine. No one else's. Tell me, Robin, would you have turned down the chance to be my partner? In life and in death?"

I groaned. "You know the answer, Sweeney." My arm stretched out to the side. Another few inches and I'd graze the third rail. Electrocution had to be better than anything else Sweeney planned.

I glanced up and saw him grin. "And so you justify the cleansing."

He reached for his zipper at the same time I bucked off the track and rammed my fist into his knee. The *oomph* he made as I made contact gave me a burst of hope. I lumbered to my feet, narrowly missing the third rail. Our eyes met and he nodded solemnly. Next time Sweeney wouldn't hesitate. He raised the gun, but I was already springing backward. Maybe Sweeney didn't know what the ringing of the rails and the rush of stale air pouring toward us meant, but I sure as hell did. I turned tail and catapulted through the tunnel toward the dim light ahead.

Sweeney shouted, "Run, but you won't get far," so certain he had me where he wanted that he took after me in a lazy jog. The distinct metallic *clink* and rattle finally woke him up. He muttered, "Shit!" and scrambled to catch up with me, this time not to take me down but simply to outrun the train now barreling after us.

We pounded along the tracks, huffing in perfect synchronicity. The conductor must've seen us at last because the horn blasted and rocked the ground under my feet. Brakes screeched along the rails like chickens being skinned alive. I made it to the edge of the tunnel just in time. The tracks opened up to the sky, a near-gale wind gusting toward me. I sprinted hard for the last few feet, then dove for the narrow walkway that ran alongside the outer tracks. The train shrieked by my ears, so close I could feel the metal's heat sweep along my arms.

Sweeney had been only two or three seconds behind me. As I hit the concrete and rolled onto my hip, I heard a muffled thud behind me, the sound of a sack of potatoes being slung carelessly into a grocery cart. And then, as my eyes flickered gratefully across the horizon, I saw him. The train must've clipped him as he attempted to leap out of the way, or maybe the decision had been his own. All I know is that for the briefest of moments, he hurtled through the thin, sweet air like a hawk surfing on a summer thermal. And then he arched and plunged to the ground, a streak of gray and crimson against an impossibly blue sky.

I never told anyone this, but at that black instant in hell, it was an image of beauty.

# *Postscript*

**Saturday, July 3**

The sun baked my cheeks, painted the insides of my lids the color of a cardinal's feathers. I shifted in the lounge chair so that Mallomar could curl up between my legs. She mewled contentedly. I smiled down at her, swallowing hard at the memory of her sister. The buzz of a hummingbird made both of us turn sharply to the right.

With a sigh I leaned back, the scent of Avon's Skin So Soft wafting around my nose, the whirr of insects a mild distraction. I waved away a mosquito and nodded to myself. Thank God for today. A simple prayer in a simple moment.

K.T. and I had agreed to spend her birthday weekend at a house we'd rented up in the Pocono mountains of Pennsylvania. She was inside puttering in the kitchen, whipping up sourdough bread, grinding up pesto and deveining shrimp. Me, I'd opted for the deck and a tall iced coffee with a splash of Hershey's, Ella Fitzgerald crooning at me from the outdoor speakers and the most recent issues of *People*. The past three months have been a period of brutal adjustment for both of us. K.T. and I both mourned the little girl we'd never get to know. For K.T., though, it's been much harder. Despite the doctor's assurances to the contrary, she worries constantly that something's fundamentally wrong with her. And now that she's turned thirty-eight, she's convinced that the last of her eggs have shriveled up like raisins left overnight in an exposed bowl. In August. In Death Valley. After a sand storm.

When she blew out the candles on her cake last night, she threw her emerald high beams at me and smiled shyly. "Guess what I wished for, honey?" As if there could be any doubt. Sometimes in her sleep, a small cry escapes from her lips and her brow gathers in pain. She never remembers the nightmares, though we have our suspicions. K.T. worries about what will happen to us if she does get pregnant again and the next instant frets about what will happen if she doesn't. No matter what, I'm determined to be around for the ride. K.T. will just have to learn to believe me.

I have another reason to grieve. My partner Tony

passed away last month. He went in his sleep, at his own home, after a day spent with friends and colleagues, which was exactly the way he would've wanted it. The funeral was small and simple. As sad as the day had been, most of the attendees seemed relieved he hadn't suffered more. But losing him was harder than I'd expected. We spent so much of the last several years cussing and battling with each other, I barely noticed how fond I'd grown of him. And how much I needed him at the helm of Serra Investigations. Of course, with Ryan on board and some serious reengineering, I'm sure SIA will survive. Some of the major changes are already underway. We made Jill Zimmerman a full partner and hired Evan Alexander as our full-time research clerk. At the last staff meeting, we agreed unanimously to keep the agency running under Tony's name. We owed it to him, me more than anyone else.

Ryan has his own demons to face. When the horror of Sweeney's betrayal and madness sank in, he'd had a short-lived but frightening breakdown. That fateful Friday in May, when he left our offices, he'd gone straight to a bar and downed his first whiskey since Mary Ryan's funeral, nine years ago. Tony tracked him to the bar around mid-morning and immediately dragged him to an AA meeting. Of course, when the two of them realized that they'd left me to confront Sweeney alone and how close I'd come to being his next victim, they were devastated. Ryan especially. I've lost count of how many times he's sworn to make it up to me.

What concerns me most, though, is the way he's been second-guessing himself as we manage the SIA transition. He'd been so close to Sweeney and so totally conned by him, he's lost some of his old, blustery confidence. Worse, he blames himself for each and every one of the black-magic deaths, which is what the two of us have since termed them.

We still have a lot of questions about how Sweeney managed to pull off his sick charade for so long. Only last week, Ryan and I sat down together to try to close out the files for good. Thanks to a diary the NOPD found at Jimmy Lee Troy's trailer, we discovered more about Sweeney than he'd ever expected the dumb egghead to know. Sweeney should have done a little more investigating. The egghead had earned a degree in creative writing from a correspondence program he'd enrolled in while in jail. Good old Jimmy Lee figured he'd write a screenplay based on his cousin's exploits one day. His writing style didn't impress me much, but his attention to detail sure did.

Troy's tattoo, we learned in the last few pages of his diary, was suggested and paid for by Sweeney. No surprise there. What was surprising was how fully informed Troy had been about his cousin's and Sweeney's activities, dating back to the time of Mary Ryan's murder. Another matter that struck us as odd was the fact that NeVille had been physically involved in the actual commission of only one murder: Mary Ryan's. In all the other homicides, his role had been simply to lure victims or distract authorities.

From Troy's notes, it sounded as if Sweeney had pegged Barry NeVille as the perfect foil for his crimes almost the instant they'd stumbled onto each other again outside Mary Ryan's hotel in San Francisco. According to Troy, that was the first time NeVille and Sweeney had seen each other since NeVille's arrest on rape charges eighteen years earlier. I still wasn't sure how they had recognized each other after so long a period. Ryan and I speculated that the supposedly chance encounter had been anything but chance. Of course, we'll never know for sure. That same day Sweeney invited NeVille out to his cabin and began stirring up the drifter's anger at Thomas Ryan and pointing him in the direction of Mary Ryan.

NeVille apparently believed that Sweeney was his great protector and that Ryan had been the sole force behind his arrest at age seventeen, as well as the subsequent beating. Sweeney convinced NeVille that the most powerful expression of revenge would be to rape and butcher Ryan's wife. When my friend read those lines, he blanched, tossed the files aside and strode out of the office without another word. He hasn't looked at the records since.

Partly through the diary and partly through our own investigative efforts, we've discovered how horrifyingly circumstantial Sweeney's selection of victims had been. Eileen Anderson's ex-husband wrote an article on his failed marriage for a prominent men's magazine, which Sweeney read and must've identified with instantly. Hope Williams met Sweeney at a hospital where he'd gone for stitches. Betty Galonardi encountered Sweeney in a bookstore on the occult and later hired him to check out a neighbor who'd been harrassing her. From Sweeney's friends on the NOPD, we discovered that he knew murdered cop Peter Strampos personally and had most likely fixated on his ex-wife Lisa after meeting her at the Strampos funeral.

One interesting side note: Troy suspected that his

cousin and Sweeney had had some kind of physical relationship as well, though we never found any evidence to confirm that.

From what we can gather, Fitzhugh Chamelle's only apparent connection to the murders was his fixation on framing NeVille, an obsession that Sweeney had hoped to use to his own advantage when the right day came. Of course, his perfect scheme never did come to pass, thanks to the impact of a speeding F train with worn brakes. On the other hand, Chamelle's body has never been found, so Sweeney was right on that one.

The two other pieces of the puzzle I managed to latch onto were small, but helped me to reach some kind of closure. Chamelle *was* the man who met K.T. at Café du Monde and followed her back to the hotel. I assume that the reason for his interest had been the final minutes K.T. had spent with Lisa Rubin, but this too will have to remain a mystery. Sweeney must've been the one who had ordered breakfast for me and worn the skeleton mask outside the Napoleon Bar. Both events bear the mark of his unique brand of game-playing.

The phone jangled inside. I heard K.T. scamper through the kitchen and snap up the receiver. After a moment, she shouted to me from inside the house. "It's Beth. She and Carol are leaving Brooklyn now. They should be here in a couple of hours."

I nodded to myself, sat up and stretched. Beth was handling Dinah's abandonment fairly well, though I feared she was focusing so much of her energy on Carol, she might not have emotions in reserve if and when a new partner appeared on the scene. Meanwhile, Dinah and I have worked out a temporary financial agreement, pending sale of the brownstone, which doesn't feel much like home these days.

K.T. stepped out onto the deck, rubbing her palms together nervously. "Honey, we better do this now, before they get here." In the full sunlight, K.T. looked more beautiful than ever. Her copper-red hair brushed softly along her bronzed shoulders, the spark in her green eyes had returned, and her full lips puckered into a sweet, tentative smile. Helen of Troy had nothing on my honey.

"Are you sure you're ready for this?" she asked.

I lifted Mallomar off the chair, then strode over to K.T. and folded her into my arms. "You better believe it. Now where is that darn tank?"

"In the bedroom, silly. Along with the syringe."

"Well," I said, taking her by the hand. "We better get going. It's baby-making time."

K.T. laughed lightly and followed me in.

As we climbed the stairs, arms around each other's waists, I wondered out loud if she'd mind giving the baby my last name. After all, I am the dominant partner. The slap on my butt was all the answer I needed.

Miller-Bellflower would have to do. For now.

A few of the publications of
**THE NAIAD PRESS, INC.**
P.O. Box 10543 • Tallahassee, Florida 32302
Phone (850) 539-5965
Toll-Free Order Number: 1-800-533-1973
*Mail orders welcome. Please include 15% postage.
Write or call for our free catalog which also features an
incredible selection of lesbian videos.*

| | | |
|---|---|---|
| OLD BLACK MAGIC by Jaye Maiman. 272 pp. 9th Robin Miller Mystery. | ISBN 1-56280-175-9 | $11.95 |
| LEGACY OF LOVE by Marianne K. Martin. 240 pp. Women will do anything for her... | ISBN 1-56280-184-8 | 11.95 |
| LETTING GO by Ann O'Leary. 160 pp. Laura, at 39, in love with 23-year-old Kate. | ISBN 1-56280-183-X | 11.95 |
| LADY BE GOOD edited by Barbara Grier and Christine Cassidy. 288 pp. Erotic stories by Naiad Press authors. | ISBN 1-56280-180-5 | 14.95 |
| CHAIN LETTER by Claire McNab. 288 pp. 9th Carol Ashton mystery. | ISBN 1-56280-181-3 | 11.95 |
| NIGHT VISION by Laura Adams. 256 pp. Erotic fantasy romance by "famous" author. | ISBN 1-56280-182-1 | 11.95 |
| SEA TO SHINING SEA by Lisa Shapiro. 256 pp. Unable to resist the raging passion... | ISBN 1-56280-177-5 | 11.95 |
| THIRD DEGREE by Kate Calloway. 224 pp. 3rd Cassidy James mystery. | ISBN 1-56280-185-6 | 11.95 |
| WHEN THE DANCING STOPS by Therese Szymanski. 272 pp. 1st Brett Higgins mystery. | ISBN 1-56280-186-4 | 11.95 |
| PHASES OF THE MOON by Julia Watts. 192 pp. ..... hungry for everything life has to offer. | ISBN 1-56280-176-7 | 11.95 |
| BABY IT'S COLD by Jaye Maiman. 256 pp. 5th Robin Miller mystery. | ISBN 1-56280-156-2 | 10.95 |
| CLASS REUNION by Linda Hill. 176 pp. The girl from her past... | ISBN 1-56280-178-3 | 11.95 |
| DREAM LOVER by Lyn Denison. 224 pp. A soft, sensuous, romantic fantasy. | ISBN 1-56280-173-1 | 11.95 |
| FORTY LOVE by Diana Simmonds. 288 pp. Joyous, heart-warming romance. | ISBN 1-56280-171-6 | 11.95 |
| IN THE MOOD by Robbi Sommers. 160 pp. The queen of erotic tension! | ISBN 1-56280-172-4 | 11.95 |

| | | |
|---|---|---|
| SWIMMING CAT COVE by Lauren Douglas. 192 pp. 2nd Allison O'Neil Mystery. | ISBN 1-56280-168-6 | 11.95 |
| THE LOVING LESBIAN by Claire McNab and Sharon Gedan. 240 pp. Explore the experiences that make lesbian love unique. | ISBN 1-56280-169-4 | 14.95 |
| COURTED by Celia Cohen. 160 pp. Sparkling romantic encounter. | ISBN 1-56280-166-X | 11.95 |
| SEASONS OF THE HEART by Jackie Calhoun. 240 pp. Romance through the years. | ISBN 1-56280-167-8 | 11.95 |
| K. C. BOMBER by Janet McClellan. 208 pp. 1st Tru North mystery. | ISBN 1-56280-157-0 | 11.95 |
| LAST RITES by Tracey Richardson. 192 pp. 1st Stevie Houston mystery. | ISBN 1-56280-164-3 | 11.95 |
| EMBRACE IN MOTION by Karin Kallmaker. 256 pp. A whirlwind love affair. | ISBN 1-56280-165-1 | 11.95 |
| HOT CHECK by Peggy J. Herring. 192 pp. Will workaholic Alice fall for guitarist Ricky? | ISBN 1-56280-163-5 | 11.95 |
| OLD TIES by Saxon Bennett. 176 pp. Can Cleo surrender to a passionate new love? | ISBN 1-56280-159-7 | 11.95 |
| LOVE ON THE LINE by Laura DeHart Young. 176 pp. Will Stef win Kay's heart? | ISBN 1-56280-162-7 | 11.95 |
| DEVIL'S LEG CROSSING by Kaye Davis. 192 pp. 1st Maris Middleton mystery. | ISBN 1-56280-158-9 | 11.95 |
| COSTA BRAVA by Marta Balletbo Coll. 144 pp. Read the book, see the movie! | ISBN 1-56280-153-8 | 11.95 |
| MEETING MAGDALENE & OTHER STORIES by Marilyn Freeman. 144 pp. Read the book, see the movie! | ISBN 1-56280-170-8 | 11.95 |
| SECOND FIDDLE by Kate Calloway. 208 pp. P.I. Cassidy James' second case. | ISBN 1-56280-169-6 | 11.95 |
| LAUREL by Isabel Miller. 128 pp. By the author of the beloved *Patience and Sarah*. | ISBN 1-56280-146-5 | 10.95 |
| LOVE OR MONEY by Jackie Calhoun. 240 pp. The romance of real life. | ISBN 1-56280-147-3 | 10.95 |
| SMOKE AND MIRRORS by Pat Welch. 224 pp. 5th Helen Black Mystery. | ISBN 1-56280-143-0 | 10.95 |
| DANCING IN THE DARK edited by Barbara Grier & Christine Cassidy. 272 pp. Erotic love stories by Naiad Press authors. | ISBN 1-56280-144-9 | 14.95 |
| TIME AND TIME AGAIN by Catherine Ennis. 176 pp. Passionate love affair. | ISBN 1-56280-145-7 | 10.95 |

| Title | ISBN | Price |
|---|---|---|
| PAXTON COURT by Diane Salvatore. 256 pp. Erotic and wickedly funny contemporary tale about the business of learning to live together. | ISBN 1-56280-114-7 | 10.95 |
| INNER CIRCLE by Claire McNab. 208 pp. 8th Carol Ashton Mystery. | ISBN 1-56280-135-X | 11.95 |
| LESBIAN SEX: AN ORAL HISTORY by Susan Johnson. 240 pp. Need we say more? | ISBN 1-56280-142-2 | 14.95 |
| WILD THINGS by Karin Kallmaker. 240 pp. By the undisputed mistress of lesbian romance. | ISBN 1-56280-139-2 | 11.95 |
| THE GIRL NEXT DOOR by Mindy Kaplan. 208 pp. Just what you'd expect. | ISBN 1-56280-140-6 | 11.95 |
| NOW AND THEN by Penny Hayes. 240 pp. Romance on the westward journey. | ISBN 1-56280-121-X | 11.95 |
| HEART ON FIRE by Diana Simmonds. 176 pp. The romantic and erotic rival of *Curious Wine*. | ISBN 1-56280-152-X | 11.95 |
| DEATH AT LAVENDER BAY by Lauren Wright Douglas. 208 pp. 1st Allison O'Neil Mystery. | ISBN 1-56280-085-X | 11.95 |
| YES I SAID YES I WILL by Judith McDaniel. 272 pp. Hot romance by famous author. | ISBN 1-56280-138-4 | 11.95 |
| FORBIDDEN FIRES by Margaret C. Anderson. Edited by Mathilda Hills. 176 pp. Famous author's "unpublished" Lesbian romance. | ISBN 1-56280-123-6 | 21.95 |
| SIDE TRACKS by Teresa Stores. 160 pp. Gender-bending Lesbians on the road. | ISBN 1-56280-122-8 | 10.95 |
| HOODED MURDER by Annette Van Dyke. 176 pp. 1st Jessie Batelle Mystery. | ISBN 1-56280-134-1 | 10.95 |
| WILDWOOD FLOWERS by Julia Watts. 208 pp. Hilarious and heart-warming tale of true love. | ISBN 1-56280-127-9 | 10.95 |
| NEVER SAY NEVER by Linda Hill. 224 pp. Rule #1: Never get involved with . . . | ISBN 1-56280-126-0 | 10.95 |
| THE SEARCH by Melanie McAllester. 240 pp. Exciting top cop Tenny Mendoza case. | ISBN 1-56280-150-3 | 10.95 |
| THE WISH LIST by Saxon Bennett. 192 pp. Romance through the years. | ISBN 1-56280-125-2 | 10.95 |
| FIRST IMPRESSIONS by Kate Calloway. 208 pp. P.I. Cassidy James' first case. | ISBN 1-56280-133-3 | 10.95 |
| OUT OF THE NIGHT by Kris Bruyer. 192 pp. Spine-tingling thriller. | ISBN 1-56280-120-1 | 10.95 |
| NORTHERN BLUE by Tracey Richardson. 224 pp. Police recruits Miki & Miranda — passion in the line of fire. | ISBN 1-56280-118-X | 10.95 |
| LOVE'S HARVEST by Peggy J. Herring. 176 pp. by the author of *Once More With Feeling*. | ISBN 1-56280-117-1 | 10.95 |

| | | |
|---|---|---|
| THE COLOR OF WINTER by Lisa Shapiro. 208 pp. Romantic love beyond your wildest dreams. | ISBN 1-56280-116-3 | 10.95 |
| FAMILY SECRETS by Laura DeHart Young. 208 pp. Enthralling romance and suspense. | ISBN 1-56280-119-8 | 10.95 |
| INLAND PASSAGE by Jane Rule. 288 pp. Tales exploring conventional & unconventional relationships. | ISBN 0-930044-56-8 | 10.95 |
| DOUBLE BLUFF by Claire McNab. 208 pp. 7th Carol Ashton Mystery. | ISBN 1-56280-096-5 | 10.95 |
| BAR GIRLS by Lauran Hoffman. 176 pp. See the movie, read the book! | ISBN 1-56280-115-5 | 10.95 |
| THE FIRST TIME EVER edited by Barbara Grier & Christine Cassidy. 272 pp. Love stories by Naiad Press authors. | ISBN 1-56280-086-8 | 14.95 |
| MISS PETTIBONE AND MISS McGRAW by Brenda Weathers. 208 pp. A charming ghostly love story. | ISBN 1-56280-151-1 | 10.95 |
| CHANGES by Jackie Calhoun. 208 pp. Involved romance and relationships. | ISBN 1-56280-083-3 | 10.95 |
| FAIR PLAY by Rose Beecham. 256 pp. 3rd Amanda Valentine Mystery. | ISBN 1-56280-081-7 | 10.95 |
| PAYBACK by Celia Cohen. 176 pp. A gripping thriller of romance, revenge and betrayal. | ISBN 1-56280-084-1 | 10.95 |
| THE BEACH AFFAIR by Barbara Johnson. 224 pp. Sizzling summer romance/mystery/intrigue. | ISBN 1-56280-090-6 | 10.95 |
| GETTING THERE by Robbi Sommers. 192 pp. Nobody does it like Robbi! | ISBN 1-56280-099-X | 10.95 |
| FINAL CUT by Lisa Haddock. 208 pp. 2nd Carmen Ramirez Mystery. | ISBN 1-56280-088-4 | 10.95 |
| FLASHPOINT by Katherine V. Forrest. 256 pp. A Lesbian blockbuster! | ISBN 1-56280-079-5 | 10.95 |
| CLAIRE OF THE MOON by Nicole Conn. Audio Book —Read by Marianne Hyatt. | ISBN 1-56280-113-9 | 16.95 |
| FOR LOVE AND FOR LIFE: INTIMATE PORTRAITS OF LESBIAN COUPLES by Susan Johnson. 224 pp. | ISBN 1-56280-091-4 | 14.95 |
| DEVOTION by Mindy Kaplan. 192 pp. See the movie — read the book! | ISBN 1-56280-093-0 | 10.95 |
| SOMEONE TO WATCH by Jaye Maiman. 272 pp. 4th Robin Miller Mystery. | ISBN 1-56280-095-7 | 10.95 |
| GREENER THAN GRASS by Jennifer Fulton. 208 pp. A young woman — a stranger in her bed. | ISBN 1-56280-092-2 | 10.95 |
| TRAVELS WITH DIANA HUNTER by Regine Sands. Erotic lesbian romp. Audio Book (2 cassettes) | ISBN 1-56280-107-4 | 16.95 |

| | |
|---|---|
| CABIN FEVER by Carol Schmidt. 256 pp. Sizzling suspense and passion. ISBN 1-56280-089-1 | 10.95 |
| THERE WILL BE NO GOODBYES by Laura DeHart Young. 192 pp. Romantic love, strength, and friendship. ISBN 1-56280-103-1 | 10.95 |
| FAULTLINE by Sheila Ortiz Taylor. 144 pp. Joyous comic lesbian novel. ISBN 1-56280-108-2 | 9.95 |
| OPEN HOUSE by Pat Welch. 176 pp. 4th Helen Black Mystery. ISBN 1-56280-102-3 | 10.95 |
| ONCE MORE WITH FEELING by Peggy J. Herring. 240 pp. Lighthearted, loving romantic adventure. ISBN 1-56280-089-2 | 10.95 |
| FOREVER by Evelyn Kennedy. 224 pp. Passionate romance — love overcoming all obstacles. ISBN 1-56280-094-9 | 10.95 |
| WHISPERS by Kris Bruyer. 176 pp. Romantic ghost story ISBN 1-56280-082-5 | 10.95 |
| NIGHT SONGS by Penny Mickelbury. 224 pp. 2nd Gianna Maglione Mystery. ISBN 1-56280-097-3 | 10.95 |
| GETTING TO THE POINT by Teresa Stores. 256 pp. Classic southern Lesbian novel. ISBN 1-56280-100-7 | 10.95 |
| PAINTED MOON by Karin Kallmaker. 224 pp. Delicious Kallmaker romance. ISBN 1-56280-075-2 | 11.95 |
| THE MYSTERIOUS NAIAD edited by Katherine V. Forrest & Barbara Grier. 320 pp. Love stories by Naiad Press authors. ISBN 1-56280-074-4 | 14.95 |
| DAUGHTERS OF A CORAL DAWN by Katherine V. Forrest. 240 pp. Tenth Anniversay Edition. ISBN 1-56280-104-X | 11.95 |
| BODY GUARD by Claire McNab. 208 pp. 6th Carol Ashton Mystery. ISBN 1-56280-073-6 | 11.95 |
| CACTUS LOVE by Lee Lynch. 192 pp. Stories by the beloved storyteller. ISBN 1-56280-071-X | 9.95 |
| SECOND GUESS by Rose Beecham. 216 pp. 2nd Amanda Valentine Mystery. ISBN 1-56280-069-8 | 9.95 |
| A RAGE OF MAIDENS by Lauren Wright Douglas. 240 pp. 6th Caitlin Reece Mystery. ISBN 1-56280-068-X | 10.95 |
| TRIPLE EXPOSURE by Jackie Calhoun. 224 pp. Romantic drama involving many characters. ISBN 1-56280-067-1 | 10.95 |

These are just a few of the many Naiad Press titles — we are the oldest and largest lesbian/feminist publishing company in the world. We also offer an enormous selection of lesbian video products. Please request a complete catalog. We offer personal service; we encourage and welcome direct mail orders from individuals who have limited access to bookstores carrying our publications.